Tame A Wild Heart

CYNTHIA WOOLF

ISBN:0983937214
ISBN-13: 978-0-9839372-1-0

Cover Photo Credits
Period Images and Storyblocks

DEDICATION

For Jim, my husband, my best friend, my lover and my rock. None of this would be possible without your love and support. I love you, Sweetie.

ACKNOWLEDGMENTS

Thanks Mom. Your story of when you met Dad is what inspired me to write this one. The only thing the same about the two is the setting, Creede, Colorado. But you believed in me. Without you I never could have written this. I wish you'd been here to see it published. Rest in peace.

I would also like to thank my critique partners, without whom this book would never have gotten finished. Thank you – Kally Surbeck, Michele Chambers, Jan Snyder, Karen Docter, Jennifer Zigrino, Louise Suit, Glenna Fernandez, Shelley Wernlein and Jenn K. LeBlanc.

PROLOGUE

John Morgan's heartbeat drummed in his ears. Keeping a tight rein on himself so he wouldn't shout with elation, he looked down and watched the sunlight sparkle off the tiny yellow nuggets resting so unassumingly in his hand. Never had he seen anything quite so deadly wrapped in such a pretty package.

He'd been looking for it for so long. Father never believed there was gold in this country, but he knew better. Too bad he couldn't have the satisfaction of saying 'I told you so' to the old man, but he was long gone now, not that it mattered. Only the gold mattered. The bright, glittering stones were the answer to everything.

Looking around again to be sure he was alone, he calmly carved his mark in a tree, so he'd know where to return. Yes, the gold was the answer to all his dreams; all he had to do was get the land where it rested. Not an easy task, for he knew he stood on the Evans' property. But the gold had always called to him and, now that he knew where it was, he could answer. It didn't matter how, he would get this land and his gold.

CHAPTER 1

Flames licked through the canvas wagon cover. Great billows of black smoke escaped through the top. Horses whinnied. Men shouted. Cattle bawled. The scene was utter chaos.

Catherine Evans shouted orders, turning as a big black stallion charged into the fray. The large man on his back countermanded her orders and barked out his own.

Duncan McKenzie.

Nudging her own stallion, Wildfire, with her knees, she intercepted them. "This is my ranch and my men. I give the orders here. Where the hell have you been? You're a week late."

"I came when I could." Duncan turned to join the men.

"No, you stay." She whipped around to face the men beating at the fire on the wagon. "Forget the wagon. It's lost. Get those cows. Now."

After the men scattered, she rounded on Duncan. "When you could isn't a good enough answer. This is a working ranch. I have to be able to depend on every man here. And if I can't, then I don't want them. I don't even know why Dad sent for you anyway. We don't need a gunslinger."

"James has his reasons for asking me to come. As for a gunslinger, the need has yet to be seen."

She disregarded his response. "You know about field dressings and I've got a man missing and probably hurt. Zeke was driving one of these supply wagons. I could use your help."

She galloped to the other side of the camp, riding around debris thrown from the supply wagon. Burlap sacks once full of coffee and beans, littered the ground beside empty flour and sugar sacks. Tinned food lay bent, smashed under cattle and horse hooves. Ignoring the destruction, she went straight to an overturned buckboard wagon.

Duncan reined in beside her. "The whole place looks like a battlefield."

"It is a battlefield, and if you're here to help, then do it."

"I don't see anyone."

She stopped rifling through loose pieces of debris and cocked her head toward the wagon. "Did you hear that?"

There was a weak, distant groan. Catherine saw a muddied, work-worn black boot sticking out from underneath.

"It must have upended during the stampede. Zeke was driving. We have to get him out." She let out a shrill whistle and Wildfire came running to her side. "Good boy."

She freed her lasso from the saddlehorn, dallying up the front wagon wheel. Duncan did the same to the rear wheel.

"Let's flip the wagon over. When I holler, you have that horse of yours pull." She made sure both ropes were tight.

"Now! Pull. You too, Wildfire, come on boy." The wagon came slowly up and over onto its wheels, wood creaking as it bounced on its axles, but the buckboard held together in one piece.

She ran around the wagon to the man on the ground, checked for bullet wounds and found none. The wound on his head bled profusely, as they are want to do, but didn't appear too deep. Running her hands over him, she found his right leg broken. "Zeke, are you all right? Zeke, can you hear me?"

She looked up at Duncan. "It's broken. It'll need to be set before we can move him. I can't do this on my own. I don't have the strength to set the leg properly. Will you help?"

"Sure. I need two straight pieces of wood and something to bind them." He took his knife and cut Zeke's pant leg open to see how badly the leg was injured. She could see the bone hadn't broken the skin nor was there any bleeding, so the injury wasn't as bad as it could have been. He could stabilize the leg enough to get the man to a real doctor.

Catherine returned with a couple of loose boards she'd ripped from the wagon as Duncan started to cut off Zeke's boot. He hesitated when Zeke moaned, clearly in agony.

"Miss Catherine, is that you? What happened?" He was in obvious pain, but still lucid.

She smiled at him and gently brushed the hair back out of his eyes. "I was about to ask you the same thing. You've got a broken leg and I know it hurts, but before we set it, tell me what you remember. All I heard was the cattle rushin'. By the time I got out of the timber, it was all over."

Zeke closed his eyes. "It happened so fast. Roy Walker and his men rode in. Next thing I know, I hear gunshots. I tried to control the team, but the wagon got pounded by the herd and tipped... I'm sorry, I don't know what happened after that." He closed his eyes then opened them wide. "The team! Where's Abel and Bessie?"

She shook her head, "Don't worry, they're fine."

Zeke nodded then looked at Duncan. "Who's this? A new ranch hand? Replacing me already?" He tried to smile, but winced in pain instead.

She patted his hand. "Don't be silly, Zeke, you know you're irreplaceable. Besides, I can't let your Sarah and little Jacob go, so I guess you have to stay, too. This is Duncan McKenzie."

"Mr. McKenzie, any friend of James Evans' is a friend o' mine." Zeke lifted his hand. "But if you continue cuttin' on my boot, I'm goin' to kick you with my other leg. They're the only boots I got."

"Pleased to meet you. I've got to get this boot off so I can set your leg. And if you kick me I'll have to knock you out."

"No way." Zeke ripped his hand from Duncan's and tried to rise, but Duncan held him down.

Catherine grabbed Zeke's hand and gently held it. "Don't worry. I'm gonna buy you the best boots in Creede. I'll make Gordon send all the way to Chicago if I have to. I'll even make sure that Jacob has a pair to match his daddy's."

Zeke stopped struggling and relaxed. "The best, huh?"

"The best, I promise,"

"Catherine's promised and I'm a witness. Let's set your leg and get you home." Duncan looked up at Catherine. "Can you hold him down while I set it?"

She took a deep breath and nodded.

Duncan turned to Zeke and said calmly, "This is going to hurt like hell, but I've got to do it. I'll be as quick as I can. Yell, if you want."

"Here, bite down on this, it'll help." Catherine handed him the leather sheath from her knife.

"Just get it done." Zeke closed his eyes, put the leather between his teeth and locked his jaw.

"Wait a minute. You'll need something to bind it." She pulled her shirt from her pants and tore two strips from the bottom. She laid the cloth next to the boards within Duncan's reach.

"All right, hold him still."

Duncan pulled hard with both hands to set the bones back into place, while Catherine put all her weight on

Zeke's shoulders to hold him down. Placing one board on either side of the leg, he tied them tight with the strips of cloth from her shirt.

Zeke had not uttered a sound. He'd fainted.

When her concentration was on Zeke and his problem, she was fine. Now that it was over, she could let go. She sat back and trembled.

Duncan leaned forward and touched her shoulder. "You all right? You look a little pale."

"I'm fine." She grasped her knees to her chest and rested her chin on them.

"Are you?"

"I couldn't have done it alone. Thanks for that."

"You're welcome."

She hated to admit she needed help. Especially *his* help, but she was glad he'd come when he did.

He extended his hand to her.

"Thanks." She shook his hand, but only briefly.

Taking a deep breath, she got to her feet and dusted herself off. She was not the vulnerable girl she'd been. She was a woman. A woman determined to make her way in a man's world. One little stampede wasn't going to change that.

"We'll have to make a travois to take him back to the ranch. Even though the supply wagon didn't break anything when we flipped it back on its wheels, Wildfire doesn't take to pulling a wagon."

"Jake can pull the wagon. Tie Wildfire to the back and I'll drive while you take care of Zeke. Fair enough?"

"Fair enough."

He harnessed Jake to the wagon and Catherine gathered all the blankets and other soft stuffs to pad it. Together they managed to load Zeke.

As they pulled into the ranch yard several hours later, Catherine's father, James, slammed out of the house followed by a very pregnant, young blond woman and a little boy.

"Did you find him?" James called as the buckboard pulled to a halt. "Did you find Zeke?"

"We found him. He's got a broken leg, but he'll be good as new in a few weeks," Catherine said as she jumped to the ground. "He's going to need some tender lovin' care, Sarah."

Sarah ran to the end of the wagon and clamored up despite her bulk. "Zeke, honey, are you okay?" She knelt beside him, grazed his cheek with her knuckle, while tears rolled in streams down her cheeks.

Tenderly, Zeke wiped the tears from her face. "Here now, we'll have none of that. I'm going to be fine."

"Papa! Up!" demanded Jacob.

Duncan set the brake and went around to the back to help lift Zeke from the wagon bed. Instead, a curly haired blond boy, confronted him, pulling on his pant leg.

"Up mister. Pease." Jacob held his arms up for

Duncan to lift him.

Duncan didn't want to lift the sweet child. He didn't want to hold this tiny body in his arms for even a moment, but it looked like he had no choice. Catherine, the only one near enough to do it, just stood there with her hands on her hips, and a grin on her face, waiting.

This small child was not going to defeat him. He'd faced desperate men; men willing to kill to save themselves from Duncan McKenzie, bounty hunter. None of them frightened him as much as this one little boy, who couldn't be more than two or three years old. All Duncan had to do was bend down and lift the child, but his knees shook and he felt himself quiver inside.

"Oh, for goodness sake, Duncan. Just lift him up so he can see his Papa is all right."

Catherine knew. He didn't know how she knew, but she did. His only real weakness...children.

Getting a grip on himself, he bent and hoisted the anxious little boy up and over the wagon's gate. He was light as a feather, so tiny...so innocent.

Catherine was beside him. "That wasn't so hard now, was it?"

He didn't miss the laughter in her sparkling silver gaze or the smile formed by her perfect rosebud lips. Without answering, he stalked toward the house and the front door.

Duncan closed the door behind him and took a deep breath. He could still smell the fresh bread that Alice baked that morning. He glanced around the foyer, glad to see it hadn't changed. Directly in front of him, stairs led to the second floor where the bedrooms were. Down the hall to the right of the stairway he knew he would find James' study and a storeroom. The formal parlor, which still looked like it hadn't been used, was to his left. The Queen Anne chairs and overstuffed divan looked as new as when he'd helped James haul them in.

Beyond the parlor was the formal dining room. A massive oak table and chairs dominated it, in stark contrast to the lace curtains covering the windows. They hadn't used the room when he'd lived there, preferring instead, the comfort of the kitchen.

Duncan shook the memories from his head, turned and started for the storeroom where he heard James muttering expletives.

"Dagnabit," James said. "I've got a canvas stretcher here I got for just such an emergency. If I could just get it out from behind these steamer trunks."

"Here, let me help." Duncan quickly moved the trunks and freed the stretcher.

"Good to see you, son. You've come at the perfect time."

"To help with this maybe," he said, lifting the stretcher, following James out. "But not soon enough to keep this incident from happening, or keep your daughter from jumping down my back for being late."

"Things happen for a reason, son. You've got to find the reason."

"From what Zeke said, the reason is named Roy Walker."

"He's only part of it." James walked out the front doors, over to the wagon. "Sarah, let's get you down so we can get your husband out of there." James lifted the pregnant woman easily. He looked good to Duncan. He was still as tall as Duncan's own six feet four inches, and had remained fit and strong, despite his advancing age and the graying of his brown hair and mustache.

"Catherine, you and Sarah take Jacob here and make sure the way into the house is clear." James ruffled the lad's hair then lifted him from the wagon. "You go help your Ma and make sure to pick up all your toys, okay?"

"Yup, Big Jim. I pick up toys."

The youngster ran off as fast as his chubby legs would carry him across the yard toward the small house. Catherine followed with Sarah, who still wept and moved much slower now that she knew her husband was all right.

He watched Catherine settle her arm around Sarah's shoulders to calm her.

"Come on now. If you don't settle down, Doc's going to have to deliver that baby instead of check on Zeke's leg."

Sarah laughed and wiped her tears away. "You're right, and Doc would not be a happy man. I'm not due for another couple of weeks."

When they lifted Zeke onto the stretcher and off the wagon, he let out a groan. Duncan knew he tried to keep it in, but a broken leg is a painful thing. "Catherine, do you have any laudanum? Zeke could use some until the doc gets here."

"Sure thing. Be right back."

Before they entered Zeke's house, James said to him, "Don't worry about a thing. We take care of our own here on the JC. You and Sarah have a home here as long as you want it."

"Thanks, Mr. Evans. I really appreciate knowing that. I didn't know how I'd provide for them while I'm laid up." Zeke raised his head from the stretcher. "I'm really sorry about this, Mr. Evans."

"Pshaw. Think nothing of it. None of this was your fault. I'm just glad you weren't hurt worse."

Zeke nodded and laid his head back down. They got him settled him on the bed and walked out of the house, leaving him to Sarah's tender ministrations.

At the front door, James turned to Duncan. "I've sent for the doctor and, after you get cleaned up I'd like for you to come to my study. We've got some talking to do."

That sounded ominous to Duncan, but he nodded. "Where do I clean up?"

"In your room. I've had it cleaned for you."

"I can stay in the bunkhouse with the rest of the men."

"Don't be ridiculous. You're family. You'll have your old room." James stopped, his hand hovered above the doorknob. "This is your home, Duncan. Always has been and always will be."

Something in the dark recesses of Duncan's heart was

moved by James' declaration. Home. How long since he'd been any place he could call home? Ten years. There had never been anywhere else for him but here. "Thanks, I appreciate it."

Duncan drove the wagon the short distance to the barn where he unhitched Jake and untied Wildfire, then fed and watered them. He flung his saddlebags over his shoulder and headed to the house. When he finally opened the door to his room, he stared in wonder. Nothing had changed. Everything was exactly as he had left it ten years ago.

The massive bed that James had ordered special, so he could stretch out his long frame without hanging off the ends, still had the same quilt on it. James' wife Elizabeth had made that quilt for Duncan when he'd first come to live with them twenty years ago. He'd been thirteen, orphaned, and big for his age. None of that mattered to Elizabeth, who saw only a boy who had saved her husband's life and needed a home and family. He ran his hand over the quilt, enjoying its comforting softness.

The bedside night table and washstand were both made of dark walnut that matched the bed, as did the wardrobe and chest of drawers. They had marble tops, a luxury Elizabeth had insisted on saying, they would last forever. It appeared she was right. On the washstand were a porcelain pitcher and basin, his favorite sandalwood soap, two washcloths, and a hand towel. The nightstand held a small pitcher of water, a glass, a kerosene lamp, and an ashtray for his cheroots. At this point, Duncan wouldn't have been a bit surprised to find the wardrobe full of his clothes. He was almost afraid to look, but it turned out to be empty. Empty and stale, just like his life had been for the last ten years.

Putting aside his nostalgia, he quickly emptied his saddlebags, washed his hands and face, and donned a clean shirt before walking downstairs to see James.

Catherine met him in the hall. "Dad always said you'd be back. He made sure your room was ready for you."

"And you? Did you know I'd be back?" he asked softly.

"No. I didn't care one way or the other." She turned on her heel and opened the door to her room. "But I hoped," he heard her say under her breath as the door shut.

Duncan smiled.

CHAPTER 2

Dinner wasn't the boisterous affair Duncan remembered. They sat in the dining room. James at the head of the table, Catherine to his right, and Duncan to his left. Alice, the housekeeper and cook, told him that usually there were more people for supper. Zeke, Sarah and Jacob, and Michael O'Malley, the new foreman, normally joined them. But tonight, Sarah fixed supper in her own kitchen for her family, so Zeke wouldn't have to move, and Michael was ramrodding the search for the missing cattle.

"Tomorrow morning, I'll take supplies and join the search for the cattle." Catherine said between bites. "With any luck, we'll find most of them in a few days and can fill that army contract on time. You should have seen it," she said to her dad. "The herd wrecked everything. What hadn't been trampled had been shot up. Walker isn't going to get away with this." She slammed her fist on the table. "I'm going to make him pay."

"Kitten," her father said in his mollifying tone, "we can't prove anything. You know as well as I do, if we go to the sheriff, for everyone of our cowboys who witnessed this, Walker's going to have ten who place him on the other side of Creede when the stampede happened."

"I know, but I'm just so frustrated."

"I know. So am I."

"Anyone want to let me know what's going on?" Duncan sat back in his chair sipping his coffee, waiting for the answer.

He'd always been good at waiting. Patience was his virtue, the one reason he was so good at bounty hunting. He could wait out his quarry and take him when he was least dangerous to Duncan, himself, or the surrounding population. He prided himself on never having had a civilian casualty.

Unsurprising to Duncan, Catherine spoke first. "They're trying to run us off our land, that's what's going on."

"Simmer down and let's stick to the facts. Fact is, John tried to buy some of our property first, but I wouldn't sell."

"John?" Duncan asked.

"Buy? Buy! Steal is more like it. He offered fifty cents an acre for prime timber worth two dollars an acre. That's not an offer to buy."

"John Morgan." James ignored Catherine and responded to Duncan's earlier question.

"So what happened then?"

"Then," Catherine said, pure sarcasm lacing her voice, "the *accidents* started. We've been here for fifteen years and never lost a steer to the Ute or to poisoning. Now suddenly we have five dead from a poisoned well and another ten supposedly killed by the Ute. At least that's what someone wanted us to think."

"And you don't think it was?" Duncan asked.

"No. Never. You know White Buffalo only lets his people take cattle in the winter, and then only if game is scarce."

"That's true. But I didn't know if things had changed between you and White Buffalo in the last ten years."

Catherine got up and paced around the room. "Only twice in fifteen years has White Buffalo needed beef to feed his people, only when the women and children were starving. If his warriors had their way, they would never come; there is no honor in taking white man's cattle, but neither will they let one go to waste. White Buffalo is a great chief and knows his people are only as strong as the weakest among them. He makes sure all are fed."

"Fine. It's not the Ute. What else has happened? Any new people show up recently?"

"Yeah, Walker. Roy Walker. He's got a bad reputation, and it seems to be deserved," said James.

"The man is pure evil," Catherine spat.

Alice stood and began clearing the table. "That's enough talk for me. You all take this discussion into the study. I've got dishes to do and food to get packed for those boys up at the camp. It'll be by the kitchen door for you in the morning."

"Thanks. Supper was great, as usual. I'm sorry to have ruined the good food with poor conversation."

Catherine got up and hugged the small, buxom woman whose hair was as coal black as Duncan's. When they'd first settled here, some thought she was Duncan's mother.

"Alice, I thank you. That was the best supper I've had in a very long time," Duncan said meaning it.

Alice blushed. "Duncan McKenzie, you always could charm the socks right off me. Go on all of you. I'll bring in coffee after I make a fresh pot."

Retiring to the study, Catherine and James continued to argue. She wanted to have the sheriff arrest Morgan and Walker, but James knew they needed solid proof.

Duncan sat in one of the leather chairs in front of James' dark mahogany desk.

Catherine paced the floor.

It wasn't until after Alice had brought the coffee and departed that James finally got around to saying what was really on his mind. He sat behind the desk, in his big, soft leather chair. "I want you two to get married," he said, as if he'd just asked them to pass the butter.

"What?" Duncan sputtered as his cup clattered back to the saucer.

"You're crazy," Catherine muttered at the same time. "I've told you before I'm not getting married."

"That's too bad," said James, examining his fingernails. "Because I'm leaving the ranch to Duncan."

Outraged, Catherine lunged forward and leaned with both hands on her father's desk. "You can't do that."

"You can't do that," Duncan echoed, shocked by James' declaration.

"I can do whatever I damn well please," James shouted. Taking a deep breath, he controlled his anger and, in a softer, cajoling tone said, "Kitten, try to understand. If I leave it to you, John Morgan will find a way to force you to marry him, and we'll lose it anyway."

"Dad, he won't—"

"Yes, he will. You're a woman, and although you don't seem to realize it most of the time, it's still a fact. As a woman, you can be coerced. If I leave the ranch to Duncan, it will stay in the family."

Catherine sank heavily into the second leather chair, next to Duncan. It appeared she and James had had this conversation before.

"This isn't a good idea." Duncan paused. "What if I decide to sell the ranch?"

"You won't," James responded quickly. "I know you love this ranch as much as Cat and I do. Besides, you've dreamed of raising thoroughbreds, like that Jake of yours, for as long as I can remember. And there are conditions."

"More conditions, you mean," said a disgruntled Catherine.

Duncan narrowed his eyes. "What other

conditions?"

"You don't get the ranch or the two prime mares I have coming, unless you marry Cat. And she won't get the ranch or the palomino mare that matches Wildfire, unless she marries you. If it's going to go out of the family, I'll sell it myself."

"That's blackmail. And I don't like being blackmailed," said Duncan.

Catherine sat dumbstruck for only a moment, then she sat upright. "That's why you went to the stock show in Kansas City. It wasn't for the bull, but for horses."

James didn't deny it. "I've thought about this for a long time, before the accidents. Ever since John Morgan first started sniffing around you. I've watched him grow from an uncaring, callous boy into a greedy, selfish man. I refuse to have that bastard a part of this family, whether I'm around to see it or not."

The vehemence in James' voice startled Duncan. He'd never heard the man he'd come to respect as no other, talk like this before.

"I've told you, I...will...never...marry...John Morgan." Her voice rose with each word until she shouted the last.

"And I've told you what I think about that." James turned to Duncan, "Son, I don't like putting you in this position. I just don't know any other way to see Kitten is taken care of."

Catherine jumped up. "I can take care of myself. I've been doing just fine up until now."

"James," Duncan said quietly, though he still commanded both their attentions, "I'd like to speak to Catherine in private, if she doesn't mind."

James shoved back his chair. "Of course. I'm sure you need to talk things out between you. I'll be on the porch when you want me."

He left and Duncan watched through the window until he saw him light his cigar then turned to Catherine.

She hadn't said a word. She plopped down and sat stiff as a board in the big leather chair, her fingernails making marks in the arms, waiting for him to speak.

He said simply, "I think we should."

"No."

"I don't like this anymore than you do, but I don't want to see you lose your inheritance because your father has gotten some crazy notion in his head." Duncan leaned against the desk and stretched his legs out in front of him. "I came back here hoping to stay. I want out of the bounty business, and I have no desire to become a gun for hire. This will give me that opportunity."

Catherine leaned forward, resting her elbows on her thighs, hands hanging between her knees, and stared at her boots. "We don't love each other," she said, looking up. "We don't even know each other anymore."

Duncan squatted in front of her. "But we used to, very well, and we used to care about each other."

"That was a long time ago. We've both changed. I'm not the little girl who hung on your shirttails, or the young woman you left behind. I don't know if friendship is enough to build a marriage on."

He took her hands in his. "Many marriages have been based on less."

"I know, but—"

"Unless, of course, there's someone else you'd rather marry—"

"No," she shook her head vehemently. "There's no one else."

"Then why not me?" He rubbed small circles in her palms with his thumbs, making it extremely difficult for her to think. "We can have a good marriage, Cat. You could even grow to love me...someday."

The heat from his hands seared her. She looked into his eyes, still such a deep, dark blue, like the sky at midnight, searching for some of the Duncan she'd known. The man before her had no laughter in his eyes, no spark...no joy. Could she give that back to him? Would he again become the man she fell in love with before he'd left for the deadly life of a bounty hunter? She had to find out...had to know if the real Duncan could be saved.

First, though, she had to know if he'd meant what he said. "What about you? Someone else you'd rather marry? Will you be able to leave the thrill of the chase and the money behind you?"

He shuttered his eyes. She couldn't read anything in them but coldness.

"There's no one else, and there's no thrill in the chase. Just long, hard days in the saddle going from one rat hole to another. Tracking scum that would kill their own mother for the gold in her teeth. If you think that's thrilling, then you and I are more different than ever."

His accusation, though unstated, still stung. They'd been too different when he left. He wanted to see the world and make a fortune. She'd only wanted the ranch. That was still all she wanted.

"And the money? Ranching's not a safe life. There are plenty of times when you don't know how you're going to pay your men or the bill at the grocer. Cattle are contrary creatures, and you're at the mercy of Mother Nature."

"I'm not going to raise cattle, remember? I'm going to breed horses. Together we'll breed the best thoroughbreds and palominos in the country. And I don't need more money, I have plenty."

"Horses are more temperamental than cattle. Sure you want to risk your wealth on something so...uncertain? And if you're so wealthy, why haven't you settled down before now?" He had the means but hadn't married. Why? Hope built in her heart, unasked for and unwarranted, maybe he still cared for her.

Duncan released her hands and paced back to the window. "This is the only home I've ever known, here with you and James." As if that was enough of an explanation, he said nothing more, and she guessed it was enough, for it spoke volumes.

Catherine came up behind Duncan and set her hand on his shoulder. "Are you certain about this? There'll be no going back, and I won't have a husband who hunts bounties or hires his gun out to the highest bidder. My mind is no different now than it was before. I still only want to be here. I don't want to leave the ranch. I don't want to travel and see the world."

Duncan turned to her. "No going back, no bounties, no gun for hire ever again. I've seen all of the world I need to see and more than I wanted. I've known enough other women to know I don't want anyone else."

Then he did the strangest, most amazing thing. He wrapped his arms around her, pulled her close, and kissed her. "I'm finally home."

They told James their decision. He didn't try to hide his elation. Duncan knew he wasn't just happy about keeping the ranch from John Morgan. James talked about building a house for them and seeing his grandchildren play in the yard. He said he even knew the perfect place where a young couple could have the privacy they needed to get started on those grandchildren.

It irked Duncan to think James had duped him, but he was sure this was why James had summoned him home. He and Catherine both left the study as soon as they could. James was eager to make plans, but all either of them needed was time alone. Time to think about their decision…about the future.

Duncan stood in the shadows, leaning against the porch railing. He lit a cheroot and watched the small house across the yard. Little Jacob was playing in the dirt with his wooden horses and toy soldiers. Doc Wright had come and gone after telling Duncan he'd done a fine job of setting Zeke's leg. With help from Sarah and crutches Doc had left, Zeke sat in the glider on the porch, his leg propped on a kitchen chair, his wife beside him, watching their son play.

Duncan felt a slow ache, deep in his soul. He envied Zeke. Not his broken leg, of course, but his family, his happiness. Even though Zeke was in pain, there was contentment on his face. Duncan wanted what he saw, wanted a home and family, needed to find for himself the contentment he saw in Zeke. Of course, wanting something and having it are two sides of the same coin. He'd never thought it possible before, but James was giving him an opportunity to live his dreams, not just to breed horses, but to have the wife he'd always dreamed of...Catherine.

Someday he would be watching his own son play in this yard. He and Catherine would be sitting together, talking softly and holding hands. Bitterly, he shook his head and almost laughed out loud. They would never have that. Zeke and Sarah loved each other. It was evident for anyone to see.

Catherine had loved him once. He knew that, but he'd spurned her love; went looking for a better life over the next hill...and the next...and the next, until he couldn't see anything else but the next rise. Always hoping he'd be able to leave the guilt that haunted him over next hill, but it followed him. Never any peace, not from the guilt for the men he'd killed, not from the war memories that started him on the path he'd taken.

The closest he'd ever come to finding peace was with Catherine and James in this valley. That's why he'd come back. He knew now he would have come even without James' summons. It was time to come home.

Duncan tossed his smoke to the ground and snuffed it with his boot. He heard Sarah calling to Jacob, his attention once more to the little family he envied. Did they know how very lucky they were? Duncan doubted it. Until you lost everything you treasure, you never know how precious family was; you took it for granted.

Duncan never would.

Again.

*****

All of the dead men from his past.

The battlefield.

His stomach roiled and he could see the young Confederate. Elias Ford "Slim" Walker had been the name on the papers they'd found on him. Duncan watched as the man lay face down in the leaves of a heavily wooded thicket. He could tell by the way he laid there, he was hurt and scared. Duncan was scared, too. The battle had been God-awful.

Advance and retreat, advance and retreat. Duncan had advanced as far as possible before becoming separated from his Union regiment. Now there was nowhere to retreat to.

He'd heard someone order a charge, didn't know if it was a Confederate or Union officer.

Then it was chaos.

Men falling and screaming all around him. When Duncan had finally stopped, it seemed his powder and shot had been expended hours before. In actuality, it had been only minutes. He'd watched, unable to do anything else, as Elias attached the bayonet to the end of his rifle and advanced tree by tree until the stately oak in front of him exploded.

The cannon shot, which dropped Elias in his tracks, had been an indirect hit. The ball careened off the oak and continued through the Union ranks, which were engaged in hand-to-hand combat with their Rebel countrymen. He watched as a long chunk of bark lodged itself deep in Elias' belly. Duncan lay there, unable to move, while Elias' life ebbed into the sweet earth below.

He lay there for moments—it might have been hours. From the corner of his eye, he saw the gold braid on the shoulder of the Union officer that was surveying the devastation of the day.

The Rebel had one last chance for defiance, one last chance for revenge. Slim Walker tried to spring from the earth and drive his bayonet into the back of the enemy officer.

Two steps behind the valiant southern warrior, Duncan saw him stagger to his feet and aim the long knife on the end of his rifle toward Duncan's commander's back.

With no choice, Duncan took a quick step forward and swiped the butt of his Enfield into the back of Elias' head. The blow broke the neck of Elias Ford "Slim" Walker and laid him to rest in the leaves.

Duncan had to know who this valiant and determined soldier was. He'd never seen anyone try so hard. He checked the man's pocket. In it, along with his army papers, was a picture of a woman and little boy. On the back was written, Emma, age twenty-two and Roy, age four.

Duncan woke; sweat dripped from his brow and ran into the hair at his temples. He was tangled in the blankets. As the moisture dried, he felt cold goose bumps rise. He went to the basin and washed the sweat from his body, dressed, and went down to the kitchen. He wouldn't be able to sleep again tonight. He hadn't killed the woman and boy, but he might as well have. He knew from his own experience, with no father, they had little chance of making it on their own. They were the first three lives he'd taken.

Fragments of the dream still remained vivid in his mind. He remembered the name now.

Roy Walker.

Was it the same one? Had the child managed to survive and now come to haunt him in the flesh? No, it couldn't be. There must be hundreds of men with that name. But how many in Creede, Colorado at the same time he and James were here, too?

His concerns nagged him.

Could it be?

CHAPTER 3

Duncan sat at the table sipping a cup of coffee when Catherine came to the kitchen. "Hey, sleepyhead," he called.

"I thought you'd be the late sleeper," she yawned in response. "Still coffee in that pot?"

He nodded. "Pretty good, too, if I do say so myself."

"You made the coffee?"

He smiled at the surprise in her voice. "Yup. I've been living alone for a long time. You either learn or do without. I didn't want to do without." He watched as she poured a cup and sipped the coffee cautiously.

"Hey, this is good. Better not let Joshua, our camp cook, know you can make coffee or he'll give you a regular job."

Duncan laughed. "Trust me, unless his is just too awful to drink, I'm not saying a word."

"If you haven't eaten, you better eat fast. The men are going to want these supplies real soon."

"You go ahead, I'll get the horses."

She watched Duncan disappear. Grabbing three

left over dinner biscuits, she slathered them with fresh creamy butter and Alice's homemade chokecherry jelly. Taking a bite out of one, she couldn't stop the moan of pleasure.

Someday she would have to learn how to cook. She finished her biscuit and coffee then wrapped two more biscuits up in oilcloth and shoved them in her slicker pocket. Whistling, she stepped onto the porch next to the sacks of food Alice had prepared and waited for Duncan.

She heard the slow clip-clop of horse hooves and the creaking of the wagon rounding the side of the house and looked up, shading her eyes from the bright, rising sun. Catherine tried to hide her surprise at seeing Duncan driving the wagon with Jake and Wildfire saddled and tied behind, ready to go.

"I didn't mean for you to skip breakfast," she said.

"I didn't. I've been up for a while." He took the fifty-pound sack of beans she'd managed to balance on her shoulder and threw it in the wagon as though it was filled with cotton.

Not dressed in his usual black, he wore a soft-blue chambray work shirt and sturdy, but well-worn denim trousers. She couldn't help but admire the play of muscles across his shoulders as he hefted the sack, or the sung fit of his pants on his long legs. Long, muscular legs, she amended to herself.

"Are these two sturdy beasts I hitched to the wagon Abel and Bessie?" Bessie nickered and begged for him to rub her, butting her head against him.

Caught staring, Catherine nodded. "They came home on their own. I found them standing at the barn door when I did chores last night and put them in the corral."

"Smart horses. Came home to where they're cared for and loved."

Catherine laughed. "Where they're fed is more like it. Horses don't know about love."

"How do you know? You don't think Wildfire loves you and wants to please you? Doesn't he come up and nudge you when he wants his ears and nose rubbed?"

As if understanding what he'd said, Bessie and Abel both nudged him. He smiled and scratched behind each of their ears.

Catherine thought his smile was the most beautiful thing she'd seen this morning. She wished he'd turn those dimples her way. That smile was the first she'd seen from him since he'd returned.

"Of course. He nudges me all the time because he's spoiled rotten...but that isn't love."

"Love, affection." He shrugged. "Horses feel things the same as we do. That's why some horses and riders are so perfect together. Like you and Wildfire, me and Jake."

Shaking her head, she said, "Bounty hunter and horse philosopher... What have I gotten myself into."

Duncan's lip quirked up at the corner. "That is ex-bounty hunter, ma'am."

She laughed. "Come on, Mr. Philosopher and ex-bounty hunter, we've got work to do."

They rode together in silence on the buckboard for the hour or so, the two riding horses tied to the hitch. Catherine wanted to talk about their upcoming wedding, but didn't want to disturb the quiet companionship she was enjoying.

Duncan broke the silence. "Tell me what's behind these accidents. James said Morgan wants the ranch but if I remember right he has as much land as you do and your properties don't even connect. Why would he want to buy land from you?"

"Good question. Our land does connect in the very northeast part of our property. There's maybe a hundred feet that adjoin. The Wasson Ranch separates us. He offered to buy the property at the connection."

"But why? What use would it be to him? Buying property from Wasson makes more sense. It's prime grazing with a good water supply."

She shook her head. "I don't know. Dad talked to old man Wasson and he said John never approached him about buying any property."

Duncan slapped the reins lightly on Abel and Bessie's rumps. "You said the land he wanted is prime timber. Could he be going into the lumber business?"

Catherine put both hands on her waist and stretched her aching back, then squirmed on the wagon bench trying to get more comfortable. "It's prime land, but there's not enough timber to make a full-fledged logging operation viable. Too hard to get the trees to the mill. The timber is enough for personal use, not much more."

"Then it's something else, but what?"

"That's what you're here to find out."

"Maybe he just wants you. James told me Morgan asked you several times to marry him."

"I could never marry him." The thought of John Morgan touching her turned her stomach. She looked away from Duncan to the blue-green mountains surrounding her home. "I could never marry a man I don't love. Speaking of marriage, I think we should discuss ours."

"What's to discuss? We're getting married," Duncan replied.

Catherine sighed. This would be harder than she thought. "I need to know what you expect from this marriage...from me." She laid her hand on his knee and felt him tense. "I'm not your normal woman, Duncan. I don't cook or sew. I work the cattle, branding, mending fences. I break horses and birth calves. That's what I do and who I am."

Duncan didn't speak for a few moments, long enough for her to think he was unhappy with the agreement they'd made with James. She removed her hand from his knee and looked away. "I'm sorry you're disappointed, but I haven't changed."

"No," he blurted out. He grabbed her hand and squeezed. "I'll never be disappointed or ashamed of you or anything you do. I don't ever want you to be something you're not. I've had enough pretending to last a lifetime, saying one thing and being another. All I expect from you is your faithfulness. That's all."

She looked down at their joined hands and thought how wonderful it would be if their lives could be joined as easily. "I will always be faithful and I expect the same from you but..."

"But?" His gaze pierced her as if he could see clear to her soul...and perhaps found her lacking.

She took a deep breath. "I don't want us to become intimate right away. I want to get to know you." There, she'd said it.

"What?" He abruptly released her hand and halted the team. Setting the brake, he turned to her. "Explain yourself."

"Please, Duncan, don't be angry. Hear me out," she rushed on; afraid if she didn't she wouldn't be able to say the words. "Dad wants us to get married right away. You heard him. He's planning the wedding for a month from now. All I'm asking is that we know more about each other first. We'll still get married, we just won't do...that...for a while. Not long, a couple of months, maybe." There she'd said it. She waited for the fireworks to begin.

"No."

"No? Is that all you can say?" She was disappointed and started to climb down off the buckboard, intending to ride Wildfire the rest of the way to the camp.

"Wait," he said. She reseated herself. He touched her chin and nudged until she looked at him. "I'll give you the month until the wedding. You can always ask me anything you want and I'll answer you as honestly as I can. We'll spend all our waking hours together, working, talking and getting to know each other. But, Cat, I want children and I want a wedding night. Neither of those can happen if I agree to your plan."

Catherine jerked her chin from his grasp. "I don't have a choice, do I?"

"Cat, I'm not a raging animal. I won't take you against your will. I want you soft and willing. You're a beautiful woman, and I want us to be partners in all things and that includes making love."

She didn't hear anything after the words *beautiful woman*. "You...you think I'm beautiful?" The heat tinged her face and she knew she blushed, but still couldn't fathom that he truly thought her beautiful.

Duncan chuckled, the sound a bit rusty. "Yes. You've grown into a very beautiful woman. You're definitely not the same gangly, awkward girl who used to follow me around."

"I wasn't gangly and awkward when you left. I'd already changed a lot by then or have you forgotten?" she challenged.

"I haven't forgotten," he said quietly. "It's why I left. I wanted to marry you, but you were too young. What was I supposed to do? James trusted me, dammit."

"What about me? I trusted you. A few kisses, then you were gone without even a goodbye. You never wrote to me even though I sent letters with Dad. You never explained why you left, or even if you were coming back. I was fifteen, what did you expect from me?" Her voice broke on a sob.

Duncan hauled her into his arms. "Ah Cat. Is that what this is all about? Are you trying to get even for me leaving? Or are you afraid I'll leave again?" She nodded against his chest. He held her tighter not knowing how to reassure her. "I won't leave. I was young then, too. I'm not that same untried boy now. I want to put that life behind me. Look at me, Cat." He waited until she raised her tear-streaked face to his. "I won't leave. I promise."

She pulled away from him and wiped her face with the back of her hand. "I'll believe it when I see it. Don't ask me to trust you, Duncan. Not yet, maybe not ever." She jumped off the wagon. "I'm riding the rest of the way. See you in an hour."

He felt as if she'd slapped him and she couldn't be clearer. Not that he blamed her, he didn't. He knew he wasn't fit to shine her boots. She was goodness and light in his dark, somber existence. He thanked his lucky stars that James still wanted him as a son-in-law and didn't throw him off the ranch instead. He'd left before because he couldn't...wouldn't take James' trust and throw it back in his face.

Now he'd have to earn her trust all over again. It looked like he had his work cut out for him.

*****

Duncan got to the camp late in the afternoon, as the sun prepared to descend. Catherine was there, searching through the debris left by the stampede. The cowboys had moved on with the herd. They'd catch up to them tomorrow. But tonight, this would be their camp. It was doubtful that Walker and his crew would strike twice in the same place.

Duncan watched her every movement. She'd changed into a soft, light buckskin shirt, the perfect match to her pants; pants that accented her long, strong, well-shaped legs. It still got cold at night and the buckskin would be warmer. He wished he'd brought his. She wasn't wearing her boots, but knee-high moccasins. They resembled the ones he himself owned. They were much more comfortable than boots after a long day.

The fringed buckskin jacket she put on when the sun went down hit just below her buttocks. The jacket opened in the front, allowing him to admire the snug fit of her shirt. It was taut over her lush, full breasts. There was nothing petite about her.

"Find anything useful?" he called, bringing the wagon to a stop.

"Not much. The boys must have gotten by on hardtack and water last night. It's too late to go any farther today. There's a basket of cold chicken and biscuits in the wagon for dinner. I'll get some wood and start a fire, if you'll unhitch and rub down the team."

"Sounds good to me." Duncan hoped her businesslike demeanor meant she had put her other worries behind her. They would be married, would be husband and wife...completely...or his name wasn't Duncan McKenzie.

Their camp had been used many times before. The ring of rocks used for the campfire was black with soot. On two sides of the ring were large fallen logs, used as seats. The other two sides were left open, so if it was cold, you could sleep next to the fire.f

He sat next to Catherine on one of the logs and took a bite of what was probably the best fried chicken he'd ever had and washed it down with a swig of coffee. "My business is here. I'm staying."

"Yeah, you say that now. But I know you, or at least your type. There's always something calling from just over the next hill, the next horizon. I have a hard time believing you'll give that up. Not when you gave..." She stopped and shook her head. "Never mind."

Duncan nearly choked on his coffee. "No, go on. You were going to say when I gave you up, weren't you?"

"It doesn't matter. Our lives took different paths."

"And now they've crossed again. We have a second chance, Cat."

"Look, I didn't get where I am by believing in happily ever after. I got here with hard work. You think it's easy being a woman in this country; doing a man's job? Well, it's not." Catherine put her plate aside and leaned forward, resting her elbows on her knees and warmed her hands in the warmth of the fire. "Everyone is just waiting for me to make a mistake; waiting for me to mess up, so they can say 'I knew she couldn't handle it.'"

He'd wondered what else had her so jaded. He knew it couldn't only be him. He had no idea she felt so strongly. "I get your point. Life hasn't been easy for you. I never said it was. Life isn't easy for anyone out here, man or woman. You chose a path that's even harder. I get that."

"Dad's the only one who's ever believed in me. He's given me a life I could only have dreamed of. Easy? No, it hasn't been easy. But it's been worth it. I'm proud of who and what I am. Dad's proud of me, and that's why this business with John Morgan is so frustrating."

"Tell me." Leaning forward, he put his hand on her leg. "Why's this so important, other than the obvious?"

"I told you I don't know. There's more to it than John just wanting the ranch or to marry me. There's something else at stake here."

He didn't remove his hand from her leg, liking the feel of it there. She was strong, yes, but she still needed his help, though she wouldn't admit it. There was something about Cat that made him feel possessive. Touching her reminded him of why he left in the first place. But he wasn't that randy, young boy anymore. "We'll get to the bottom of this."

"I hope so. I want all this to be over and done. The sooner the better."

Catherine looked into Duncan's eyes. He really meant what he said, but she'd learned long ago not to trust anyone but herself. Even her father, good man that he was, couldn't help her become what she wanted to be.

And what exactly was that? You've got everything you ever wanted, don't you?

No. It was the honest answer. Being a woman in a man's world didn't give her the joy she always thought it would. She wanted more. She wanted it all; a family of her own, children, and a husband she loved. One who loved her as much as she did him. That was the crux of the problem with Duncan. She could have the family, the children, but if he didn't love her, there was no point. It was a hollow dream.

Catherine had melted the moment Duncan looked in her eyes and touched her shoulder after helping Zeke. She'd had beaus over the years, even some that had made her feel——special. None of them had ever made her melt, though. Only Duncan could do that. She was in big trouble.

"Are you so anxious to be rid of me, Kitten?" His voice was deep and husky, so soft, it seemed to caress her very being.

Stay here? Settle down in her valley? Be a real husband and father? For a moment her heart jumped at the thought. She mentally shook herself. There was no need to be thinking that way. After all, he was a gunslinger, gambler, bounty hunter, and who knows what else? But he sure as hell wasn't a rancher. He'd never be happy settling down on a ranch, like a normal man. After the exciting life he led, it would be too dull.

"No. I'm not. I think you're doing this for Dad, that's all." She got up, took her plate and coffee and moved away from him, to the other side of the fire. It was too tempting to look into those beautiful blue eyes; too easy to get lost in them.

She sipped the now-warm coffee and picked at her chicken. "Why do you call me Kitten?"

He chuckled. "Your father always called you that when you were little. He still does. But I think you've got the beautiful gray eyes of a cat, not a kitten." He moved to sit next to her. "Why didn't you marry

40

Morgan? You could've avoided this mess. It would've been a lot easier."

Stunned, she looked at him. "I couldn't."

"Why?" he persisted. "Lots of women marry for worse reasons."

Gazing at the fire, her answer was barely a whisper. "I don't love him. He's not the one."

"Do you know who is?" His voice, barely a whisper, caressed her like a lover's hand, made her long to meet those smooth lips with her own.

She didn't answer. Raising her gaze to his, dark sooty lashes framed deep blue eyes twinkling in the firelight, she wondered. *Did he know? Was she that obvious?*

A half-smile lit his face just enough for her to see the dimple in his right cheek. "Do you know your eyes flash silver when you're angry and sparkle when you laugh?" He became serious. "You don't laugh enough."

She shivered, though she wasn't cold. "There's not much to laugh about these days. Not since Morgan started his little war."

"Well, in that case, I want this little war, as you call it, over. You see, Cat--" he placed his fingers under her chin, gently lifting it until she looked into his eyes; "I like to hear you laugh and see those beautiful gray eyes sparkle."

He slowly lowered his head to hers until their lips met ever so gently. When she didn't pull away, he increased the pressure slightly and caressed the side of her mouth with his thumb. "Open for me, my little Cat, let me taste your sweetness," he murmured.

Giddy and a little afraid, she didn't want to stop; she wanted to explore this pleasure. Other boys and men had kissed her but usually all she felt was a pleasant pressure at best. As a girl, Duncan's kisses had thrilled her. But this kiss was a whole different kind of feeling. It reached clear down to her toes.

Tentatively she put her hands on his shoulders and then full around his neck, bringing him closer. She opened her mouth at his gentle prodding. Duncan's tongue plunged in, tasting of warm coffee and sweet honey. He feasted on her and she let him.

"So sweet," he murmured into her mouth as he wrapped an arm around her waist, bringing her up solid against his chest.

She liked these new feelings, but they frightened her. Even though it was years ago, she still remembered his leaving. He'd abandoned her then. She wasn't going to give him the chance to do it again.

Like she'd been doused with a bucket of cold water, her sanity returned and she pushed him away. "We...we better get some sleep. The men will be here in the morning, and we'll have our work cut out for us finding the cattle." She stood, walked away from him, and laid down on her bedroll, on the other side of the fire, turning over away from the flames, away from temptation…from him.

Sleep would be a long time coming.

*****

She and Duncan had a lot of work to do. Five men from the ranch showed up the next morning. Even with their help it would take at least a week to locate the herd. The cattle had scattered when they hit the trees and gone in all directions.

True to his word, he answered every question she had. He told her about his life since he'd left; about the easy bounties and the hard ones; the near misses and the ones that still tortured him. Little by little, they got reacquainted. They didn't indulge in any further kissing, which Catherine regretted mightily. Though they were friendly, she was careful not to put too much stock into his staying. She'd just enjoy their time together for now.

Surprised at how quickly he remembered the ranch work, she noticed he knew what needed to be done, even before she said it. It bothered her that the men looked to him for guidance and orders. She couldn't berate them for it; they were just doing what came naturally. Still, it was hard to tolerate.

The days wore on and the men continued to defer to Duncan and not her. She heard Joshua, the camp cook, ask Duncan if they were about done rounding up the herd, or if he should go get more supplies.

Duncan.

Not her. That was the last straw.

She was the trail boss, not Duncan. Well, if he wanted her job, he could have it. She was tired of the quick baths every morning and night in the river. She wanted to wash all over and relax. There were enough men to look for the remaining cattle, and they didn't need her--they had Duncan. Digging her heels into

Wildfire's flanks, she took off.

Duncan watched as Catherine lit out, riding like the wind, while Joshua continued his tale of old times in the valley.

"I tell you, son, them were some wild times. White Buffalo was a young man and had just become the chief. He was a little wild, don't you know, but he was never a bad man. He just liked to stir up the settlers a little.

"He'd go around to some of the homesteads and pop up at the window while some poor woman was in her kitchen, scaring the hell out of her. Then he'd make her cook food for him. Of course, she would 'cause she was scared out of her mind. But he'd never hurt her." Joshua cackled with glee at the memory. "He'd eat what she fixed and leave, laughing all the way back to his camp. It's a wonder he didn't get shot.

"After doing that a few times, though, folks here around got wise to him, and the women would already have food fixed and ready when he showed up. He said it took all the fun right out of it." He slapped Duncan on the back and laughed.

"Excuse me, Joshua. Catherine just left. I better follow her."

He started to turn away, but Joshua stopped him. "No point, son. She looks madder than a wet hornet, and if I were you, I'd let her be."

"Why would she be mad? We've found most of the cattle, the ones still missing have been replaced, and the drovers are leaving for Durango with the herd tomorrow."

"Did you tell her that?" Joshua glanced down at his boots before he spit his tobacco juice away from them.

Duncan took off his hat and scratched his head. "Well, no. What difference would that make?"

"Well, I've been watching Miss Catherine, and I don't think it sits too well, all the boys cozyin' up to you for their orders and all. She's been boss around here for going on five years. Must eat at her craw, all those years for nothin'. The first man that shows up and takes an interest, and all her hard work is down the drain." He spit again. "So to speak."

"But I never meant—"

"Don't matter what you meant. It matters what she saw."

"Where's she going?"

"Probably up to the springs. It's her special place."

"I don't like the idea of her going off alone. Tell me how to get there?"

"Can't do that."

"Why not? I won't bring her back here kicking and screaming, you know." Duncan was trying very hard to keep from strangling the old man, but with every word out of his mouth, it was becoming more difficult.

"Don't know where they are."

"Who does?"

"No one here abouts. Only she and Gray Wolf know where them springs are. Found 'em when they was kids and never told another soul."

"Well, crap." Duncan slammed his hat on and went to get Jake.

"She'll be all right, son. Why she's probably safer than you are. Ain't no one can track her when she don't want to be found." Joshua called out to him as he mounted Jake, and headed in the direction Catherine took.

"We'll see about that."

*****

Hours later, Duncan returned to camp.

Without Catherine.

He'd lost her in the rocky area at the bottom of the bluff.

"Didn't find her, did ya?" Joshua said.

Duncan shook his head and Joshua handed him a plate of the savory beef stew he'd cooked for dinner. "She'll be back tonight. I sent word to Gray Wolf to go get her. He's the only one who can."

"How could you send word to him? You don't even know where he is. Do you?" He stared hard at the old man.

"Don't have to know. I got my ways of contacting him or his father, White Buffalo." The old man gave Duncan a look of pure satisfaction.

"What? Smoke signals?"

"I'm just funnin' you, son." Joshua cackled in that irritating way he had. "Gray Wolf came by while you were gone. Told him he needed to bring her back."

He handed Duncan a cup of coffee and fresh baked sourdough bread to go with the stew. "Why don't you eat your supper before it gets cold? The boys already ate and are beddin' the herd down for the night. Tomorrow's going to be a mighty rough day for you."

"No worse than today."

"I wouldn't put money on that, young fella." Joshua replied with a snort.

"I won't." Duncan shoved a bite of the stew in his mouth. "Hey, this is good," he said around his food.

"Ain't nobody cooks as good as me on the trail," Joshua answered with pride. "'Course I don't hold a candle to Alice. That woman can make biscuits so good, they don't need no butter to melt in your mouth."

Duncan nodded his head in agreement, remembering the cold biscuits his first night out here with Catherine. Where was she?

It was his last thought. The supply wagon where Catherine usually slept erupted in flame. All hell broke loose.

*****

The hot springs were about an hour's ride southwest into the hills—the little glen well hidden. A deep, blue pool edged up to the soft grassy shore on one side, enormous boulders on two sides, and a high cliff on the last. Several smaller pools were downstream and each a little cooler the farther away they got. This pool was the largest, deepest and hottest. It was the one she loved best.

"This is what I needed," Catherine said, sliding off Wildfire's back. It was mid-afternoon and still warm, so she took off his saddle, bridle, and blanket, letting him wander free. She didn't hobble him, Wildfire always stayed within whistling distance.

"It's beautiful, isn't it, boy?" She patted Wildfire and brushed him down with some sweet grass.

Not able to stand it a moment longer, she shucked off her boots and the rest of her clothes in record time. Grabbing the soap she always kept in her saddlebag, she ran to the pool and dove in. She scrubbed the dust, dirt, and sweat from her body and her hair. The lavender scented soap bubbles floated gently toward the stream, flowing to the lower pools.

Throwing the soap back to the grassy shore, she floated on her back then dove under. She felt like a mermaid in an enchanted sea. Her troubles slowly left her body, leaving her with a deep feeling of peace and contentment.

She surfaced with a shout, "Yes! God, I love this place."

"If you keep shouting like that, everyone in the mountains will know where you are." A familiar, masculine voice sounded from the high rocks behind her.

"Gray Wolf." She turned and smiled at her

friend, secure in the fact that her hair floated about her like a cloak. "I didn't expect you to be here. You should be with Laughing Waters; you are still newly married."

"Autumn Sun, you know we do not have 'honeymoon' as your people do. We are married, but I still must hunt, and Laughing Waters must prepare the meat for winter. Much is happening in our mountains." He squatted down on the rock, but did not come closer. It was their unspoken agreement that they would not bathe together, and had been since they'd found the springs.

"There's a lot happening in the valley, too. But I'm sure you already know that."

"We know. Found some J Bar C cattle wandering close to our camp. We had great feasts." Gray Wolf smiled and rubbed his belly. He knew she and her father didn't mind his people taking a few beef now and then.

"Thought you might, after Walker stampeded them. We found most of them." She splashed the water in front of her, muttering, "I guess. How would I know? Does anybody tell me anything? No."

"Stop talking to yourself and get dressed. I will meet you by Wildfire." He stood and disappeared from view. She swam back to the shore and dried off with the small towel from her saddlebags. She'd dressed and was untangling her hair when Gray Wolf rode up.

"Took you long enough." She spoke to him without looking.

"There is only one way in on horseback, as you know."

She grinned at him. "Yes, that's the beauty of this place. You never hunt around here, so what brings you?" Braiding her hair into its usual single, long plait, she waited while he sat next to her.

"You."

"Me? I didn't even know I was coming myself until a few hours ago."

"Your camp is in trouble. The 'big' man worried about you. Joshua sent me to get you."

"Joshua knows I'm fine. The big man is Duncan McKenzie."

"McKenzie? Old friend McKenzie?"

"Yes. One and the same."

"You should go back now. Walker has many men watching your herd. He's going to cause more trouble very soon. He's sending a message to McKenzie."

Catherine scrambled to her feet, whistling for Wildfire. "No! Dang it, we don't need any more of this…" She bit her tongue. As she saddled her horse she said, "He's not sending Duncan a message. He's sending us, Dad and me, a message."

Gray Wolf shook his head. "No. He sends message to McKenzie. No mistake. Walker talks in his sleep." Gray Wolf winked at her. "He says much in his sleep with Otter Woman. The message is definitely for McKenzie."

"I don't have time to argue. I've got to go."

Wildfire pranced as if sensing the urgency in his mistress.

"I am not arguing." Gray Wolf swung up on his paint's back. "You are. But I will go with you anyway."

"Suit yourself."

*****

Catherine and Gray Wolf galloped into camp just as the wagon's last flames were being extinguished. The Rio Grande was close enough they'd been able to put the fire out with a bucket brigade. They were lucky. Had they been further along the trail with no water source close, they'd have had no choice but to let it burn itself out. Another wagon lost. Damn!

She jumped off Wildfire and was immediately grabbed by the arm and whipped around.

"Where the hell have you been?" Duncan shouted.

"What? You would prefer I was here? In that bed? Is that what you wanted?" she snapped, pulling at her arm.

"No, but you could've been." He didn't release her arm but tried to draw her closer.

"Well, I wasn't."

"Who would've known? You didn't tell me where you were going."

"Oh, that's right. Since you're the trail boss, I should have checked with you." She cocked her head, "What? You're not?" Up until then she'd kept her

51

temper, "Damn straight you're not!" She let loose her anger, wrenching her arm from his grasp, and shouted back at him, "And you aren't my keeper. I'll go anywhere I please, whenever I please."

He moved closer, forcing her to look up at him, his voice low and menacing. "No you won't. Not as long as I'm around."

She stood her ground, refusing to be intimidated by him. "Yes, I will."

The two of them stood toe to toe, each refusing to give an inch, until Gray Wolf spoke.

"Autumn Sun?"

"What?"

"Did you ask him if he got the message that Walker sent?"

"Who's had a chance?" she said, crossing her arms over her chest.

Duncan's head snapped toward Gray Wolf. "What message?"

Gray Wolf stood apart from the two combatants, next to his horse. "Walker sent you this message." He nodded at the burned remains of the wagon. "No one you care for is safe."

Duncan frowned, but said nothing.

Gray Wolf continued, "You know he wants you. Autumn Sun is also his target. You know the reason for this, do you not?"

Duncan turned and walked away from them.

"Don't you walk away from me," Catherine yelled, running to catch him. "Duncan, what's going on? Why does Walker want you dead?"

CHAPTER 4

Duncan rode hard not slowing until the terrain forced him to. Jake could handle the pace—that wasn't a problem. He was from racing stock, with a deep chest and long legs. But, Duncan didn't want to risk him breaking a leg in the dark.

Stopping in a small grove of aspen, he slipped from the saddle, leaving Jake to graze, and plopped down at the base of a tree. What was he going to do now?

Walker was here for him and would do anything, even use Catherine to get to him. There had to be a way to keep her safe and dispose of Walker at the same time.

Leaving wasn't an option; he promised Catherine he wouldn't leave. Besides, Walker would use it as an excuse to try and kill James or Catherine. He wasn't a coward, he wasn't afraid for himself, but for them.

That Walker hadn't tried harder to kill James surprised him. Duncan had saved James by killing Walker's father, though the father wouldn't have survived regardless of what Duncan had done. Walker had to know this, if he knew that Duncan delivered the final blow. But none of that mattered. Roy blamed Duncan.

Duncan heard the crack of twigs long before he heard the horse and rider stop.

Catherine slid from Wildfire and looked toward an empty saddled Jake. "Duncan? Where are you?"

Blending into the shadows was his specialty; it was why he usually wore black. But he was changing his ways, at least he was trying to. He shot to his feet, coming up silently behind her.

"What are you doing here? Do you have any idea the danger you're in?" he whispered in her ear just before he grabbed her shoulders and spun her around.

"Do you?" she replied.

Hearing the click of a hammer sliding into place, he looked down at her Colt pointed straight at his belly. When had she pulled her gun and why hadn't he known it? He was losing it. Maybe James was right...it was time to retire.

Catherine uncocked and holstered her weapon. "Care to explain?"

"There's nothing to explain." He walked back to his place at the base of the tree and sat.

She followed him. "Nothing to explain?"

"That's right." He got up and whistled for Jake.

"You just ride out in the middle of a conversation—"

"It's a free country, remember?" He mounted his horse and then turned to her. "Coming?"

"I'm not going to let this drop, Duncan. We have to talk." Mounting Wildfire, she added, "There's a lot you aren't saying."

"Nothing that concerns you."

"First, you said you would answer any questions I had. Second, everything on this ranch concerns me. Get used to it." Catherine took off, Wildfire knowing the way, leaving Duncan to follow, alone with his thoughts.

As they returned to camp, he realized she still meant more to him than he wanted to admit. He'd watched her, riding the herd, commanding the men, working alongside him from sunup to sundown.

She had gumption and drive, like he'd never seen in a woman before. She always considered what was good for the ranch before making a decision, but never put that consideration over what was good for her men. She didn't ask any of the men to do something she wouldn't do herself; was fair in the extreme and her men respected her. He respected her, but he wanted her more.

That scared the hell out of him.

He'd been betrayed and hadn't trusted a woman since. He couldn't trust women and yet, a man needed to be able to trust his wife. He'd never have a wife…or so he thought.

Catherine was proving him wrong. She was honorable and dependable...trustworthy. When he thought of her, his mind just naturally went on to things like a home and children. She'd turned into a beauty. Her man's clothes certainly didn't hide that fact. But, Lord, she was his best friend's daughter, and he was going to marry her.

But what was marriage without trust? The thing was, Catherine was worthy of trust. It was himself he didn't trust.

Marriage, ha! If it was up to her, they'd have a business arrangement. She was everything he didn't like in a woman. Independent, opinionated, a damned hellcat. She was...his.

What was he thinking? He shook his head. What the hell was the matter with him?

Catherine.

He'd already begun to think of her as his wife.

*****

Catherine sent the herd on its way to Durango with extra men to protect it. That left the ranch short handed, meaning she had to take up the slack.

She worried about Duncan and his connection to Walker, but had little time to dwell on it. There was something there, but try as she might, she couldn't figure it out, and Duncan refused to discuss anything with her.

He'd made sure to keep his distance since the night of the last wagon incident, only talking to her when necessary and making sure they were never alone together. Every time she'd start toward him, he'd suddenly remember something that couldn't wait. The other thing that had changed was his relationship toward the men. If they asked him what to do, he'd tell them to ask her. She didn't know what had happened, but this new attitude was almost more irritating than the other. He was appeasing her, having the men go to her; she knew it but she didn't know why.

This day seemed especially long. After an entire day of branding, she stunk of sweat, smoke, and leather. She needed a long, hot bath, and intended to do just that when she got home.

Alice was on the porch waiting for her.

"Where's Dad?" she called as she passed on her way to the barn.

"He's inside, and let me tell you, there has been no living with the man. You better get in there now."

Catherine stopped, pulled back up to the porch and slid from Wildfire. "What's happened?" Taking the steps two at a time, Catherine ran into the house with Alice following in her wake.

"Something about a letter he received. He's been ranting since he opened it. Duncan's with him now."

She stopped short. "Duncan's here already? He was supposed to be—"

Alice halted in front of the door to James' study. "Your father sent Joshua to get Duncan as soon as he finished the letter."

She started to ask why, but Alice opened the door, shooing her inside. "You better get in there. Like I said, your daddy didn't like it at all. Tell them I'll have dinner ready in an hour and can serve it in here if they want."

Dinner in the study? Catherine stared after Alice's retreating form. They'd never had dinner in the study. It was James' one tradition from their Philadelphia days. They always dressed for dinner, even if that didn't necessarily mean she wore a dress, and even if it was in the kitchen not the dining room.

James called to her. "Catherine, come in. We've got new problems."

"New? Don't we have enough old problems?" She flopped on to the big overstuffed davenport and stretched her legs. "Ahhh, that feels good."

There were two dark brown leather wing chairs in front of the large mahogany desk. Duncan sat in one. He turned to face her, his arms resting on the arms of the chair with his hands clasped over his belly. "This isn't funny. You could lose the ranch after all."

She shot to her feet and charged across the room. "Lose the ranch?"

"Thought that might get your attention."

"Look, I've spent all day in the saddle or burning the flesh of calves." She stood over Duncan, forcing him to look up at her. "Forgive me for trying to get a little break. When I get home, I don't even get a chance to catch my breath before I'm summoned because of another crisis."

"Stop it, both of you." Her father rose, walked around the desk and sat on a corner. "This is serious."

Chastised, Catherine sank into the chair next to Duncan. "Sorry, Dad. Duncan," she nodded in her father's direction. "Tell me what's happened."

James reached over, grabbed the letter from the top of his desk and handed it to her. "It's from Sam down at the courthouse. There's been a deed come through for part of our ranch. Says it's from Roy Walker to Tom and Beth Peterson."

Startled, she repeated, "Roy Walker!"

James continued. "Yes, Walker. It's not legal, but that's not going to mean a thing if we get a lot of settlers down here thinking they own part of our property. We'll end up in a real range war."

"But what can we do? We can't stop people from coming if they think they own the land. Walker must need money. Why else would he risk selling property he doesn't own?"

"I don't know," Duncan said. "This is something new. I've never heard of Walker being a swindler, but then, I don't know everything about him."

Catherine leaned toward him. His heat assailed her and goose bumps rose on her arms. "What exactly do you know about Walker?"

Duncan closed the gap between them and whispered, "Nothing I know about him is going to help us now. Leave it alone."

"Let me be the judge of that," she spat back, more angry with herself than him. She hated how his nearness sent every logical thought careening out of her head.

"What are you two whispering about? Speak up!" James walked back to his chair behind the desk.

"Nothing important, Dad." She sat back in the chair, as far away from Duncan as she could get. But it was still too close to him for her comfort. All of her nerves tingled. She rose and paced the room, hoping it would help her feel normal again. Besides, she always thought best on her feet. "So, what do you want to do about this?"

"I don't know. Sam says I don't need to worry because it's not legal, but I wonder how many of these things Walker has sold. This could cause us real problems."

"I think we're overreacting." Duncan stayed in his chair and looked relaxed.

How can he relax? Doesn't he understand?

"These could be the only people he sold to. Maybe Catherine's correct and he needed some quick money. In my opinion, that's what we should be worried about. What does Walker need five thousand dollars for?"

"Five thousand dollars! How much of the ranch did he sell?"

"Three thousand acres," Duncan and James answered at the same time.

"Oh my God! Where? What part of the ranch?"

"Smack dab in the center," James went to the map covering the wall behind his desk. "See here," with his finger he traced a triangular section, "from Bristol Head Mountain, northeast to Shallow Creek, southeast to the Rio Grande and west back to Bristol Head."

"Well, at least it's not prime grazing land," Catherine noted. "That property is practically worthless, except for the timber, and it's too steep to cut much of that."

Duncan rose from the chair with the grace of a mountain lion. "You're missing the point. Walker's selling property based on landmarks he knows from his short time here. It doesn't matter to him what the property is suited for, and he's not selling it local. It's just a fluke we even found out about it."

Duncan paced the room with her. She could feel the power radiating from his every pore. It nearly overwhelmed her. If they kept pacing like this, her father's rug would have holes in it.

"Why can't we just write these..." she searched the letter in her hand, "Petersons, and tell them they don't own anything?"

"If you read a little further," her father nodded at her hand, "you'll see that Sam says they included a letter of their own with the deed, saying they were coming down from Denver right away. They could already be in Creede, for all we know."

"We can try. The stage for Del Norte leaves at dawn, and I'm going to make sure our letter is in the mailbag for Denver."

Duncan stopped pacing and turned to her. "I'll take it."

"No need. I'm going to town anyway. I have to get Zeke those boots I promised him. I'll write it while I'm at Mrs. Peabody's tonight."

"You can't go to town alone," he insisted.

"Why not? I do it all the time. Unless there's

some reason you haven't told me about, I don't see why I shouldn't go."

"Catherine," her father said, "listen to Duncan. I don't want you out riding by yourself. It's too late. It's too late. You won't get there before dark. A lot could happen between here and there."

"Dad, I've done it hundreds of times. It'll only take a little more than an hour to get there if I canter fairly often, long before dark sets in. Besides, Wildfire knows the way, even in the dark."

"I don't know..." Her father glanced at Duncan, as if he was hoping for assistance.

"Dad, I'm going. Nothing, and no one, is going to stop me from doing my job protecting this ranch." She started for the door, all thoughts of a relaxing bath forgotten. The ranch was in danger. Nothing else was more important than the ranch. It was everything.

"You're not going anywhere." Duncan blocked her way. "Riding out by yourself is just foolhardy enough to give me gray hair."

"What do you think she's been doing to me for years?" James asked.

"Get out of my way."

"You can't go by yourself,"

"Hide and watch," she said, skirting him and striding out the door. She didn't wait to see if he followed, but went to the kitchen. "Alice, I'm going to town, and the way I'm feeling right now, I may be there for a couple days."

Catherine didn't stop or give Alice any opening to ask questions. She walked straight outside, jumped on Wildfire and took off.

James watched his daughter leave from the window of the study. He knew her ire was up. She always rode like the devil when she was mad. He wondered if Duncan saw her leave, then saw the young man running for the barn and knew he had. They'll be fine, he reassured himself, heading to the kitchen.

James found Alice rolling out dough for biscuits.

"What's for dinner? There'll be just you and me."

"I figured as much," Alice answered. "Catherine came through before she lit out."

"Did she say anything in particular?"

"Just that she may be gone a couple of days. I don't think she was too happy when she left."

Hearing hoof-beats, he watched Duncan race out of the barn hot on Catherine's heels. James chuckled. "I know. Duncan's trying to tell her what to do. He doesn't realize yet that you can't deal with Catherine that way."

*****

Catherine was angry at Duncan...at her father...at life. But that was no excuse to take it out on poor Wildfire who she'd run at full gallop for more than a mile. She slowed the stallion to a walk, and as he cooled off, so did her temper.

Why did she let Duncan affect her? She knew

better than to let her anger get the best of her. She worked very hard to keep her temper under control, but whenever he was around, she went off like a firecracker.

She pulled Wildfire up in front of Peabody's Boardinghouse, tied him to the hitching rail, suddenly remembering the first time she'd seen this boardinghouse and Mary Peabody, the owner. She, her father, and Duncan came to Creede. They didn't know anyone and needed a place to stay, while James saw a man about property. Mary was a small, round woman with perfectly white hair and the friendliest face Catherine had seen in months. She'd bustled with energy then, and fifteen years later, she still did.

They'd stayed at the boardinghouse until their house was built. Not the big house they had now, but the small one they called the South Ranch. Duncan had left not long after the big house was finished.

Catherine smiled when she saw Mary sitting at the dining room table working on her ledgers. She looked up when Catherine came in the room and hurried around the table to greet her.

"Why, Catherine Evans. What in the world are you doing in town in the middle of the week?" She enveloped her in a big hug.

Catherine hugged the small woman back. "Hello, Mary. How are you?"

"I'm fine as frog's hair. Even finer, now that I see you here. But what are you doing in town? You never come in except on Sundays."

"I have to put a letter on the stage tomorrow and need a room for the night. You have any available? I may stay for a few days."

Before Mary could answer, the front door of the boardinghouse slammed open, hitting the wall, making them both jump. Duncan stood there, hat in hand, his blue eyes black with anger.

"Make that two rooms, Mrs. Peabody," said Duncan.

"Duncan!" Catherine exclaimed before regaining her composure.

Mary extended her hand to the man looming in her doorway, sure her eyes were deceiving her. "Duncan...?"

"McKenzie, ma'am. Duncan McKenzie." He took her tiny hand in his big one, shaking it.

"I thought so. It's been a long time." She retrieved her hand, eyeing him suspiciously. "I still run a respectable place, so if you want to stay here, you better slow that anger of yours to a walk, if you get my meaning."

"Yes, ma'am. It's been a real long time, and I do understand your meaning. I apologize for barging in." He lifted one dark brow at Catherine, who had the good grace to blush. "It seems Catherine wanted to come to town and was too anxious to wait until I could accompany her. I assure you," he walked over to Catherine, resting his hand possessively at the small of her back, "neither of us will cause you any trouble."

"Call me Mary, you're fully grown now and we're friends. Remember?"

Duncan nodded. "I do. And I promise we'll be a lot less trouble now than we were all those years ago."

Mary looked up at Catherine, ready to throw Duncan out if she saw the least little bit of fear in her eyes. Mary Peabody may be small, but she didn't take any guff off anybody. "Catherine, do you agree? You two won't do no fighting while you're under my roof?"

Catherine glanced at Mary, then at the devil that had chased her from her home. He'd calmed down. His eyes were no longer angry-black, but turned to a beautiful dark blue. They even twinkled a bit. That made Catherine wary, but she nodded her head. "I agree. We won't fight or cause trouble while we're here. But I want our rooms as far apart as possible."

Duncan shook his head at the older woman. "I need to assure Catherine's safety, even if she doesn't want me to. If you have adjoining rooms, it would be best." He winked at Mary, then smiled at Catherine.

Mary wasn't going to get into the middle of whatever was going on between these two young people. Though she loved Catherine dearly, she felt it was high time the girl had a sterner hand in her life, someone to keep up with her and keep her out of trouble. From what she remembered, and what she'd seen so far, Duncan McKenzie was the man to do just that.

She looked again at him. A handsome man, strong and sure of himself, he reminded her of her beloved Mr. Peabody, God rest his soul. When he looked at Catherine, his expression showed exasperation more than anger, as if he was dealing with a willful child. Mary smiled. She remembered looking at Catherine with the same exasperation herself a time or two.

Catherine, though, was still very angry. If looks could kill, Duncan would surely be dead. But she said nothing, just looked at him. That was all Mary needed to see. Her decision made, she handed Duncan the keys to both rooms.

"Here you go, Duncan. Top of the stairs, last two doors at the end of the hall. You two go on up and, remember, dinner's in one hour, six sharp. See you then." Dismissing them, she went back to working on her books.

Duncan took Catherine by the elbow and walked up the stairs.

She hissed at him, "You may think you've won, Duncan McKenzie, but let me tell you this has just begun. I won't be dictated to or dominated by you or anyone else. Do you understand me? I won't be treated as less than a man just because I'm a woman. You're not going to walk all over me."

They reached the door to the first room. Duncan unlocked and opened the door, gently shoved her inside and locked it behind him. He casually stood leaning up against the doorjamb with his arms crossed over his chest, waiting for her to finish.

Catherine started pacing the room as soon as he pushed her in. "Don't push me. You're treating me like a child. I'm an adult and I expect to be treated like one."

He sighed and shoved away from the door. "Are you quite through?"

She nodded.

"Then I have a few things I'd like to say. First, I don't want to walk all over you. I don't want you to do anything you don't like. You say I treat you like a child...well, you act like a spoiled brat. I swear James should have taken you over his knee a long time ago and I warn you, you are this close," he held his thumb and forefinger an inch apart in front of her face, "to having me put you over my knee right now."

Catherine looked squarely at him, chin held high. "You wouldn't dare lay a hand on me. Dad would have you drawn and quartered."

Duncan smiled. "Wouldn't dare, huh? I'll show you just how much I dare." He walked slowly toward her.

Catherine backed up until the back of her knees touched the side of the bed. With nowhere to go, she rolled over the bed to the other side and put the bed between them.

It was a mistake.

Fast as a panther, Duncan followed her over the bed and cornered her between it and the wall. Placing one hand on the wall on either side of her head, he had her effectively trapped.

"Now, you were saying?" His eyes glittered, dark and stormy as he lowered his head to hers. As he touched her lips softly with his own, Catherine froze, locked in the clear reality of everything she'd dreamed of for so many years.

Duncan slanted his mouth over hers once more and traced her lips with his tongue. She gasped, the slight tickling sensation took her by surprise. He took advantage of the opening to slide his tongue into her mouth.

He tasted like mint. His hands moved away from the wall and cupped her face. Gently, his thumbs caressed her cheeks, soothing her. Slowly he pulled away until he looked her in the eye. She didn't know when or how, but her hands had found their way around his neck and tangled in his silky hair.

"See how much I dare?" his voice was rough and husky. He removed her arms from his neck and set them at her side. "You tempt me." He turned toward the door between their rooms.

"What are you talking about? I didn't do anything," she finally sputtered. Her breath and senses were slow to return.

"You're right. There's nothing about you that's the least bit tempting. Why, you're about as tempting to a man as a porcupine, only they're a lot less prickly." He quietly closed the door.

Catherine couldn't have been more surprised by what had just happened or more insulted. "Porcupine! Less prickly!" She raged at the closed door. "Of all the nerve. Not tempting to a man, huh? Well, I'll just give him something to be tempted about."

*****

Duncan threw his hat on top of one of the high knobs on the top the straight-backed chair then flopped on the bed.

What the hell was he thinking, kissing her like that. Her response, hesitant at first, then fully participating, overwhelmed him. Never in his life had any other woman kissed him like that. With such passion, yet not even aware she was doing so.

Only Catherine.

The glazed look in her eyes, her arms around his neck, fingers entwined in his hair, told him all he needed to know. Her rosy mouth still pursed for kisses almost made him do just that.

Again.

But he knew kissing wouldn't be enough, so he'd pulled away. Kissing Catherine would never be enough. Not when he knew the passion that lay dormant inside her, just waiting for release. It was a tangible thing and, Lord, he wanted to unleash her passion. Just the thought made his trousers more uncomfortable.

The door to Catherine's room slammed shut. She was just as passionate in her anger as he knew she would be in her loving. He smiled, grabbed his hat and followed her.

It would be a rocky ride, but he was determined he would tame her wild heart.

CHAPTER 5

Catherine headed directly for the mercantile just down the street. Duncan joined her and walked close by her side. He kept his senses tuned to what was going on around them. He was surprised when Catherine drew his attention to the left, toward the saloon, and asked, "Duncan, did you see that man get on his horse when we came out?"

"Yeah, I saw him. What about it?"

"I think he was watching the boardinghouse. He's one of Morgan's men, Charley Sloan. Do you think he was watching us, hoping to find the ranch unprotected?"

"Maybe, but somehow I don't think it's the ranch he's hoping to find unprotected. We'll have to keep our eyes open."

"What do you mean? That he hoped to find Dad or me alone? So, what if we are?"

She stopped cold, suddenly realizing just how much danger she could be in. "Oh God, how could I be so stupid? If Morgan got to Dad or me, he knows the other will do exactly what he wants. What are we going to do? Dad's not as young as he used to be, and he's alone."

Duncan laughed, but there was no humor in it. "James is hardly alone. There are more people on that ranch than here in town. Your father can take care of himself, believe me."

She looked up at him and nodded. "I know you're right. I just wish he wouldn't fret so much about me. I'm not a weak, simpering little female, you know."

Smiling down at her he said, "I know, but let us men worry a little anyway. It makes us feel manly." He put his arm around her shoulders. "Morgan is not interested in your father. He wants you. Whether you believe it or not, he has always wanted you, with the ranch."

They walked together in silence. If Morgan had managed to catch her unaware and taken her, her father would have given up everything. And it would be her fault.

"Let's get Zeke's boots and go home."

"No, we'll get the boots, have supper at Mrs. Peabody's and head back in the morning. It's going to be dark soon, and I don't want to travel at night, not with Morgan's men hanging around."

"But with everything we've just figured out, shouldn't we get back as soon as possible? If we stay here, we could be playing right into Morgan's hand."

"I think that's more likely if we travel at night."

"But—"

"We stay. It's safer."

His voice and the squeeze he gave her brooked no argument. There was no getting around him when he made up his mind. "You're right. We'll stay. The horses need a rest anyway."

The store was large but still crammed to the ceiling with goods. Three rows of freestanding shelves formed aisles from front to back. The shelves on one wall overflowed with cans of food, milk and tobacco.

Barrels full of flour, sugar, dried beans, and peas stood in front of the counter. Jars of stick candy glinted in the fading sunlight, their colorful presence a rainbow on top of it. The freestanding shelves held ready-made pants, shirts, boots, and hats.

In a corner, hidden from the sun during the day, was a table piled high with bolts of material of all kinds, cottons, linens, velvet and even a couple of silk. This was Catherine's favorite table. She may not know how to sew, but she enjoyed the feel of the soft fabric beneath her fingers.

The large items, like wheelbarrows, shovels and plows, took up another wall. Catherine was always amazed that they could cram so much stuff into the relatively small space. The store was filled with everything that a rancher, miner, farmer, or even a lady might need.

The smell of coffee on the stove caught Catherine's attention, making her stomach growl, reminding her she hadn't eaten since breakfast. Their boots sounded loudly on the wooden floor, alerting the owner to their presence, if the bell sounding when they opened the door hadn't.

"Hello, Sadie." Catherine smiled at the woman

behind the counter. "I need a new pair of boots for Zeke."

"You barely caught me. I was just getting ready to close up and go home." Sadie wiped her hands on her dusty apron as she came around the counter and gave Catherine a hug. "Zeke, huh? I heard about his accident. How's he doing?"

Catherine returned the hug. "Healing. Not as fast as he'd like, but in another couple of weeks, he'll be back to making us crazy as usual. I want the best pair of boots you have. He deserves it, and I promised him. And a pair for his little boy, too."

Sadie nodded, her eyes landed on Duncan and she smiled admiringly. "Who's this fine looking gentleman? Aren't you going to introduce us?"

"Oh, Sadie, uh, this is Duncan McKenzie. Duncan left the valley before you and Gordon came to Creede."

Duncan tipped his hat. "Ma'am."

Sadie's eyes widened. "*The* Duncan McKenzie? The one I read about in the Denver Prairie Gazette a few years ago?"

Duncan looked uncomfortable, but nodded. "Yes, ma'am, I suppose so."

That was enough pleasantries for Catherine. "Duncan, why don't you go check out those boots over there and see if there's a pair of size tens for Zeke while I talk to Sadie."

"Sure thing." Relief was written all over his

face. He tipped his hat again and went down the aisle to the boots.

"Sadie," Catherine said quietly.

Sadie stared after Duncan, her tongue practically hanging out of her mouth. It didn't set well with Catherine, watching someone else lust after Duncan.

"Sadie!" she said sharper than she'd meant to.

"Uh, yes. Sorry. That's just one fine looking man, but then you already know that. So what else do you need?"

"I want a dress." Catherine looked over at Duncan, making sure he wasn't listening. "Something pretty. Something like I've never had before."

"You want a dress? But you never wear dresses. What's the occasion?"

Catherine felt herself flush. "Keep your voice down. I don't want the whole world to know. I need to prove to a certain someone that I can be tempting, be a real woman."

"Oh." Sadie nodded, and smiled, clearly pleased to be included in such a secret. "I know just what you mean. Something pretty, but not overtly so, a Sunday-go-to-meeting type of dress. Right?"

"I guess." Catherine shrugged. "You know I don't know much about fashion. I want something I could wear to a party. Maybe our annual barbecue." She kept looking over her shoulder to make sure Duncan wasn't returning. "Something that will knock someone clean off his horse."

Sadie burst out laughing. "Why, Catherine, this is marvelous. Oh, my dear, come with me. I have the perfect dress. I just couldn't resist ordering it, even though Gordon said we would never be able to sell it. Come on. It's in the back room. Mr. McKenzie," she shouted, "if you'll watch the store, I'd be obliged. If anyone comes in and needs help, give me a holler." The shopkeeper pulled on Catherine's arm, hauling her into the back room.

Catherine looked over her shoulder one last time. Duncan watched them go as he made himself comfortable in a chair next to the big pot-bellied stove. He smiled at her and winked, sending shivers up her spine. She ignored the shivers, she stiffened her back, and her resolve as she followed Sadie.

In the back room, the other woman opened the cedar storage closet. "Here is where I keep the better ready-made dresses."

Now it was Catherine's turn to gawk with her mouth open.

Hanging on the back of one of the double doors, all alone, was the most magnificent dress she had ever seen.

Sadie said, "The royal blue will look wonderful with your hair. The high collar and long puffy sleeves, with long satin cuffs will cover all that brown skin you've acquired working in the outdoors. The bodice is satin from the waist to just below the low sweetheart neckline. That will show off your bosom nicely. The soft, sheer lace from the neckline up to the high satin collar keeps it modest. And look at this, seed pearls adorn the bottom of the collar and outline the neckline, then eight larger pearl buttons run up each of the long satin cuffs.

"Oh, Sadie, do you think it will fit me? I am so damn tall." She stared down at her chest in disgust. "And full."

"Don't you worry. The skirt hasn't been hemmed yet so it will be plenty long. And they always make these dresses a couple of sizes bigger than normal, so there is plenty of room for alterations. Here, try it on."

Catherine was out of her buckskins in nothing flat. Sadie helped her put on the dress and buttoned her up. Turning around to the mirror, she gasped. She actually looked like a girl. No, a woman. She twirled. The dress was perfect. It would need a small hem, but no other alterations.

"It's so beautiful, like it was made for me. I'll take it."

"You'll need shoes and undergarments. I'd try to sell you a corset, but seeing you in that dress, I can tell you don't need one. Will Alice be able to hem this for you or do you want me to get it done and have it sent out to the ranch?"

"I'm sure she will. She's real handy with a needle and thread. Help me get out of this, will you? I don't want to ruin it before I get a chance to wear it."

Before she took off the dress, she looked at herself again in the cheval glass Sadie had back there just for the ladies. She cocked her head to the side. "What about something for my head?"

"The picture in the catalogue showed the model

with flowers in her hair. Maybe you can wind some ribbon in your hair."

"Or pearls?" She cocked her head, lifted her braid up and wound it around her head in a makeshift coronet. "Mama had a beautiful strand of pearls. Maybe I could sweep my hair up and pin them in. What do you think?"

"Beautiful," said a deep, familiar voice. She let go of her hair and spun around to find Duncan leaning against the doorjamb, arms crossed over his chest and a devilish smile on his face.

She felt points of color rise on her cheeks. "Thank you. But you should have knocked. I could have been undressed."

"So?"

"So? It's improper..." She looked around for something to throw at his fat head. Damn the man.

Duncan laughed and held his hands up in a gesture of surrender. "Okay, okay, I'm going. Just came to tell Sadie she has customers out front." He beat a hasty retreat, still laughing.

Sadie smiled. "That's a mighty handsome man you got there. Take care you don't lose that one."

Catherine yanked her buckskin pants up over her hips, irritated with Sadie, wishing that Duncan really was her man. "He's an old friend, nothing more." That wasn't true and she knew it. Duncan was so much more. "Well, I guess a little more," she conceded to Sadie.

Lifting her eyebrows, Sadie snorted. "If I wasn't

a married woman, I might make a try for that one myself, seeing as how you're just friends and all."

"You are a married woman, so just forget it," Catherine snapped. "Sorry. I'm a little on edge. Let's get this on my tab."

Sadie chuckled, mumbling under her breath, "On edge? Just friends? I don't think so."

Duncan stood near the door to the back room waiting for Catherine. There was a small blond woman, about twenty or so standing at the counter. Her companion intently examined something on one of the shelves and had his back to him. Duncan figured him to be in his late twenties or early thirties. Catherine rushed out of the back, came to a dead stop and stared at the young woman at the counter.

"Cassie?"

The woman was dressed in a long, black skirt with a bustle and plain white shirtwaist. But it wasn't the clothing that claimed Duncan's attention. She was so pale. Too pale. As she turned and looked up at Catherine, he could see dark purple circles under her eyes.

"Cassie, it is you," Catherine squealed. "How are you? It's been so long. I'm so glad to see you."

The blond woman ran up to Catherine and hugged her like a drowning person holding on to a life boat. "When John suggested a trip to town, I didn't really want to come. But now I'm glad I did."

Catherine stiffened, her voice cold as ice. "John? Is your brother with you?"

"But, of course I am, Catherine." Morgan tipped his hat, stepping out of one of the aisles. "Do you think I would let Cassandra come to town unescorted? She is a lady, unlike..." he let his gaze roam up and down Catherine, "...others."

Catherine ignored the not-so-veiled reference to herself and glared at him. "Tell me John, did you decide on this trip to town before or after Charley Sloan told you I was here?"

He stepped forward, as if trying to threaten Catherine with his mere presence.

Duncan moved in front of her. "Don't believe I've had the pleasure. Aren't you going to introduce us, my dear? It would seem I owe Mr. Morgan quite a lot."

"What in the world could you possibly owe him?"

"Think of it, Cat," he drawled. "If Mr. Morgan hadn't started this feud, your father would never have asked for my help. I might not have come home, and we wouldn't be engaged, now would we?" His smile was smug.

Eyes widening, Morgan answered, "You're Duncan McKenzie? I've heard about you." His lip curled and he sneered. "Taking advantage of Catherine's generous nature it seems, though I hadn't heard you got engaged. When did that happen?"

"A week or so ago." Duncan wrapped an arm around Catherine's waist, snuggling her up to his side, as though he'd done it millions of times before.

She knew he was trying to fire Morgan's temper,

force him to make a mistake and end this charade.

"Catherine!" Cassie shrieked and hugged her again. "Is it true? I'm so happy for you! You must be ecstatic."

"Uh, yes. It's all happened rather suddenly. I'm still not used to it." Catherine glanced from Cassie to Duncan. Feeling ridiculous, she batted her eyelashes at Duncan, trying to play the adoring fiancée.

Catherine watched, her nerves on edge, as Duncan and Morgan sized each other up like two bull elk in rut, ready to butt heads. John was no match for Duncan, either in size or skill, but the rancher was a dirty fighter and she couldn't help but feel a twinge of concern for Duncan. Shaking it off, she decided it would do no good to worry. She'd just have to make sure he took no chances.

Cassie took Catherine aside and whispered so her brother couldn't hear, "I'm glad John wanted me to come to town with him. This feud between our families is so stupid. I don't know what's the matter with John. I've never seen him like this."

Catherine glanced over her shoulder and saw a look on Duncan's face she'd never seen before—he was every bit the bounty hunter. "Of course it's stupid. John's hiring every piece of vermin he can find and causing chaos. Can't you talk to him? Make him see he'll never get the ranch, now that Duncan and I are...engaged?"

"I wish I could. I want this to end. I miss you so much." Cassie's voice sounded so forlorn.

"I miss you, too." Catherine took Cassie by the

shoulders, hugged her, then set her at arms length, looking her up and down. "What's happened to you? You've lost weight and you're so pale. You look like you haven't slept in days."

Cassie looked away, over her shoulder at her brother, then shook her head. "It's nothing, really. I'm fine."

Catherine didn't believe her, but let it go. "When you're ready to talk, I'm here. You're not alone, as long as I'm around."

Cassie nodded. "I know. I wish, I...." She shook her head, changing her mind. "Oh God. I'm so sorry about all of this. If there was only something I could do...but John won't listen to me. Unless there's something he wants, he doesn't even acknowledge my existence. Never has, you know that. The only reason he wanted me to come today is because it would give him an excuse to talk to you and meet Duncan." She glanced at the two men. "We've heard about him, you know. He doesn't look anything like I expected him to, based on his reputation. He lived with you and your Dad at the ranch for awhile, didn't he?"

"Yes, he did and, no, he doesn't look like you think he would, does he? He's too darn handsome for his own good, but I'd never tell him so." She laughed, giving him a sidelong glance.

Duncan caught her eye and winked.

She felt herself start to blush and lowered her head with a smile.

Cassie didn't miss their exchange. "Why, you're blushing! I've never seen you blush before."

Catherine felt her face grow hotter. "I am not blushing," she stammered, turning her back to Duncan and Morgan, taking Cassie with her. "And do you have to shout it so the whole town knows?"

When she'd gotten several feet away from the men, she leaned down and whispered, "Sometimes just looking at him...it takes my breath away."

"What takes your breath away?" Duncan asked from behind her.

Catherine nearly jumped out of her skin. He'd come up like a cougar, with nary a sound.

"Dang it, will you quit sneaking up on me? It makes me crazy!" She looked around him. "Where's John? Did he leave Cassie here or is that too much to hope for?"

He wrapped his hands around her waist, pulled her close, and whispered in her ear. "Sorry, Cat. I didn't mean to scare you. It's just my nature to walk quietly." He looked over at Cassie. "He went back to the Hotel Creede; said you could meet him there later."

Pushing him away, Catherine went to the counter to settle with Sadie and sign her tab. She didn't look back, knowing he would be grinning at her if she did.

Cassie started laughing. "Oh, Duncan, you two are a pair. Catherine's going to marry the only man I've ever seen that can get close to her without her knowing. Whether you know it yet or not, she's a very special woman. I think you may have your hands full. Both of you."

Catherine heard the remark and grimaced at Cassie.

"Now, don't look at me like that. You're my best friend and I love you dearly. But you are too independent for your own good, and you know it."

Duncan nodded to Cassie and smiled. "Miss Cassie, I believe I like you, despite your brother. We can't choose our family, can we?"

"No, we can't. But we do choose our spouses and our friends. See that you take care of the one you've chosen."

"I intend to, ma'am. I'm very protective of what's mine."

The laughter gone from her voice, she said, "Don't ever hurt her. I'll make you very sorry if you do."

Her pale complexion and dark circles suddenly made sense. Duncan wondered who had hurt Cassie. "I'll never hurt her. You have my word."

"Good." Cassie's smile faltered and she wrung her hands. "Thank you. I want you to know that I don't side with my brother. He's not a good man, but he is my family and, for the time being, I must rely on his generosity."

Looking at Catherine, she said wistfully, "Perhaps if I were as pretty as Catherine, I'd be married now and not have to depend on him."

He couldn't believe his ears. "You judge yourself too harshly, Cassie. You're a beautiful woman." He lifted her chin with his knuckle. "Don't let anyone tell you different."

She looked up at him, her eyes wide with disbelief.

He took her hands in his. "Trust me, Cassie, I never lie. You just haven't found the right man yet."

"I believe I could learn to like you, Duncan, especially if you keep up those compliments."

As Catherine returned with her purchases, Cassie waved them off. "You two had better get going. Mrs. Peabody doesn't hold supper for anyone. I've got to get back before John decides to leave without me. We brought the buggy, but he might make that terrible Roy Walker drive me home. I can't stand that man." Her body shook. "He makes my skin crawl."

"I know what you mean. He does the same thing to me." Catherine hugged Cassie one last time. "Take care of yourself."

Cassie held her hand out to Duncan. "Goodbye. It was very nice to finally meet you. Don't forget what I said."

He enfolded her small hand in his. "I won't forget. And if your brother does leave without you, I can take you home."

"That's very kind of you, but not necessary. John will be too anxious to find out what I learned, to leave without me."

He nodded in understanding. "By the way, how did you know we're at the boardinghouse? Does your brother have somebody watching us?"

"I wouldn't be a bit surprised if he does. But I know you're at Mrs. Peabody's because Catherine never stays anywhere else. Everybody knows that, including John." She smiled and walked out the door.

Duncan turned to Catherine. "Did you find everything you need, Cat? I got Zeke's boots. They're the best to be had in Creede."

"I think so." Smiling at him, she grabbed his arm and headed out the door. "See how accommodating I can be?"

"Why is it I feel like the more accommodating you are, the more trouble I'm going to be in?"

"Why Duncan, I haven't any idea what you're talking about. After all, we are engaged." After they reached the boardwalk, Catherine shoved away his arm. "What was that all about? Engaged? Are you crazy? He wasn't supposed to know until after it was a done deal."

"Now, Cat. Don't go getting all riled up." He grabbed her hand and tucked it back into the crook of his arm. "It was the best thing I could think of at the time. Maybe Morgan will get the hint that no matter what he does, he'll never get the ranch, and quit trying."

"This isn't going to stop him. Engagements can be broken, fiancé's can die. Or didn't you think of that?"

Duncan let go of her and ran his hand through his hair around to the back of his neck. "I thought of it, but it doesn't matter. If Morgan calls me out, it will just end this that much sooner."

"Not if he wins."

CHAPTER 6

Arriving at the boardinghouse just in time for dinner, Catherine and Duncan washed in the kitchen before joining the others at the massive mahogany table. It could easily accommodate twelve, and when she was a girl Catherine had seen as many as twenty seated around it. But tonight there were six already seated and chatting when they emerged from the kitchen.

"Come on, you two," said Mary, who always ate with her boarders. Meals were family-style. Mary said it was a boardinghouse not a restaurant, and she wasn't a waitress. "Sit down and get some of this food while it's still hot."

Catherine and Duncan sat next to a young man dressed in a clean but slightly shabby suit; across from them were a young couple and two young men. Mary always sat at the head of the table and introduced everyone.

The first man was a lawyer, on his way to Lake City, just stopping for the night. Next were two brothers from Ohio, out to work in the mines. They'd be moving up to the mining company housing in a couple of days.

Last was the young couple across from them—Tom and Beth Peterson from Denver. Catherine let out a silent groan. She wouldn't be sending her letter after all.

She almost left the room, but it would have been cowardly and she was made of stronger stuff. Besides, she needed to find out if they were in with Walker or innocents, used by him.

Beth was about Catherine's age and expecting a child. Soon, if her huge, round belly was any indication. Tom was older, maybe thirty, and definitely a cowboy, from the faded but clean, chambray shirt to his well-worn Levi jeans. His clothes could have been those of any one of the men back at the ranch. The big hand he closed over his wife's was tan, callused and had seen hard work.

Too bad, they were innocent. Unlucky enough to be ripe for picking and Walker had plucked.

"Oh!" Beth grabbed her stomach.

Conversation stopped.

Tom paled. "Beth? Is it the baby? Is it coming now?" Concern laced his voice and Catherine's heart smiled. He confirmed her first observation. No one that concerned with another person's welfare could be in cahoots with Walker.

After taking several deep breaths, Beth nodded at her husband. "It's all right. Only a big kick. He's going to be a rancher, big and strong, just like his daddy."

Catherine glanced at Duncan. The color was returning to his face, much as it was Tom's, and she smiled behind her hand. Big strong men and they got all shook up about a baby coming.

"When is the baby due, dear?" Mary asked.

She'd risen from her seat, as they all had, but resettled herself. "You gave us all a little scare there."

"I'm sorry. He's not supposed to be due for another six weeks or so, but I've heard you just never know with babies—especially first ones. We'd hoped to get here and settled before he came." She smiled and looked down. "I'm not sure we'll be able to now, though. He seems to be getting anxious to meet us."

"So, Mr. and Mrs. Peterson, where are you planning on settling?" Catherine hated to ask, afraid she already knew the answer. It was too much to hope there was another couple from Denver by the same name.

"We bought some land on the Rio Grande from Roy Walker. We never actually met the man, bought it through a newspaper advertisement." He took his wife's hand and kissed it. "It's our dream to start a ranch of our own. I won't have to drive cattle anymore. I'll be home to see my son grow up." His eyes clouded over, his voice was hard. "I won't have my kids raised like I was. They're going to have two parents. Parents who love them."

"That's very commendable, though not always possible," said Duncan quietly.

"It is possible. It has to be," Tom replied. He looked at Mary. "I'd hoped to have the house built before the baby comes, but Mrs. Peabody has assured us that we can stay here if it's not finished by then."

"I was hoping you wouldn't say that," Catherine said, her voice echoing the sadness she felt.

Tom Peterson looked confused. "Why would you say that, Miss Evans? I hear there's plenty of land for everyone."

Catherine felt sick to her stomach. "Mr. Peterson, I don't know how to tell you this, but the land you bought wasn't Walker's to sell. My father and I have a ranch about fifteen miles northwest of here and the property you think you bought is ours."

His jaw dropped, but he managed to remain calm. Probably for his wife's sake, for she was now pale as a sheet.

"But...well...I've got this deed and a map," he argued. "I bought the property sight unseen which was probably foolish, but it was just too good a deal to pass up."

The deed Catherine had seen had clearly showed the property to be part of their ranch, but maybe Peterson's map would show something different. She hoped so. "Let me see your map. Maybe there's been a misunderstanding and we'll be neighbors," she said lightly.

Tom handed Catherine the map of his property. She looked at it and felt the blood drain from her face. "Mr. Peterson," she kept her voice soft, not wanting to alarm them, "I'm very sorry, but this is part of my property. Walker had no right to sell this to you. Sam Johnson, down at the courthouse, sent a copy of your deed to us. He said it wasn't legal. Duncan, look at this." She handed him the map. Marked out was the three thousand acres smack dab in the middle of the Evans Ranch.

"You're right. This is part of the J bar C." He turned his attention back to the young man and his wife. "I'm sorry, but it would appear you've been duped. Roy

Walker is a liar, cheat, and some say, murderer. Now I guess we can add con man to the list."

The young would-be rancher was obviously distraught. He rose from the table and began to pace the room.

"Oh, Tom," Beth cried. "What are we going to do? We don't have enough money to get back to Denver." She began to weep.

"I can't believe it. I don't believe it. You're lying. I don't know why, but you are! This just can't be true. We gave him almost all our life savings for that land." He knelt beside his wife's chair and took her in his arms. "Ah, don't cry, honey. I'll think of something. It'll be all right. I promise."

The lawyer cleared his throat. "Perhaps I can be of some assistance. My practice is to be in Lake City, but I am familiar with the property laws here in Mineral County. I could check the deeds at the courthouse if it would make you feel better."

"Before you do that, young man," Mary looked directly at the Petersons from her position at the head of the table, "you should know I've known James and Catherine Evans ever since they came to this valley. That's pert-near fifteen years now. If they say that deed is for part of their land, you better believe them. You'll find no finer folks anywhere. They're honest. Walker on the other hand..." her mouth formed a thin line and her body shook. "...snake in the grass," she spat.

"Mary!" Catherine interjected before Mary could continue. She was touched by the young couple's plight, especially with a baby on the way. "We know the kind of man he is, no need to get worked up over him."

She turned to the Petersons. "Please believe me, I'm truly sorry. Maybe something can be worked out."

Tom's anger erupted. "How can anything work out? We're broke, so we can't even go home. Dammit." The glassware shook when he pounded the table. "I was too eager to have my own place. I should've checked the man out, come to see the land before giving him our money."

He stood beside Beth and wrapped his arms about her. She pressed her face into him and cried. He rubbed the small of her back while she continued to cry. After her sobs abated, he sat back down and raked his hands through his hair, then propped his elbows on the table and buried his face in his hands.

"Please, Mr. Peterson, Tom. I think I've a solution, if you'll hear me out." Catherine thought and spoke fast, hoping he wouldn't explode again before she finished. "We're terribly shorthanded right now. One of our men was injured in a stampede and several others have left as well. I'd like to offer you a job. The money's good, and it includes a house."

Catherine glanced at Beth Peterson, who was sitting up, listening, and wiping her tears with her napkin. Catherine took a breath and worried her bottom lip before she rushed on. "I know you didn't want to work for anyone again, but I don't know what else can be done. We can try to get your money back, but that's not going to be easy. You can talk to the sheriff. Maybe there's something he can do, but Walker has probably already spent it."

"I know," Tom snapped from behind his hands.

She took a deep breath. "Before you decide, I

need to tell you why those other cowboys left. The man you gave your money to works for my neighbor, John Morgan."

Mary snorted. "Morgan's the real snake. Never did like that boy, and his father was just as bad. Only good thing come from that man was Cassie."

Catherine frowned at the older woman. "John is trying to run us off our land. I don't know why, but he's decided he wants our ranch and won't take no for an answer. My father and I refuse to leave and there have been...accidents. It could be dangerous for you."

Tom started to shake his head, but his wife laid her hand on his sleeve. "Please."

They needed this job and Catherine knew it. She didn't want Tom's pride to prevent him from taking it, so she tugged on Duncan's sleeve. "Well, be a fiancé here and help me out. He has to accept. We need him and they need us. Convince them."

He shrugged. "Just what do you want me to do? Hold my gun on them until they say they'll go with us? That'll surely show them our good intentions."

"Oh, you..." she sputtered. "Is this what I can expect from you anytime I need your help? Sarcasm?"

"Now, children!" Mary slapped the table, sending coffee over the rim of her cup into the saucer. "Enough bickering. We have more important things to discuss." She turned to the Petersons, her eyes kind and her voice soft. "Catherine owns half the ranch, so if she says she needs you, then she does. There are no better souls here in the valley to work for."

Mary wagged a finger at Catherine and she felt about twelve years old again.

"And you just remember your promise to me. No fighting under my roof. I swear I've never seen two more mule-headed people. And what's this about a fiancé?"

"Nothing. A slip of the tongue..." Catherine hedged. She'd hoped her slip would go unnoticed. She wasn't sure about this engagement and the fewer people who knew, or remembered, the better. It would be hard enough when Duncan left again, without having to deal with everyone's pity.

Mary narrowed her eyes and shook her head. "Don't give me that, young lady. I've known you too long for you to start telling tales to me now."

Catherine ignored her.

Duncan had no such inclination. "Yes, we're engaged," replied Duncan, easily repeating what he'd told the Morgans. "As a matter of fact, we're going to have a party in a few weeks to celebrate. James wants to be able to tell the whole valley at once. I'd be very pleased if you all would come."

Catherine looked at him, wondering how he could come up with these outrageous lies so easily, but he needed her support. "Oh yes, we'd love it if you'd come," she said, giving weight to Duncan's offer. What else could she do? "You can stay at the ranch house until the baby comes, and by then we'll have your belongings settled into the South Ranch. Please say yes." Catherine looked from Tom to Beth.

Tom looked over at his wife. Her eyes were still

sparkling from the tears, but she nodded her head. Catherine thought he was so gallant, as he took Beth's hand and raised it to his lips. "Very well, we'll come with you. It's been a long, hard trip from Denver, and my Beth needs some cheering up."

"Good. I'm so glad we got that settled. Now we can enjoy our supper."

Tom shook his head. "This has been one of the oddest meals I have ever had. I lose a ranch, gain a job, and," he looked at them, "new friends all in one evening."

Duncan chuckled. It sounded rusty, but rich and deep, striking a chord in Catherine she'd thought long dead. She hoped there could be a future for the two of them. Together. "I hope so. Since I do have some say..."

"Not as much as she would like, though." Duncan said.

His eyes twinkled, like he was privy to some funny story she wasn't. She knew he didn't laugh much. He didn't have the deep lines around his eyes like her father did. Seeing the crinkling when he smiled now increased her pleasure of watching him.

She turned, looked into the deep, dark-as-the-ocean, blue of his eyes and found herself lost. Her mouth fell open and she leaned forward before she caught herself. Shaking her head to clear it, wishing for the world she wasn't blushing, when she knew she was, she stiffened and straightened in her chair.

"Uh...yes." She forgot what she was saying.

"Hey, wait just a minute," she cried, realizing

what Duncan had said. "Are you saying I'm bossy? I am not bossy. I'm just...conscientious."

"Yes, sweetheart," Duncan smiled, the endearment rolled easily from his lips. "Anything you say." He leaned close and whispered in her ear, "At least while we are partaking of Mary Peabody's hospitality." He nodded to Mary, who smiled in return.

The look he gave Catherine promised things would change. He was not going to let her wear the pants in their family.

Their family?

For a moment she let herself be caught up in the thought. She'd dreamed of it too long not to enjoy living it, if only for a sweet moment.

The evening ended much too soon. Before she knew it, Duncan was saying goodnight to the Petersons and taking her elbow, leading her toward their rooms.

When they reached her door, Duncan opened it but didn't come inside as he'd done earlier. She turned to him, hoping he would take her in his arms and kiss her senseless like before.

"Goodnight,"

Duncan raised his hand to her face, lightly grazing her cheek with his fingers. The movement so soft, so tender.

She closed her eyes and leaned her face into the heat of his hand, absorbing his scent, relishing the roughness. Then, it was gone. Opening her eyes, she saw his door close.

He hadn't made a sound.

CHAPTER 7

Catherine lit the kerosene lamp on the bedside table and laid back on the bed, her arms propped under her head. She stared at the ceiling. What kind of man was Duncan? Would he really have come home even if Dad hadn't sent for him?

She got up and paced the room, too keyed up to rest. An old newspaper on the dresser caught her eye. Maybe if she read something she'd relax.

*****

Denver Prairie Gazette

November 29, 1880

What follows is our weekly excerpt from the new dime novel "Tall, Dark, and Lethal" by Jimmy 'The Pen' Pennebaker.

THE SAND HILLS

As you well know, my intuitive and sophisticated reader, I am not a mercenary type of fellow, but could you believe my luck? In through Delilah's saloon doors had rolled a novel on the hoof, Duncan McKenzie. Six feet four inches of slow talkin', fast drawin', drop dead western action. I was beside myself with glee and trying real hard not to show it. After all, a man had just been removed from existence. Not a very nice man to be sure, but a human being just the same. Few would miss 'Mean Jack' Slade, but it would have been unseemly to dance the jig I had bubbling inside me.

Duncan had let 'Slow Hand' inspect the warrant that was issued for Slade so the sheriff was simmering down. Hanson was no fast gun but he took his duties seriously. Except for the occasional harmless drunken drover, Arthur was a peaceful little community. The sheriff intended to keep it that way. Sheriff Hanson inquired, "Tell me, McKenzie, what makes a man do what you do to make a living?"

"If the truth be told, Sheriff, the money is good, the landscape changes, and there are a lot more bad men than law men. Essentially, I'm an unpaid officer of the court. Unpaid, that is, until I bring the man in."

Hanson persisted, "How many do you bring in alive?"

"What's the problem, Sheriff? You were a witness. I gave Slade every opportunity to have his day in court. He chose the time of his death, not me. I've brought in forty men and one woman. Twenty men and the woman were alive. With 'Mean Jack' here, I guess that puts me at half-and-half. That should be proof enough that I'd just as soon not kill. Now, if you're satisfied as to the legality of all this, I need to find the proprietor of the general store and then hit the trail."

Said proprietor just happened to be standing at the bar. "Mr. McKenzie, I'm Wilbur Wooten, owner of

Wooten's Mercantile. What can I do for you?"

"Mr. Wooten, I left Denver in kind of a hurry. I'm in need of burlap, beans, and bullets. If you would be so kind as to reopen your establishment, I've got a twenty dollar California gold piece for you."

Wilbur brightened. "That will be the fastest twenty dollars I've made all week. Follow me."

I followed Wilbur and Duncan out of the saloon while, unbeknownst to me at the time, two hard looking sodbusters slipped out the back door. Upon arriving at Wooten's Mercantile, Duncan turned and addressed me. "Have you got some reason for following us around, stranger?"

"A thousand pardons, Mr. McKenzie. James Alouicious Pennebaker, at your service. I wonder if you would be terribly upset if I were to tag along with you for a spell?"

Duncan was incredulous. "Jimmy 'The Pen', a.k.a. Pennysworth, a.k.a. Penny Dreadful. Are you that Pennebaker?"

"Yes sir, I am."

"Mr. Pennebaker, I suspect I will provide more service to you than you will to me, but we'll see. I saw what you were doing when I walked into Delilah's. I think your new nickname will be 'Penny Poker'."

"I protest, Mr. McKenzie, that was paper money on the table, no pennies involved."

Duncan rejoined, "'Dollar Poker' has no ring to it, and it doesn't fit you. 'Penny Poker' it shall remain,

Jimmy, unless you prefer 'Penny Ante'."

"You're a hard man, Mr. McKenzie."

"So I've been told, Mr. Pennebaker."

Wilbur had a ten-pound bag of beans and a bolt of burlap laid out on the counter as we walked in. "How much burlap and what caliber of bullets do you need, Mr. McKenzie?"

"I'll take all that burlap. Mr. Pennebaker, do you really intend to ride with me back to Denver?"

"I would like to ride with you at least as far as Denver."

"Tell me, Mr. Pennebaker, do you know how to handle a Winchester?"

"No sir, I've never so much as picked one up. Why would I need one now?" I was starting to get nervous about where this conversation was leading.

"Let's drop the formalities. I'm going to be honest with you, Jimmy. At the best of times, I'm not a safe man to partner up with, and now is most certainly not the best of times."

I had no idea what he was talking about. "What's so dangerous about now? You've already got the man you came for."

He looked at me and shook his head. "Did you happen to notice the two cowboys at the bar that headed for the back door while we walked out the front?"

I admitted I had not.

"*I know those men. I took their brother in some time back. He had his trial and was hanged in Omaha six weeks ago. I'm pretty sure to hear from them long before I get back to Denver. If you're gonna ride with me, you need to be armed.*"

I was in a quandary. "*Are you sure I need to have a weapon? I've always felt that it was the men with guns that actually got shot. Those without guns rarely get shot at.*"

"*This is the way it is, Pennyworth. If those cowpokes kill me, they're not going to leave you as a witness. You might as well go down fighting. Here's what I'll do. I'll buy the rifle and the shells. If we live long enough, the rifle will be my gift to you. I might even teach you how to shoot it. We can hunt some elk in the foothills west of Denver. Now is the moment of truth, Penny Poker. Are you in or out?*"

"*Shit, I'm in. Mr. McKenzie, uh... Duncan. How come you're being so generous? Winchesters aren't cheap.*"

"*Nothin' generous about it, Jimmy. A lot of these desperadoes are like woman beaters. They can't stomach a real fight. They prefer to ambush a lone man. If they see two well-armed hombres ride out of town together, maybe there won't be a fight. Mr. Wooten, that ten-pound bag of beans won't get it. I need six fifty-pound bags and a Winchester.*"

"*I got the beans, Mr. McKenzie, but I sold the last Winchester I had. Will a Henry do?*"

"*You bet your buckskin it will. We'll need about a hundred rounds for it. Jimmy and I are going huntin'.*"

Wilbur sort of danced from one foot to the other. "Mr. McKenzie, all this stuff comes to more than twenty dollars."

"Don't fret, Mr. Wooten, I got a pocket full of double-eagles. Give me the tally, I'll treat you right. Just don't tell anyone what you heard in here tonight. I don't want my bluff stepped on, if you know what I mean."

"You don't have to worry about me, Mr. McKenzie. I don't talk to anyone but my wife, and I don't talk to her much."

"I forgot to inquire, Mr. Wooten. How is the lovely Mrs. Wooten?"

"Mean as a snake, Mr. McKenzie. Mean as a snake."

Duncan looked around the general store one last time. He selected several fagots of sticks used for weaving baskets, a slab of bacon, and ten copies of the Arthur Star Tribune.

Wilbur looked at the quantity of goods stacked on his counter and interjected, "This is a lot of stuff, Mr. McKenzie. I got a buckboard out back I'll let you have for one of those double-eagles. There's some hay in it I'll throw in for free."

"Good idea, Mr. Wooten. I'm sure my packhorses will appreciate it. Slade's apt to get a touch ripe before we get back to Denver."

While Wilbur was loading the buckboard, McKenzie instructed me in the loading of the Henry. He pulled on a small catch and the barrel swiveled at the muzzle, revealing the magazine tube located underneath the barrel. He inserted a number of .44-40 caliber rounds, and then pulled up on the barrel. The weapon closed with a satisfying click.

McKenzie elucidated, "The Henry holds thirteen rounds, one less than my Winchester. One less round shouldn't make much difference to you. If you fire all thirteen it will be time for you to haul spurs through the sagebrush." He handed me the rifle. I nearly toppled under the load.

"As you can see, it's a mite beefy. Weighs about nine pounds unloaded and is a good five inches longer than my Winchester Yellowboy. You crank the lever to chamber a round. Don't chamber a round 'til we get to camp tonight. That will keep you from shooting your horse, yourself, or me by mistake. When it comes time to pull the trigger, make sure you have a good grip on it. This bad boy is similar to a mean horse—it likes to kick."

I felt compelled to show that I knew a little bit about guns. "I thought you were supposed to squeeze the trigger, not pull on it."

"I'll teach you how to use the sights and squeeze the trigger when we hunt elk. Tonight, you just point the barrel in the general direction of the fracas, pull the trigger and crank the lever to chamber another round. Point, pull, and crank. Got it?"

"Oui, Mon Capitan."

Duncan picked the burlap off the counter. "Stuff your pockets with as many of these cartridges as they will hold. I've got an extra bandoleer in my saddlebags. I want you to fill it with the shells and then drape it across your chest. You need to look like a desperado as much as possible. I need to get Slade ready to travel."

Tall, dark, and lethal walked out the door of the general store, and I followed. I wondered if a new novel and a Henry rifle were worth the risks I was about to take. In for a penny, in for a pound. Jimmy 'The Pen', a.k.a. Penny Ante, had entered a high stakes game.

'Mean Jack' Slade lay on his back in the street in front of the saloon. One of the spectators informed us that Delilah offered to buy the house a round if her clientele would be so kind as to take out the garbage littering her floor. The barkeep was still working with a mop and pail collecting Slade's life essence, removing the last evidence that he had ever darkened Delilah's doorstep.

McKenzie rolled the burlap out next to the body. He had a large leather sheath strapped to his left calf from which he extracted a twenty-four inch Bowie knife. He cut a length of burlap that was twice as long as Slade was tall. After unfolding the material he rolled Slade onto it, and then folded it over him. The body was now covered top and bottom with burlap.

He went to his saddlebags and tossed me the spare bandoleer. For himself, he extracted a ball of twine and a large needle that was probably used originally on sailcloth. Expertly, he stitched the material to enclose the corpse in the biggest burlap bag I had ever seen. What we had was a one hundred ninety-pound bag of punctured and drained Slade. I was standing there with my full bandoleer draped as ordered, and my Henry in my hand. (Don't snicker. I said Henry, not Johnson.) I was feeling more like a buffoon than a desperado.

McKenzie looked at me and once again shook his head. "I'll take the pack horse and go collect the wagon."

I contemplated going back into Delilah's for a quick belt, then thought it through. I'd be better off with a clear head tonight. I thought it through again; I'd be better off if I didn't feel so weak in the knees. To hell with it. I went back in and had two belts of the not so good stuff. My knees felt better and I did feel tougher standing there with my Henry leaning against the bar.

When I walked back out front, Duncan sat astride the big black stallion. The wagon was loaded with all the goods from Wilbur's, all Duncan's equipment from the packhorse, and the sack of Slade. A third horse was tethered behind the wagon.

He gazed at me sternly. "Have you changed your mind, Mr. Pennebaker?"

"No sir, I'm raring to go."

"Good. You handle the buckboard, I'll ride shotgun."

I collected my hay burner from the hitching post and tethered her behind the wagon with the mare. Climbing up into the seat of the wagon, I kept the Henry in my lap. As we rode out of town I asked him, "Is elk any good to eat?"

"It's the best stuff there is, Jimmy. Better than buffalo or rattlesnake."

We had been moving southwest along a trail winding through the sand hills for about an hour. It was 9:00 p.m., Tuesday, November 12, 1878. The moon had cleared the horizon behind us, and was nearly full. The planet Jupiter was directly in front of us, about ten degrees above the hills that rolled in front of us. I didn't recall ever seeing it that large. It could have easily been mistaken for the evening star, Venus, which wouldn't be seen until tomorrow night. (Yes, gentle reader, I had been reading my Star Almanac *while waiting for the poker game at Delilah's to begin). The constellation Aquarius was up and to the left. The Milky Way was a wispy cloud to the right, near vertical, stretching from the horizon to just past the zenith. All in all, it was a beautiful, crisp, clear, fall evening. I didn't notice the approaching storm clouds. McKenzie rode up close beside the buckboard and spoke in a voice just loud enough to overcome the noise from horse hooves and the creaking wagon.*

"Bad news, Jimmy. Five men are shadowing us. I've been catching a glimpse of them from time to time between the sand hills. I don't think they'll hit until after we set up camp. In about a quarter of a mile, we'll come to a dry creek bed. Take it to the left. We'll take it a little ways down and then set up camp. As soon as you stop the wagon, put on the brake and chamber a round in the Henry. Leave the horses hooked up. Take the Arthur newspapers and that bunch of sticks and build a fire that's not too large. Make a pot of coffee and stick it in the fire. I'll set up the rest of camp."

"What rest?" I wanted to ask.

"Better yet, cock that Henry now."

We took the turn onto the creek bed and went about a hundred yards. Duncan held up his hand and I stopped the wagon and jumped down. There was already a ring of charred rocks from a previous campfire. The

*ashes were still warm to the touch. While I built the fire
and made the coffee, the big man was busy. He removed
the Winchester from his saddle and gave Jake a gentle
swat on the hindquarters. The horse sauntered down the
dry wash, munching delicacies he found along the way.*

*Two at a time, McKenzie retrieved the six large
bags of beans and placed them in two piles, eight feet on
either side of the fire. He arranged the bags end to end
and then covered each pile with a blanket. Our chores
done, he led me to the left side of the wash and set me
behind a large rock hidden amongst the sage and cedar
that blanketed both sides of the creek bed. He knelt
behind a large oak, ten feet from my rock. He put his
finger to his lips.*

*I guess he wanted silence. He didn't have to
worry about me; I was too scared to fart.*

*I have to admit that the setup was elegant. We
had what appeared to be two sleeping men, one on
either side of the fire. They were so tired, they hadn't
even bothered with the horses. The subterfuge was
complete with the smell of coffee in the air. Both sides of
the wash were thick with dry brush. We couldn't be
approached from the front or the rear without someone
making a great deal of noise. If they came from behind
the wagon, the horses tethered there would get nervous
and we would be alerted. The only quiet approach to our
camp was along the wash to our left.*

*We didn't have long to wait. The fire had burned
down to a third of what it had been originally, but
between it and the moon, there was enough illumination
to highlight the two sleeping figures. Across from us we
could hear rustling in the dry brush. Four men crept in
from the left with their guns drawn, slow and careful.*

They were ten feet from the sleeping beans when they opened fire. As they pounded round after round into the prone parcels, the fifth man sprang from the brush across from us and contributed to the fireworks with his revolver.

As the Winchester exploded into action to my left, I pointed in the direction of the villain across from us and pulled the trigger. I missed <u>him</u> clean but I nailed his hat; it flew off into the dark. I must have scared him rather badly because he dropped his piece and raised his hands.

"Don't shoot! Don't shoot!" he implored.

I levered the Henry and kept it pointed at him.

The other four lay face down in the dirt, arms and legs akimbo. Duncan had fired four rounds. The first man was hit in the right temple, the left side of his head was gone. The second was hit in the chest; by the size of the hole in his back, his heart was probably laying somewhere in the brush. The other two were neck shots, almost removing their heads.

Duncan ordered the fifth man to put his dick in the dirt. He tied his hands behind his back and checked him for additional weapons. He then yanked him to his feet.

"You're going to stand trial for attempted murder, Jackass!"

The man had nothing to say. His pants were wet.

Duncan let out two short shrill whistles. Jake galloped up the wash from the south but stopped just shy of the bodies. The big man took the saddle off the big black horse, then got a bale of hay out of the back of the wagon, giving a quarter of it to Jake. The paint pulling the wagon was given another quarter after being unhitched. The rest of the bale was divided between my filly and the mare.

Meanwhile, I had thrown some more sticks on the fire; once again it burned brightly. I wanted some coffee, but it had boiled dry. Our prisoner sat in the dirt with his head hung low.

Galloping horses and torches were approaching down the wash from the north. More folks from Arthur were joining the party, apparently. I picked up the Henry and started to head back to my rock when Duncan held up his hand.

"Don't bother, Jimmy. Men after us are not likely to ride in with torches." Nevertheless, he picked his Winchester back up.

From his bandoleer, he slipped four shells into the side of the Yellowboy. It didn't look to me like Duncan was convinced this was a harmless situation. I slowly backed up in the direction of my rock.

The riders slowed to a walk as they passed the buckboard. Sheriff Hanson led nine citizens from Arthur; he surveyed the devastation. "Damn, McKenzie, you're a one-man slaughter house."

"C'mon, Sheriff, it was five to two and they came in with guns blazing. You can't parlay with bushwhackers."

"Yeah, you're right. We saw these morons follow you out of town. It took me awhile to raise this posse. Half the town is smashed at Delilah's, cussing

and discussing the spectacle you put on there earlier. Looks like they missed the big show. These were the only sober men I could find. Who's under the blankets?"

"Those are the Bean Brothers, Frank and Judge Roy."

Duncan removed the blankets. All the men from Arthur roared with laughter, save the sheriff.

The sheriff was not amused. "This looks like a perfect place for an ambush, and you damn sure set it up for one. How did you find a spot this good in the dark?"

"I stopped here and had supper before I went into Arthur. When I noticed those men following, I figured this was the best place to meet them. If they had announced themselves and come in with guns holstered, they would be alive right now. To be honest, I saw two of them in the saloon and figured they'd come after me. Their brother was hanged in Omaha because I took him in. I didn't know they were going to have help, so I was real glad to have found this place beforehand."

Hanson appeared satisfied, but continued, "I assume the live one was the one Pennebaker was shooting at."

"Hey, I shot his hat off!"

McKenzie addressed the sheriff. "Speaking of the live one, you can take custody of him if you like. He's guilty of attempted murder, if nothing else. If there's a poster on him, you can take the bounty and spread it amongst yourself and your posse. I appreciate you coming out here to help. If these fools hadn't been in such an all fire hurry, maybe none of this would have happened. Wire me in Denver and let me know if you need me to testify."

"I'll do that. We have a traveling judge, but he's not due for more than a month. It would be best if 'Penny Dreadful' came back as well. This saddle tramp needs to cool his heels in the territorial prison for a spell. Let him consider his foolish choice of traveling companions."

Hanson and the posse took charge of the silent, nameless would-be murderer and headed back to Arthur.

"Okay, Jimmy, do you want to do the routine with the burlap or look for these gent's horses?"

"Since you're giving me the choice, I'll look for the horses. I don't see why we need them, though. We can just throw this debris into the wagon."

Duncan shot back, "We need the horses for a couple of reasons. One—horses, saddles, guns, and equipment can be sold in Denver for good money. There may or may not be bounties on these men, but their possessions, at least, have value. Two—we need to ride straight through to Denver. These five bodies are going to start to stink before long. We need to rotate the horses so we can keep going."

I had some more questions. "Why do you bother with the burlap? Why don't we just dump the bodies in the wagon and haul ass back to Denver?"

"It's like this, Jimmy; there's almost always kids playing on the streets of Denver. Kids are real curious, and I don't think they need to see the fruits of my labor. I don't think it's proper for a child to witness this much destruction. I saw a lot of death and devastation before I even hit my teens. I think it changed me, maybe not for

the better. After all, look what I do for a living. Never mind, it probably won't be a problem. By the time we hit town, the smell will most likely keep everybody away from the wagon. By the way, don't put anything in the wagon you want to keep. It's near impossible to get the smell out. On occasion I've had to wash horses with skunk which is better than the smell of a man long dead."

That was more damn information than I wanted. I went to find the horses. They were tethered all together about a quarter mile from our campsite. When I returned, Duncan had the buckboard loaded with our sacks of death and the Bean Brothers. Jake was saddled again. We were ready to roll.

The ride back to Denver was uneventful. Luckily, it was cold and rainy most of the way. The smell of the dead became noticeable, but not unbearable. We had to stop Friday night. Men and beasts were exhausted. At sunset, Duncan spotted a herd of antelope in the distance. They were near the limit of our visibility in the light downpour. He borrowed my Henry and dropped one with a single shot. If you couldn't say anything else about Duncan McKenzie, you could say the man was frugal with bullets.

We set our camp upwind from the wagon. The antelope was excellent, and we had plenty left over to jaw on for the remaining ride. He also fixed beans with bacon. Tolerable, once you worked around the lead slugs. We hadn't seen a soul since the shoot-out at the dry wash, so we didn't bother with guard duty. We just slept. Slept well past sunrise. We had beans and antelope for breakfast, then finished the ride to Denver.

I never did find out the names of the four

additional dead men, but they must have been ornery. Duncan collected two thousand dollars a piece on all five, including Slade. The would-be murderer taken back to Arthur was one Jesse Torrence. We didn't have to go back to testify. He set fire to the jail and was shot dead trying to escape. Sheriff Hanson and the posse collected a thousand for Torrence. He was wanted for murder as well.

Duncan told me I was entitled to half of the bounty for the four men outside of Arthur. "Damn, Jimmy, you stood up with me and barked like a big dog."

I declined. "I didn't kill anybody, and I don't think I want the notoriety. To tell the truth, I didn't really believe there would be any trouble when we rode out of Arthur. It was all over so fast, I didn't even have time to think."

I have to admit the money was tempting. McKenzie made ten thousand dollars in less than two weeks. He said that was a first. Most times, he tracked a man for a month or more, usually for a thousand or two. He wouldn't pack a horse for less than that. Five hundred dollar outlaws weren't worth the risk.

He did teach me to use the sights and squeeze the trigger of my Henry. I got me an elk in a pretty little valley in the foothills west of Denver. We hunted with William F. Cody. Buffalo Bill said he loved that little valley; said he would like to settle down there one day.

I was tickled when I shot that elk. "Duncan, I love this rifle! I should think up a name for it."

"Penny-wise, don't be a fool. This is the west. We might name our horses but we never name our guns

or our dicks."

Little Jim and the twins were sorry to hear that.

*****

Catherine giggled. The story was very entertaining and if she believed it, there was still some of the old Duncan inside the cold, hard man he'd become. If he could take a complete green horn stranger under his wing, then he couldn't be as cold-hearted as he let on. Could he?

The excerpt from the novel gave her hope, more than she cared to admit. If a stranger could see past the exterior to the heart of Duncan, why couldn't she?

CHAPTER 8

The trip home from Creede was much longer than the trip out. They'd gotten a late start. First she'd slept late, something she hadn't done since she was a child; then they'd had a marvelous breakfast of eggs, bacon, sausage, grits, fresh bread and baked apples at the boardinghouse. Catherine loved breakfast, and Mary always served the best.

After breakfast Tom and Duncan went to the sheriff's office and reported the fraud. Catherine insisted she and Beth go to Doc's place, to make sure it was safe for Beth to travel. Even the short distance to the ranch would take hours. The Peterson's wagon, pulled by four old but sturdy mules, was loaded high with everything they owned.

Doc said Beth was in good physical condition and he was glad to know she would be at the Evans's. He assured them Alice could handle things until he could get there when the baby decided to come.

When they finally were loaded up, Catherine sat next to Beth and drove the wagon, while Tom rode Wildfire beside Duncan. It was nearly ten in the morning.

Half the day was gone.

She really liked Beth Peterson. Seeing Cassie

yesterday made her realize how much she missed having a friend, someone she could talk to, maybe even confide in. After all, she reasoned, Beth was a married woman. She ought to know how a man's mind worked. And, heaven knew, she wished she understood Duncan better.

"You know, in a way I'm kind of glad things have worked out this way," Beth said. "I was so afraid we'd come here and be alone. I don't like being alone, especially right now." She lovingly touched her swollen belly.

Catherine took her hand and gave it a reassuring squeeze. "Don't worry about anything. This will all work out fine. I like the idea of having another woman my age to talk to. It can get lonely out here, especially for women. How long have you been married?"

"Just a little over a year. Tom courted me for four years, but wouldn't marry me until he had a home. I finally told him that anywhere we are is home, as long as we're together. Don't you feel that way?"

Do I? Would I really be happy with Duncan anywhere or just here in my valley?

"I don't know," she hedged. "Duncan and I have only been engaged for a few days and haven't talked about it."

Beth looked stunned. "You sound like you don't know if you love Duncan, but I can tell by the way you look at him, you do. Don't you want to admit it?"

"As a little girl, I'd always dreamed of the day I'd marry him. He's been my knight in shining armor, my Prince Charming, ever since I can remember. But I always thought..." Catherine sighed. "I don't know what

I thought."

Liar! I always thought he'd love me as much as I love him.

She looked out over the landscape, hearing only the clip-clop of the mule's hooves hitting the rutted road. Taking a deep breath, she filled her lungs with the crisp, clean air. Wildflowers; columbines, bluebells, Indian paintbrushes and many others she couldn't name, carpeted the valley. As always, when she took the time to notice, the beauty of her land took her breath away. Would she give all this up if Duncan truly loved her?

"I'm sorry." Beth laid her hand over Catherine's. "It's none of my business."

"It's nothing. No reason to be sorry. We just have a lot of things to work out, that's all." She slapped the reins on the mules' rumps, suddenly anxious to get home. "Giddy up, you two. Come on, getup."

*****

As they cleared the rise, five hours later, the ranch came into view. Beth gasped in delight and amazement. "Oh my. It's beautiful and so grand."

Catherine cocked her head at Beth, and then looked at her home, trying to see it as Beth did. The house was two stories in the center with a steep pitched roof. Both ends were single story. One housed the kitchen, dining room, and Alice's bedroom. The other side was her father's study, the formal parlor, and a storage room. The entire structure was made of rough-hewn logs, varnished and oiled before they were laid together. It cost more and took longer to do it that way, but her father had insisted, saying, "The house will stand forever if we build it right."

A wide covered porch surrounded the house on all sides and had hitching rails in front of it by the main and kitchen doors. The porch, made of boards not logs, matched the house in color, but hadn't been oiled. "Too slick to walk on," her father had said. She smiled at the memory.

He'd put in a porch swing for her, and a couple of rockers for him and Alice. Sometimes they'd all sit out there after supper and never utter a word. Just watch the sun go down, the animals, wild and domestic, head for the river for their evening drink, and revel in the view.

The barn was big, bigger than the house, with a new coat of red paint done just this past fall. There was the little house that they'd first lived in, now occupied by Zeke and his family. The second structure they'd built, the barn was the first. Her dad said the animals came first. Without them there wouldn't be a ranch, so they'd stayed at the boardinghouse and built the barn.

All the out buildings looked the same to her. The hay shed, bunkhouse, tool shed, outhouse, all just rough-hewn pine with wood shingles on the roof. Not so grand, but good. Sturdy.

Home.

Before she realized it, they'd rolled through the gates to the ranch. The sun was just beginning to set and James was on the front porch smoking his pipe, waiting for their return.

Duncan and Tom tied the horses to the hitching rail at the end of the porch. "Hello," Duncan said. "We, uh, brought home some folks for you to meet."

"So I see." James rose out of the rocker and came down the porch steps. Standing close to Duncan, he whispered, "Well, my boy, judging by the look on your face, it would seem things are going to be all right between you and Kitten. Am I right?"

"Dad." Catherine said from behind them. "Things between us are between us, not you."

James almost dropped his pipe. "Tarnation, girl! Are you trying to give your old dad a heart spell, sneaking up on me like that?"

Catherine laughed. "You're certainly jumpy." She kissed his cheek and hugged him. "I love you too much to give you a heart attack. Besides, we have some news that may please you."

Catherine, ignoring her father's questioning gaze, moved to Beth's side and introduced everyone.

"Real pleased to meet you, Mr. Evans," Tom said while vigorously shaking James' hand with both of his own. "Catherine says you will be able to help us out of this predicament we're in."

"Tom, calm down and let Mr. Evans have his hand back." Beth smiled at James. "He tends to be overly enthusiastic about everything he does. Don't pay him no mind."

"I'm pleased to meet you." James returned the young man's handshake. "Though, I don't know how I can help you."

Catherine shook her head at her father.

He arched a brow in question, but followed her lead. "Come on in the house. We'll let you get cleaned up and talk about this after supper."

Catherine showed Tom and Beth upstairs to the guestroom, leaving James and Duncan alone.

"Son, would you join me in the study? I'd like to talk to you," said James.

"Sure, but I'd like to get some of the trail dust off me first though."

"This will only take a minute. You'll have plenty of time to wash up." James walked into the study. "Shut the door behind you, would you? Sit and have a drink."

"No, thanks." Duncan stood next to the door, his arms crossed over his chest. He didn't think he would like what came next. "What's on your mind?"

"What the hell is going on with you and Catherine? What's this news, and why did you bring those people out here?" James raked his fingers through his hair.

Though he was expecting something, the older man's outburst still took Duncan by surprise. He wouldn't lie to him. James was already worried, so Duncan was mindful of his words.

"We ran into Morgan in town. I told him Catherine and I are engaged. Catherine backed me up but she was not happy. Didn't want him to know until after it was done." He rubbed his chin with his hand, noticing the whiskers. "She's the most headstrong, stubborn and brave woman I think I've ever known. Anyway, I hope it will stop the accidents."

"How in the world is that going to stop Morgan?"

Duncan went to one of the chairs and slumped into it, stretching his legs in front of him. "Damned if I know, but that's what I told Catherine. We saw him at the store and he tried intimidating Catherine, so I stepped in and announced we were engaged. I know it was a fool thing to do, but I couldn't stand the thought of him touching her and—" Duncan stopped, realizing he'd said too much. His reasons for doing it didn't even make sense to him; how in the world could he expect them to make sense to James?

"Son," James said, gripping his whiskey glass, "an engagement is not going to stop John Morgan. If there is any chance he can get this ranch, he'll keep going. I'm not even sure your marriage will stop him, but at least she'd have some legal protection."

Duncan felt he'd been punched in the stomach. "What are you saying?"

"I want you and Kitten to get married sooner rather than later."

Duncan didn't move or say a thing. He was afraid he'd regret it later.

"I know this isn't what you wanted to hear. It's something I've wanted for a long time, and I won't pretend otherwise." His words hung in the air.

"I don't think—"

"I do." He rose, turned his back to Duncan, gazing out the window. "You've wanted to settle down for a while, and I know that's one of the reasons you came when I asked. I'm not getting any younger, and as much as Catherine thinks she can run the ranch and hold on to it when I'm gone, I know she can't. She needs you."

He turned back and the look in his eyes told Duncan he wasn't going to give up on this idea.

"It's got to be this way. We both know it. I know she wants to wait, and if you can see any reason to postpone the wedding, let me know. Think on it. Otherwise, you two will be married on Sunday."

Duncan got up to leave. Anger made finding his voice difficult. James might not want to force them, but he would if he had to. Duncan knew it and so did James. He owed James so much, and for that reason alone, he said, "I'll think on it."

*****

Camping gear filled her saddlebags, her bedroll secure behind the saddle. She rechecked the cinch, it was tight. She was ready. Alice came out the kitchen door carrying a sack of food.

"Tell Dad I'll be back in a few days. I'm going to the hot springs."

Alice sighed. "You shouldn't be going alone. Catherine, we all discussed this. You can't go off by yourself. It just isn't safe."

She took the bag of food and hugged Alice. "I'll be all right. Besides, no one can find me at the hot springs. I'm safe there. I'm not even off the ranch for the most part, and I've been fine while I'm working on the property."

"You saw what happened to Zeke. He was still on the ranch, too," Alice pointed out.

She smiled at her friend. "Look, I have to go. You have Beth and Sarah, to help you, and for you to mother. They need it more than I do with them both expecting at anytime.

"I need time to think, to be by myself. I never take anyone with me to the springs, you know that." She hugged Alice again, swung up on Wildfire and took off at a dead run, leaning over the horse's neck and clutching his mane in one hand and the reins in the other.

Duncan rode around the far side of the house just in time to see Catherine take off. He was mesmerized. Even after watching her for the last six days, her skill on a horse still amazed him.

Alice's shout brought him out of his stupor. "Damn, that girl! She's going to get herself killed. So sure she can take care of herself. You have to go after her."

"I can see that. Where's she going in such a hurry?"

"To her hot springs. Hurry Duncan, if you lose her you'll never get her trail back."

"I'm going." He turned Jake and rode after Catherine.

It was a good thing Jake was fast. He would need all of his speed to catch her. She rode like the wind.

When he caught up to Catherine, she had stopped to rest her horse. She looked up at him and laughed. "I thought Jake was faster than that. It took you long enough to catch me."

"Jake is fast, but Wildfire is the devil, and has a witch for a mistress." He got off Jake and strode purposefully toward her. He was not smiling. "You scared Alice half to death, and didn't do my heart any good either. If anything happened to you, James would never forgive me."

I would never forgive myself.

She looked more angry than scared, but backed up a step. Her eyes flashed icy silver. "I'm safe on our land. Why are you so angry? Since you and Dad decided that John's after me, I can't go anywhere alone, and except for the stampede and the wagon fire, nothing has happened. Alice worries about me if I go to the barn by myself. It's too much."

Her face flushed red. She swung away from him and started to mount Wildfire. Grabbing her by the shoulders, he spun her around.

Her hat went flying and so did her hair. She hadn't put it in her usual long braid, but had wound it tight and tucked underneath the hat. It fell about her shoulders and down her back in a dark red cascade. He wanted to run his fingers through the silky tresses.

"I'm angry because you're acting like a child. A willful child. It's time you started thinking about someone else besides yourself."

He pulled her close and kissed her. Hard. It was a kiss meant to punish. She struggled and pushed at him, but he deepened the kiss and tightened his hold. He heard her sigh and eased his hold on her. She melted into his arms.

He applied gentle pressure to her mouth and knew when she opened her lips to him, he'd won this battle. Wasting no time, he took her sweet offering, plunging his tongue into her honeyed warmth.

She moved her tongue to meet his. The slight movement took him by surprise. Pleasant surprise. Memories assailed him. Memories from a happier time, when he'd held this woman in his arms.

Catherine wrapped her hands around his neck and leaned her body until it collided softly with his. This felt so right. He wanted to kiss her forever, but couldn't trust himself not to make love to her. It frustrated the hell out of him, but he did his best to make sure they took it no further.

He knew she wanted to explore her feelings. He'd learned a lot since that long ago day when Jimmy 'The Pen' Pennebaker had called him naïve about women. He'd been so careful to keep away from her after the last kiss they'd shared, she probably thought he didn't like kissing her. Boy would she be wrong. Hardly a moment went by that he didn't relive having her in his arms.

Her hands unwound themselves from his neck and traveled down to his chest. Feminine fingers worked his buttons free and tangled in his chest hair. Soothing, caressing as they went.

All his hard-won reserve flew out the window at her sensual onslaught. His hand moved to her hip, caressing her as he went. Up across her firm belly and slowly higher, to her breast. He undid the buttons on her shirt, then the laces on her camisole, half revealing her to the waist. Her creamy white skin stood in pale contrast to his dark hands as they moved upward and over her breasts. Her camisole and shirt still shielded her nipples, to his consternation.

He kissed her lips and then lowered his head to nuzzle her throat, trailing soft, wet kisses in his wake. All the while, one hand held her close, caressing her back, the other moved slowly over and around her breast. Exploring, feeling, memorizing every curve. She was more lush than he'd imagined. Her breast would have overflowed a smaller man's hand, but it was perfect for his.

Her undisciplined nipple pebbled with need before he even touched it. He cupped her breast, circling ever closer, and finally teased her with his thumb.

She gasped with pleasure.

Ever forward toward his goal, he kissed and caressed her flesh wherever he touched it. Moving ever downward until his lips touched her breast. He kissed all around her perfect nipple, took the small bud into his mouth and sucked.

Catherine clung to him. She threw back her head, holding on to his shoulders for support, arching her back to get closer to his mouth. He caressed her aching nipple with his tongue. She gasped at the shock of what he was doing, then moaned with pleasure.

"Well, now ain't this a pretty site."

Catherine grabbed her shirt together with one hand. Duncan tightened his hold on her, keeping his back to the intruder.

"If it ain't the high and mighty Miss Evans and some cowboy. I guess the boss was too good for you, huh?" Roy Walker stepped his horse out of the shadow of the trees.

They'd been so caught up in each other, they never heard him approach.

Catherine spun away from Duncan. "Roy Walker you son of a... I ought to kill you right now for what you did to Zeke. What are you doing on our land?"

Though she and Duncan had turned simultaneously, when her hand went for her Colt, his gun was already out, pointed at Walker's chest. She'd moved fast, but he was faster. He now stood in front of Catherine shielding her from Walker's view.

"You'd better answer the lady, Walker, if you want to keep breathing. Though it would give me great pleasure to remove your sorry ass from this earth."

Walker turned his attention to Duncan. Something flickered in his eyes, but she couldn't say what. Excitement maybe.

"I heard you were in these parts. It's been a long time, McKenzie. I see you haven't lost any of your speed."

Walker shrugged, ignored Duncan altogether and spoke to Catherine. "I came to see if your men gave you my warning, followed you up here from your camp. I'd hoped to find you alone."

His gaze raked her and Duncan started forward. Catherine put her hand on his arm and he stopped.

Walker continued, oblivious to the danger he was in, "...but then I saw McKenzie coming after you and figured I'd tell you both at the same time. That stampede was just a warning. I mean to see you off of this ranch sooner or later. It would be better all around if it was sooner."

She buttoned her shirt and stepped from behind Duncan to stand at his side, but had holstered her gun. "Running off a few cows? Hurting one of our ranch hands in the process? Is that what you consider a warning?"

"I told your men to get off this land. It isn't going to be yours much longer. Just thought I'd save them some trouble, letting 'em leave now."

"Or what? You'll give us another warning?" She was furious. "Let me tell you something. My father owns this land, and there is nothing John Morgan can do to change that. You tell Morgan if he doesn't leave us alone, I'll come after him myself. If he wants war, he'll have it. You tell him."

"Oh, I'll tell him all right. You can be sure I'll tell him everything about our little meeting today. Don't you worry your pretty little head about that."

Walker turned his horse and galloped away. They could hear his laughter long after they could see him.

Duncan knew exactly what he meant. James was not going to be a happy man. He wouldn't like it when the talk got back to him.

Catherine was so angry she was shaking. "Damn, what've I gone and done now? Dad's going to be pissed that I declared war on Morgan. And what did Walker mean when he said it's been a long time? Do you know him?"

"We've met," was all he'd say. He took her by the shoulders, "Declaring war on Morgan is the least of your worries where your father is concerned. Don't you understand? Roy Walker is going to use what he saw here tonight to try and ruin you and your father."

"Duncan, think for a minute. Nothing he saw is going to mean anything to anyone. We're engaged."

He sighed. "Cat, no one knows we're engaged except Cassie and John Morgan. Do you think that he will allow anyone to know that? He'll be the first to use this as a way to embarrass and disgrace you and your father in the eyes of the town. Think about what Walker saw. We'll push up the wedding to Sunday. Your father and I already discussed it." He didn't tell her he hadn't given James an answer. The answer was forced on them now, like it or not.

She faced him, hands on her hips. "Like hell we will. I have a month, two weeks left and I'm not letting Dad or anyone else force me. How could you? How could you agree with Dad before even talking to me?"

"Listen." He ignored her questions and moved away, shoving his hands through his hair, trying to come up with the right words. "Walker just caught us in a...situation. You're my best friend's daughter. You will not be ruined because of me. Nor will I have your father's reputation tarnished because you're too stubborn, or just plain blind, to the way of the world and a woman's place in it."

"A woman's place?" she croaked. "That's what all this is about, isn't it? Hang my reputation. No one will believe Walker, least of all Dad."

"He will believe him," he said very softly.

"Why? Why should Dad believe anything that he says? He's a liar, a cheat, and probably a murderer."

"Because he's a fair man, and before he makes up his mind about anything, he listens to all sides. He'll ask me what happened, whether what Walker says is true. I'll tell him the truth."

"Why? Why are you doing this to me?"

"I don't lie to James."

"Don't give me that. Everybody lies. It's part of human nature."

"Maybe, but I won't. Not to him. He's my friend and I have too much respect for him, even if you don't."

Her voice quivered, "How can you say I don't have respect for Dad? I love him. He's all I have. I wouldn't do anything in the world to hurt him."

She paced, angry and upset at the turn of events. She turned away, not wanting him to see her tears, her weakness. "You don't know anything about me," she said softly. "I'm not the same young girl you left brokenhearted so many years ago." She slumped down to the ground next to Wildfire, hugged her knees and lowered her head to them.

Duncan walked over, sat down next to her, and put his arm around her waist and brought her head to rest on his shoulder.

His voice was soft and low. "You don't know me either. I'm not the same boy you knew. I'm a man, and a man has only his honor. I won't destroy mine, or your father's. We'll be good together, Cat. You'll see." He put his fingers beneath her chin and gently lifted her face to his.

She knew his mind was made up. He would marry her on Sunday, just four days away. That was it, and she'd better get used to it. When she'd started out this morning, she'd already known. Duncan was the love of her life. She didn't believe her father would really keep the ranch from her if she didn't marry him, but this wasn't the right way for it to happen.

She looked into his eyes. Maybe he didn't love her now, but she'd do everything in her power to make him love her.

She lifted her hand and stroked his cheek. "Oh, Duncan, don't you see, I don't want a husband, not this way. Men want a wife. Someone to cook, clean, and sew, all those female, wifely things. I can't do any of those things. I like being free. Free to make my own decisions. My own mistakes." She lowered her eyes.

"Cat, look at me," he commanded gently.

She looked up, no longer able to keep the tears from escaping.

"Cat, I don't lie or cheat. I'm good with a gun and at cards, but the only thing I know about ranching, I've learned from you and James. I don't care whether you can cook or sew, never have. We'll share, Cat. I'll make you a good husband. I take care of what's mine.

From now on, Catherine Evans, you are mine." He held her face in his hands, stroking her cheeks with his thumbs. "Trust me. I'll protect you with my life, and everything I have is yours. I'll do my very best to make you happy."

She blinked and the tears ran down her cheeks. He caught one on his finger and put it to his mouth.

Maybe she had been waiting for Duncan to come back. Perhaps that was why she'd always turned down every proposal she got. She'd had a few. Some were men who wanted her ranch, some wanted her body, but had any wanted just her? She loved Duncan. That wasn't something she could say about any other man.

She sniffled and rubbed her tears away with her palms.

"Trust me," he said softly.

As she looked into his gorgeous blue eyes, she knew she would trust him.

Wiping her tears again, this time with her sleeve, she couldn't answer him now, not yet. She hiccuped. "I'm doing something I never thought I'd do. I'm taking you to the hot springs. I haven't changed my mind about going so you can come, or leave now."

Duncan looked at her. "That's not wise, Cat. Your father'll be fit to be tied after he gets wind of what Walker has to say."

"Dad will be elated. It's what he wants. What he doesn't want is for anyone to question *my* reputation. That will make him livid. So, since you're with me for safety and he's going to be mad anyway, it won't matter if it's a day or two longer before we face him. I may not have a chance to come this way again, since I'm to be a married woman."

He was stunned. He didn't want to assume anything when it came to this. "Does this mean you're not going to fight me on this? That you'll marry me on Sunday?"

She shrugged. "I guess we don't really have much choice. I'm not naïve enough to believe it wouldn't matter what Walker says, and I don't want to cause Dad any more trouble than he's already got. The only other choice I have would be to leave the valley. I can't...I won't do that. I've never run from anything in my life and I don't intend to start now."

She'd like nothing better than to run and never look back, but her heart wouldn't let her.

CHAPTER 9

Catherine led the way to the springs. She was careful, taking a roundabout route, making sure Walker wasn't still tailing them. When she was certain, she turned Wildfire west and urged him to a gallop.

Duncan, on Jake, had no problem keeping up.

"Sure you want to go with me? I might try to drown you and solve all my problems," she shouted to be heard over the thud of the horses' hooves hitting the ground.

He laughed. "You couldn't drown a kitten. Besides, I've always wanted to see the hot-springs."

"I'm only taking you because I don't have a choice. You're going to be my husband, and I expect you to keep the secret."

He twisted an invisible key against his lips. "You've got my word."

Working their way through the narrow canyon one at a time, Duncan was glad it was a short one. He didn't like enclosed spaces, and the rock overhangs in this canyon made it seem more like a cave than a canyon.

Holding his arm in front of his face so the

branches wouldn't smack him, the canyon opened up into a beautiful, tiny valley. Green and lush with vegetation, the valley wasn't more than ten acres total.

"Wow."

"Is that all you can say?" They walked the horses to the last pool where Catherine slid off Wildfire to the grass covered ground near the edge of the water. She loosened the saddle and put it on a downed aspen tree, laying the blanket over the top to dry. Duncan followed suit, setting his saddle next to hers, like it belonged there.

"Come on. The water is heavenly." She was already removing her moccasins, heading toward the water.

"Sounds great to me. I could use a bath. Want to go first while I keep watch?" Duncan was doing his best to be a gentleman about this whole thing, though he desperately wanted to watch.

"There's no need to keep watch. Even Walker couldn't track us the roundabout way I brought us here. No one has ever found this place except Gray Wolf and me. We can bathe together, provided, of course, that you have something on under those pants of yours."

"What if I don't?" He raised one dark brow and grinned.

She blushed. "Well, I guess you'll just have to stay at one end of the pool and I'll stay at the other. That should work."

Lord, he hoped so, but he wasn't so sure that his body wouldn't get carried away, even if his mind didn't.

He grabbed her hand. "Sure. Let's go get clean."

They walked down to the largest pool. She pulled off pants and shirt. She was still wearing her drawers and camisole.

When she lifted her arms and began to wind her hair into a long coil atop her head, Duncan sucked in his breath. He was beginning to think this wasn't such a good idea after all. Her camisole pulled tightly across her full bosom, it was all he could do to turn away before his body betrayed him.

Catherine watched as he turned away and pulled off his boots, then his shirt. When she saw the broad expanse of his back, she couldn't breathe. Her hands stilled in her hair and she just stared. When he started to remove his pants, she stifled a gasp, dropped her hair, grabbed her bar of soap and dove into the pool. When she surfaced with her back to him she heard a splash as he dove into the water.

Grinning, he surfaced about three feet from her and shook his hair out of his face.

"This feels great. Who could imagine swimming in hot water out here in the mountains?"

"It is wonderful, isn't it? I've got some soap if you'd like to use it. We're starting to smell like the cows." She laughed as she lathered her hair, then tossed him the bar.

She scrubbed the long mass and then ducked down to rinse it out. When she surfaced again, Duncan was nowhere in sight.

"Duncan?" she turned a complete circle in the

water. "Duncan, where are...?"

He grabbed her ankles and pulled her down, then let her go.

She bobbed to the surface, sputtering and spitting water out of her mouth. "Why you ornery..." Scooping up water with her hands, she sent a small wave in his direction. Laughing, she swam away.

He caught her easily, pulled her into his arms, lifted her high and tossed her into the deep, clear blue water. She came up smiling and swam back toward him, fully intending to push him under water. She hadn't played like this since she was a child and wondered if he ever had.

When she got close enough to touch him, he pulled her into his arms again. This time he just held her there. His eyes were black with desire. Through her thin bloomers and chemise, she could feel his nakedness. It sent shivers down her spine.

She wrapped her arms around his neck, pulled him closer and whispered, "Would you kiss me, Duncan?" She knew it wasn't a wise thing to do, but no one had ever accused her of being wise.

He answered by pulling her tight to him, closing his mouth over hers. The kiss was gentle, tender. He traced her lips with his tongue, teasing, tasting.

While he treaded water, she wrapped her legs around his waist, putting his hard erection right at the opening in her drawers. She could feel the tip of his cock, touching her flesh. She started to throb down there and moaned with pleasure.

Oh God!

They nearly drowned!

Duncan had been so stunned when she wrapped her legs around him, he stopped treading water and they sunk like stones. They both came to the top sputtering and laughing.

"Well, that was quite a kiss, Mr. McKenzie. Remind me never to do that again."

"Next time I think we should try it on dry land. I can't seem to remember what to do when we're in water." He shoved his hair back from his face. "You better get out of here and dry off before I forget that I'm a gentleman and continue what we started."

When she hesitated, he splashed her and said, "Go on, get."

Catherine laughed and swam away. She didn't know what in the world had possessed her to wrap her legs around him like she had. But my goodness, the feel of him, the tip of him touching her down there.

Lordy, she was hot and she didn't think that it had anything to do with the water.

CHAPTER 10

"There's somewhere else I have to go before we go back to the ranch." Catherine said the words quietly while saddling Wildfire.

"I saw you were packed for more than a day trip. Where were you going?"

"I'm going to White Buffalo."

"Why? What does the old chief have to do with any of this?"

Duncan's voice stayed low and calm but she knew he wasn't happy with the idea of not returning to the ranch right away.

"I won't get to see him or Gray Wolf, or any of them, for probably a long time. It's only a matter of time before the army roots them out and sends them back to the reservation." She rested her head against Wildfire's neck, smoothing his mane. "I want to say good-bye."

Duncan nodded in understanding.

Arriving late in the afternoon, they entered a camp of fifteen tepees arranged in a circle. The camp, located in a small box canyon surrounded by high mountains, had only one way in or out. Duncan sensed they'd been watched while entering, though he never saw or heard anyone.

The chief stood in front of the largest tepee, his arms crossed over his chest, his legs apart. His appearance was not that of a happy man.

He wasn't tall—actually Catherine was tall as he was—and he was quite portly. White Buffalo's height told Duncan the man hadn't had enough to eat in his early life. He knew enough of the Ute people to know they were a tall, sturdy people when they got enough food. Gray Wolf was a good example. He was a full head taller than his father, covered with sinewy muscle. Joshua's story about the young White Buffalo suddenly took on new meaning.

Duncan saw that despite his lack of stature, White Buffalo commanded great respect from his people, and from Catherine. She slid easily from Wildfire's back and rushed to greet White Buffalo.

He clasped her shoulders in greeting. "It has been a long time since your last visit, Autumn Sun." Glancing at Duncan, he asked, "Who is this with you?"

"Chief White Buffalo, this is Duncan McKenzie." she answered in his native Ute. "You called him Night Eyes. It has been a long time since he went away. And," she stopped, looked over at Duncan and held her hand out to him, "we'll be married when we get back to the ranch."

White Buffalo moved Catherine away from him and walked to Duncan. He held his hand out to him as a friend. "Night Eyes. It has been many seasons since you have been to my camp. I have heard many stories about the man called Duncan McKenzie. One of my warriors came into camp just a short time ago with a new one—

one I do not want to believe. Morgan's man is telling all that you and Autumn Sun were found in the way of a husband with a wife. Is this true?"

"Yes, it is true," she answered before Duncan could respond, her voice laced with shame.

The shame on her face and in her voice angered Duncan. She had nothing to be ashamed of. It was him. He was the one who pushed the limit, who'd forgotten.

"She did nothing wrong. I was the one—"

White Buffalo silenced him with a wave of his hand. His attention still on Catherine, he said, "Because of your actions, your father will lose face with the other whites. You will marry Night Eyes to save your father from the shame." His eyes narrowed. "Do you wish this man for a husband? If you do not, I will make it so he is not your husband, and your father is not shamed." He walked around Duncan looking him up and down from head to toe. He never took his eyes from him, sizing him up to find any weaknesses.

"No, White Buffalo, please," Catherine replied. She didn't want Duncan to know what she was saying, so she continued in Ute, even though White Buffalo spoke perfect English. "This problem is my own making. Duncan is a friend to me and I do want him for my husband. I love him. He is an honorable man. I've agreed, given my word. I'm an honorable woman."

"Well, Cat, is he ready to slit my gullet for taking advantage of you?"

"Not entirely. I've explained the situation we find ourselves in is my fault." She stopped and stood stock-still. Her heart fell to her stomach and together they continued on to her feet. "How do you know what he said?" She was just going to fall down and die. Did he know she'd said she loved him? "Do you speak Ute? You didn't used to."

"Some. Enough to know he was trying to find out if you wanted me as a husband. I think he's deciding whether or not I'm worthy."

White Buffalo raised his hand. "Enough. We will speak English. This one is to be your husband and should understand all that is being said." He stood before Duncan, looked him squarely in the eyes. "You will take care of this woman? You will be a good husband to her?"

"Yes," Duncan replied, returning White Buffalo's direct gaze. "I will take care of her. I protect what is mine, and Catherine is mine."

White Buffalo, hands clasped behind his back, and circled Duncan again, as if judging the veracity of his words. Finally, he looked over at Catherine. She pleaded with her eyes with White Buffalo to believe him.

"Good," White Buffalo said, his decision made. "I am glad you have returned, Night Eyes. You will be a good husband for Autumn Sun." It was a statement not a question. He slapped Duncan on the back. It showed his approval, and at the same time gave Duncan clear warning what would happen if he was not a good husband.

Duncan turned and smiled at Catherine. "Autumn Sun. I'd forgotten that they called you that."

"Yes, my hair was much lighter when I was

younger. Like the red of the leaves in the autumn sun. Don't you remember what I looked like when I was a little girl?"

"Oh, I remember. You followed me everywhere I went. Or don't you remember?"

"You make it sound like I was a pest. I'll have you know, I worshipped the very ground you walked on when I was a child." She raised one eyebrow and the corner of her mouth crooked up. "Obviously, I'm not that naive now."

Suddenly serious, she looked solemnly into his eyes. "Well, Night Eyes, it seems White Buffalo has made his decision about you." She smiled, teaseing him again, "Maybe Dad will decide to kill you first."

"Not a chance, Cat. Your father knows me too well. He'll listen to what I have to say, before he thinks about killing me."

"We'll see about that, now won't we, Night Eyes."

White Buffalo was quiet for a long time. When he finally spoke, it was with a solemnity that Catherine hadn't heard in a long time. "Autumn Sun, you will be married here, tonight. You cannot spend another night with this man until you are wed."

"But White Buffalo, I've already told you we will be married when we get back home. There is no need—"

"No. You will not return home together unless you are married. James Evans is my friend, and I will not have him put to any more shame. You will marry,

145

here, tonight or you will return to the ranch alone. The choice is yours, Autumn Sun."

Catherine stared at White Buffalo, unable to stop her eyes from tearing. He simply shut his eyes. She had to make this decision on her own.

"It will be as you wish."

White Buffalo smiled. "Good. Go with Laughing Waters to my tepee. There you will be prepared. The ceremony will take place at sundown."

A young woman came to Catherine, touched her arm and pointed. "Come, Autumn Sun, we have little time."

Duncan started toward Catherine.

"No. Night Eyes, you come with me." White Buffalo turned to a young brave standing near. "Leaping Fox, find my son. He will want to be present at the marriage of his sister."

Catherine went to White Buffalo's tepee. Her saddlebags were brought to her. From them she took her brush and brushed her hair until it crackled, then dressed in a beautiful white buckskin dress. It belonged to Laughing Waters, who'd worn it at her own marriage to Gray Wolf six months ago. Catherine, taller and bustier than Laughing Waters, needed it altered to fit her.

The sides were slit underneath the arm and laced with softened rawhide strips to accommodate Catherine's ample bosom. It couldn't be lengthened, so it hit her just below the knees, the long fringe falling at mid-calf rather than the ankle as intended. Laughing

Waters tied a beautiful beaded rawhide strip around her forehead. It held her hair in place and enhanced her eyes. Laughing Waters said her eyes shimmered in the light of the small fire.

Duncan, in Gray Wolf's tepee, was given clean clothes to wear. Gray Wolf's mother, Little Bird, put two small braids into his shoulder length black hair, one at each temple. She held them in place with a soft rawhide band around his forehead.

He dressed in the softest buckskin pants he'd ever worn, with his moccasins on his feet. An elaborately beaded shirt with fringe along the back of each sleeve completed his wedding attire.

At sundown, the entire tribe gathered in the center of the camp to watch the ceremony take place. Catherine was a friend to all of the people, not just White Buffalo and Gray Wolf.

Gray Wolf moved through the crowd and entered his tepee.

Duncan watched the young man stand in the tepee. He was tall, about six feet, with coal black hair half way down his back. He wore it tied back with a single rawhide strip. His chest was bare and muscular.

"So, McKenzie, I hadn't expected to see you again so soon. Father says you're going to marry Autumn Sun." He sat at the fire across from Duncan.

"Yes, I am. Do you think I'd be going through all of this hoopla if I wasn't?"

"Do you love her, Night Eyes?" Gray Wolf asked softly, using his Ute name for the first time.

Duncan hesitated, choosing his words carefully. He didn't know Gray Wolf and didn't need him as an enemy. "She's very special to me. I've known her for many years. Her father is my best friend, and I care about her very much. That's enough."

"Enough for you maybe, but is it enough for my sister, I wonder? She's a willful, strong woman who needs a strong man to guide her. Are you strong enough to be that man, Night Eyes?"

"I protect what is mine, Gray Wolf. No one will ever harm her. She will obey me."

Gray Wolf snorted. "You may have known her for a long time, but I can see you do not really know her."

Duncan grimaced, knowing Gray Wolf was right. He didn't know Catherine, but he was determined to make their marriage work. For better or worse. "She'll learn. You said she needs a strong man and, I would add, a firm hand. I am that man."

Gray Wolf laughed loud and long. When he finally regained control of himself he said, "Well, your firm hand will be kept busy, if I know my sister."

"Why do you keep calling her your sister? You're as much her brother as I am."

Gray Wolf's eyes softened. "Night Eyes, I didn't know you before but many things change. The People are no longer free. We hide from the bluecoats, but soon they will find us. James Evans has kept our secret for many years. He and Catherine know we are here, yet they keep us safe. Soon our life here will be done. By the time the snows come, we will be gone from here, back to the reservation."

"I know this, Gray Wolf, and I am sorry. I would see The People free."

With sad eyes, Gray Wolf continued, "Many years ago, when James and Autumn Sun first came here, white men captured my father and were about to kill him when James Evans stopped them. He saved Father's life and they became blood brothers. She is blood sister to me.

"We watched the ceremony, it is a great honor among our people, but we did not understand the responsibility that went along with the ceremony. Only that it was a good thing, and if our fathers did it, we should, too. So we cut our palms and exchanged our blood, becoming blood brothers."

He proudly showed Duncan the scar on his hand. Laughing, he continued, "Our fathers were not happy, but decided we would grow up, blood brothers as we had chosen. Since that day, Autumn Sun has been my sister."

Where was I when this happened, Duncan wondered. *I don't remember James and Catherine going anywhere*...then it hit him. Catherine had insisted on riding the perimeter of the land. James hadn't done it himself yet, and thought it would be a good idea, but Duncan stayed behind to supervise the building of the house. He thought Catherine had just wanted time alone with her father, which he understood. They'd been gone for a week and both were closed lipped about the trip. Now he knew why.

Gray Wolf stood. "It is time for us to go. I will accompany you to the circle of life. There you and my sister will be wed. Then, Night Eyes, we will be brothers. I believe you will be good for her." He slapped Duncan on the back, the gesture one of comrades.

With a chuckle he added, "I'm not sure she will be so good for you."

Stepping out of the tepee, Duncan's eyes immediately found Catherine. She was more than a head taller than the women surrounding her and more beautiful than anyone he'd ever seen. Her hair hung loose to her hips and shone like burnished copper in the firelight. Her eyes sparkled, though whether it was with fear or excitement, he didn't know.

White Buffalo took her hands and walked with her to the circle in the center of the village. There she waited.

Gray Wolf brought Duncan to stand beside her. She couldn't take her eyes off of him. She'd never seen him look so handsome.

The buff colored buckskin pants were tight and showed off his well-muscled thighs. He wore Gray Wolf's marriage clothes, just as she wore Laughing Water's. The elaborate beaded shirt was white, as was the band around his forehead. Together they accentuated the deep tones of his skin, making him darker, more handsome, if that was possible.

He was, in fact, everything she'd always dreamed.

Tall, dark, and handsome.

The absolute epitome of a man.

She lowered her eyes, afraid to look at Duncan.

Afraid she'd see the anger or resentment he must be feeling. The tribal medicine man began chanting and dancing to the beat of the drums. Every beat echoed through her body.

White Buffalo motioned for her to walk clockwise around the circle. Duncan walked in the opposite direction. They passed on the far side and came back face to face, where they had started. She chanced to glance up at Duncan. He smiled and his eyes glittered. There was no contempt in them. She smiled back.

Taking first Duncan's hand, then hers, White Buffalo joined them together and clasped both of his hands around them. Entering the circle, he led them to the center, hands still joined.

The medicine man quit chanting and the drums stopped.

White Buffalo's voice boomed in the still night air. "Night Eyes and Autumn Sun have walked the circle of life and are now joined as one. They will face all the Great Spirit gives them together. Let none part them."

Catherine and Duncan walked out of the circle, their hands still clasped, though neither seemed to notice.

The entire village came to life. There were cheers and slaps on the back. The women had prepared a feast, and there was dancing and singing well into the night.

Laughing Waters came to Catherine and took her hand. "Come with me. It is time to prepare you for your husband."

Catherine's stomach turned somersaults. She bit her bottom lip, looked over at Duncan and blushed. Lowering her eyes, she said softly, "Laughing Waters, there is no need. I can prepare myself. I..."

Laughing Waters cut her off. "Autumn Sun, you will come with me now. It is my duty to see to your preparation. White Buffalo has given me this honor."

Catherine saw how important it was for her friend to help and nodded. "Very well. Let's get this over with."

White Buffalo had had a tepee prepared for them, away from the rest of the village. Laughing Waters took Catherine there. Inside, a pallet made of pine boughs and covered with soft furs was their bed. There was a small fire and a bowl for washing.

"Take off your dress and get under the furs. I will see your husband sent to you."

Catherine took off the beautiful dress and handed it to Laughing Waters. She looked around the tepee, but saw no other clothing.

"Where are the clothes I was wearing when I came?"

"They are in White Buffalo's tepee. You can change into them before you leave in the morning. I will see they are brought to you then."

"But I'm naked. I can't go without clothes. I'll freeze to death."

"You would wear clothes on your wedding night?" Laughing Waters chuckled with delight. "You wouldn't wear them long. Your husband appears to be very much a man. Trust me, Autumn Sun, you won't need clothes to keep you warm." She smiled at Catherine and left.

Catherine grabbed a fur from the bed and wrapped it around herself as much as possible. Though they were soft, they were meant as blankets, not clothing. She sat on the bed with her back to the wall of the tepee and draped another fur around her so only her arms and shoulders were exposed. Taking her hair, she pulled it forward over both shoulders to give her more coverage and a little courage. There was no getting around it though. The fact was, she was sitting naked in a tepee, waiting for her husband. Waiting for Duncan

She wiped her damp palms on the fur and tried to think of something else, but her mind kept returning to the fact that it was her wedding night. Correction, hers and Duncan's wedding night. After all these years of dreaming, she was finally married to Duncan. She smiled and her heart beat faster.

She wondered when, or if, Duncan would come.

CHAPTER 11

Duncan entered the tepee, saw her and stopped, his heart hammered in his chest.

So beautiful.

Her glorious hair, shining in the firelight. Her skin, shimmering with the flames' warm glow. His body reacted and he groaned, just looking at her. He wanted to touch her, needed to feel the passion he'd only glimpsed before.

He wanted her.

All of her.

Hardening, almost painfully, at the thought of touching her soft skin and wrapping himself in her beautiful hair, he tried to reign in his randy body. He didn't love her the way she wanted. But he wanted her and cared for her. That would be enough. It had to be enough because he'd never let her go. He moved forward, away from the entrance and started to remove his clothes.

Catherine stared up at him until she realized what he was doing. Suddenly shy, she looked down at her hands lying in her lap and said, "Duncan, I don't know if you should be doing that. Much as I love White Buffalo and his people, we're not truly married. The marriage would never be recognized back home."

Duncan removed his shirt, then knelt in front of her and reached out, gathering her silky hair in his hand. Moving slowly, caressing as he went, his hand slid along her jaw until he could lift her chin, forcing her to look at him. "Cat, you are my wife now. We are married. Just because the ceremony was not performed by a preacher doesn't make it any less binding to me. I'm your husband and you're my wife. I told you I'd do my best not to hurt you. Do you trust me?"

"Yes. Maybe I shouldn't, but I do."

She was nervous, but not frightened. She loved him. It'd taken her some time to become aware of that fact. Time to forgive him for leaving. But that was in the past. Now was the future.

Their future.

Duncan took her into his arms and rose to his feet. She gasped at the sensation of her body pressing against his. Even the fur between them didn't stop the electricity.

"You're so very beautiful." His hands skimmed her arms, sending shivers up and down her spine. "I'm going to kiss you now, my beautiful little Cat."

Slowly he lowered his head and softly brushed her lips with his. His hands glided over her body, following the curve of her back, down her buttocks.

She lifted her arms, wrapped them around his neck and returned his kisses. At her response, his kiss deepened. His tongue gently played on her lower lip. He leaned his body into hers so she could feel his sex, hard and waiting for her.

"Do you feel the effect you have on me?" He rocked himself against the soft fur separating their bodies. "Do you feel how much I want you?"

She did feel it. He was huge. As if he could feel her fear, his mouth came down on hers, hard, demanding, sending all other thoughts out of her head. All the while, his hands kept caressing her. She burned everywhere he touched and she wanted him to touch her everywhere. She tingled and something stirred deep within her.

He moved away from her, holding her to him with only his lips. The fur slid down her body and she felt the cool night air touch her hot skin. His hands stroked every inch of her back, then grasped her buttocks, lifting until she cushioned him against her body. He kissed her mouth, each of her eyelids, and the tip of her nose. He moved lower, kissing her below the ears, her shoulders and the little hollow at the base of her neck.

He slowly dropped to his knees and turned his attention to her breasts, raining kisses over them, and around her aching nipple. When he took the firm nub into his mouth, she sucked in her breath, and moaned with pleasure.

The other, he gently flicked with his finger, giving it much wanted attention. At a time like this, she wished he had more than two hands so he could touch all of her at once.

Then his tongue played in her navel and licked flames up and down her belly. One hand caressing her breasts, the other traveling lower, teasing her flesh, all the while creating a fire that slowly consumed her.

He found and caressed the soft mound at the juncture of her legs, then moved up once again to her taut belly and breasts. Slowly his hand moved, his thumb and forefinger found her nipple and gently rolled it.

The strange sensation low in her body intensified. Her maidenly response had her wanting to squeeze her legs together, but the feeling was so pleasant, she instead found herself arching toward him. She only knew she wanted to be closer, that only he could relieve her longing.

"Duncan," she called as her knees buckled. Catching her, he laid her on the pallet of furs. Rising, he quickly shed the rest of his clothes, leaving them in a heap.

She watched him, reveling in his beautiful body. He was so big and so strong. Totally without clothes, yet he was completely at ease. His shoulders were broad, his stomach firm and flat, rippling with muscle. His legs were incredible, well muscled and lean as she'd seen earlier, but now without clothes, they seemed even more so. Her eyes inadvertently went to his manhood. He stood before her fully aroused.

"Do you like what you see, little one?" He smiled, seeing the direction of her stare.

Catherine blushed and dropped her gaze, "You are a beautiful man, Duncan. I could look at you forever." Her voice trembled, "but I'm afraid."

He dropped beside her on the furs. "Why are you afraid? I know this is your first time. I'll be gentle with you." His knuckle grazed her cheek.

She blushed deeper, but voiced her thoughts. "No it's not that. I know you'll not hurt me, purposely anyway. It's just that, well, you're…"

"Trust me, Cat." He smiled down at her. "We were made for each other. We will fit together beautifully."

Kissing and touching her, he aroused her all over again. In the heat of her passion, her fears were forgotten.

"Lay back, Cat. I want to look at you. I want to fill my eyes with your beauty."

She laid back and let him look.

Slowly his gaze traveled up and down her long body. Her breasts felt heavy, her nipples ached for his touch.

"Do you really think I'm beautiful?" she asked shyly. "I'm not too tall or too big?"

"You please me very much. You're incredibly lovely. Perfect for me. Only me."

He caressed her, coming down beside her once more, resting on his elbows, he took her face in his hands and kissed her ever so softly. He slid his gaze down her long, strong legs. "I want to feel these incredible legs of yours wrapped around me as I plunge into you. Your woman's mound, with its soft, red curls, calls to me. A siren song only I can hear."

Catherine wrapped her arms around him, brought his mouth to hers, his body atop hers and rubbed her breasts against his chest.

Duncan tried to support his weight with his arms, but she would have none of it. She wanted to feel him, feel his weight against her. She arched and pulled him tighter, her body calling out to him for release. He moved his hand down until he found the entrance to her vagina. His fingers caressed her even as they touched her clitoris, hidden from his view, within the folds of her womanhood.

When he touched her, feelings so intense she thought she'd die from them, hit her. She wanted, yearned for something but she didn't know what. She moaned, arched and called out his name. She needed him closer, needed him in her, now. She was nearly frantic with her need.

"Duncan! Oh, Duncan!"

"I know, my sweet," he murmured.

He slipped his finger inside her and she felt her body close around it. He slipped a second finger inside and slowly stretched her. He removed his fingers and kissed her mouth. He left a trail of kisses as he moved farther down, ever downward, toward his goal.

She clung desperately to him, trying to pull him closer, reaching for that unknown something, when his lips kissed her mound and his tongue delved inside.

"Duncan! You can't mean to... I mean, it isn't done. Duncan, I..."

Her protest died on her lips as he caressed her with his mouth. Fingers twisting in his hair, she arched, reaching for the pinnacle she felt so near. Suddenly she screamed and bucked. Her body shattered, and the world as she knew it was gone. Her body shook with a thousand tiny tremors. The feelings so intense, she thought she surely had died. No one could survive that kind of pleasure.

He rose over her, settled between her legs and again used his finger to prepare her. Her body, still reeled with the aftershocks of her climax, convulsed along his finger. She would never be more ready for him than she was now.

She looked up into his passion-filled eyes.

"Cat, do you still trust me?" He bent to take her mouth once more and she opened for him. Grasping his hair, she pulled him closer. Her hands traced the muscles and ridges of his back and kneaded his buttocks.

"Sweetheart, this first time will hurt. But never again, Cat. I promise after this there will only be pleasure. Do you believe me?"

"I believe you, Duncan. I trust you." She smiled up at him.

He entered her, slowly at first, letting her get used to him. She felt herself stretch to accommodate him. As he pressed up against her maidenhead, he withdrew almost completely from her.

He kissed her. "I'm sorry, Cat," he said, plunging, burying himself to the hilt, with one swift thrust.

She gasped softly, but didn't try to remove him. He pressed his weight upon her and remained still. She watched sweat break out on his forehead as he struggled for control.

"Hold still, love, it'll be all right. Just hold still for a few moments longer, and then the pain will be gone."

Catherine knew there would be pain, but it wasn't what she'd expected. She'd ridden horses all her life, maybe that prepared her, because this was nothing, a tiny scratch, a piercing, nothing more. She shifted under him, waiting for the pain to start. But there was none. Just an incredible feeling of fullness.

"Don't, sweetheart, please, don't move yet. I must give your body time to adjust."

Something in his voice, almost like pain, made her stop. She became very still. His heart beat against hers and she looked up at him, tears welling in her eyes.

"Duncan? Are you stopping?"

"Darlin' I couldn't stop now if I wanted to, and I definitely don't want to. The pain will go away. Just be still. It's getting better, isn't it?"

Catherine didn't want to be still. The pain was gone, what little there had been, now she wanted to move. She arched, rubbing herself against his chest and felt the sensations begin to build.

That little movement sent him out of control.

"Oh God, Cat." He began to move slowly in and out of her.

Thrusting deeper and deeper until he was buried so deep she felt he was truly a part of her and she a part of him. One being, one thought, one soul.

She picked up his rhythm, moving with him. Thrusting upward toward him as he plunged into her. Her movement brought him to the brink and then over it. He threw his head back, calling her name. Then his body went limp on top of hers.

"Cat, my love. You're incredible," he said as he kissed her.

He rolled to his side, keeping her with him, locked in his embrace. Holding her tight, still buried deep inside her, he fell asleep.

He had called her 'my love'. Could it be? No, it was just a saying. Just words murmured in the aftermath of their lovemaking. Nothing more.

Listening to his soft snores, she was exhausted and exhilarated at the same time. They were married, and try as she might, she could not regret it.

CHAPTER 12

"You've really done it this time, Catherine Rachel Evans."

Catherine groaned. Whenever Alice used her full name, she was always in big trouble.

"Oh dear." She worried her lip. "I really was hoping he'd have calmed down by now."

"Calmed down? Are you out of your mind? You've been gone for five days, while Walker is telling anyone and everyone he saw you two..." Alice stopped, looked at him and blushed. "Well, you just get yourself off that horse and march inside before..."

"All right." She rolled her eyes. Her father always overreacted as far as she was concerned. "I'll see him right away." She sighed.

Catherine saw determination written all over Duncan's face. Neither of them wanted to talk about confronting James, so they hadn't mentioned it during the three days of heaven they'd taken to get back to the ranch. They always made camp early, making love long into the night and sleeping in each other's arms. As far as Catherine was concerned, it had been perfect, but now it was time to pay the piper. She dreaded it.

"I guess I better go talk to him." She slipped

from her horse, not waiting for Duncan to come help her down.

"No, Cat, let me talk to him first. This whole situation is my doing, after all."

She shook her head. "It takes two. I'm as much to blame as you are." Catherine couldn't help but think her Dad wanted this, wanted them married, but not this way.

"Maybe," he shrugged. "But I still want to speak to your father alone."

Placing her hand on his thigh, she looked up at him and nodded. "Very well. I'll wait, but not for long."

Duncan dismounted and walked into the house. James waited in the study, his back to the door. He turned and spoke as Duncan entered.

"I've heard some rather disturbing rumors concerning you and two. Are they true?"

"Yes."

"I see," James said.

Duncan saw his disappointment and for a moment, a flicker of something else. "What do you intend to do about it? I take it you two decided I was right and are going to get married."

"We are married." He waited for James' response, letting it sink in.

James continued, "I hope you realize that you don't have a choice... Married?" He swung around from the window, a huge grin on his face. "You got married?

At White Buffalo's village?"

Duncan nodded.

James' smile faltered. Narrowing, his eyes he asked, "What does Catherine think about all this? Did she do this willingly? I know White Buffalo, he'd have done anything to protect her...and me. Did either of you force her to marry you? Because if you did, I'll have both your hides, everything else be damned. I want her to be happy, darn it, and if..."

"No." He paced in front of the desk. "Neither of us actually forced her." When James' mouth formed a grim line, he hurried to say, "She told him she loved me and wanted to marry me but wanted to wait until we came back. He said she would come back alone, if she didn't marry me then and there. Besides, you were going to force her to marry me. What are you so upset about?"

"That's different." James' voice was just shy of a roar, "I'm her father."

Duncan had to bite his tongue. "I'll admit she didn't like the choices, but she agreed. It's done. She's my wife and nobody, not you and not Morgan, is going to change that." He dropped his Stetson on the desk and ran both hands through his hair. Damn, he was tired and this was just the beginning. "She told him she loves me. I'd appreciate it if you didn't tell her I know. Not just yet."

James' smile turned to a grin. Duncan knew his friend, knew he wanted to jump up and shout for joy, but restrained himself.

"Well, if Kitten told White Buffalo she loves you, she must, or she'd never have gone through with the ceremony. She's a stubborn woman. Much as I hate to admit it, I don't think any of us could force her into something she didn't want. She could have called his bluff, or mine, we would have backed down. She knows it, too. Said she loves you, did she? Well, she's never said that about anyone before."

Both men turned as Catherine walked through the door. "I thought you might have killed him by now, Dad. Guess I was wrong."

James walked over and hugged her tight. "Duncan told me you two are married. I couldn't be more pleased; my two favorite people. We'll have a reception on Sunday, prior to which Reverend Black will marry you legally. I don't want there to be a question in anyone's mind."

Catherine interrupted, "But Dad..."

Stepping back from her, he looked her up and down, rubbed his chin, then frowned. "You better go to town and get yourself a dress and anything else you need for a wedding reception. Maybe some dresses for everyday wear, too. You can't go around in pants all the time, now that you're a married woman. Just have them put it on my bill."

Catherine tried again, "I already have a dress, and Dad, I don't..."

Duncan interrupted her. "She's my wife and I'll pay for her clothes from now on. I take care of what's mine, including Catherine. As to what she wears, I'll be the one to make that decision."

Catherine listened to both of her men and saw red. She turned on Duncan, left hand on her hip, poking his chest with her right index finger. "You'll make that decision?"

Poke.

"Like hell you will."

Poke.

"You two are the most arrogant...self-serving..." She stalked to the door. "You're talking about me like I wasn't even here. I'll decide what I'm going to wear and when. If I feel like strutting around in my birthday suit, I will." With those words, she ran out of the room and up the stairs.

"Oh damn. Catherine! Come back here." Duncan started after her.

James called after him, laughing. "You two are going to have a rousing good time...if you don't kill each other first."

Duncan took the stairs two at a time. When he reached the door to her bedroom, he stopped, started to knock, and then thought better of it. She was his wife. She wasn't going to get away with this flagrant disregard for his wishes. He'd have to set her straight now, or never get any peace. Expecting it to be locked, he turned the doorknob. It opened easily and he walked quietly into the room.

Catherine, seated at her dressing table, had removed the pins from her hair and was yanking a brush through it.

"What do you want?" she said without turning.

"We need to talk." He walked up behind her and gathered her hair in his hand. He sifted it through his fingers, enjoying its silky texture. He expected her to pull away. She didn't.

"I don't want to talk."

"Cat, I don't want there to be any misunderstandings between us." He stroked her neck with his fingertips. "All I want is to care for you. Look at me, sweetheart." When she turned toward him, he lifted her chin so she had no choice but to do as he bid. "You're mine, Catherine McKenzie. Don't ever forget it."

He pulled her up into his arms and kissed her so hard he thought they might never breathe again. Then he released her nearly as abruptly and left the room.

Catherine was dazed. It took a moment for her heart to stop racing and her breathing to return to normal. She shook her head to clear it and tried to make some sense out of the last few minutes.

Then she got mad.

Glaring at herself in the mirror, she said, "Try to tell me what to do, will he? Well, no one tells me what I will or won't do. I may be married to that...that braggart, but I'll be damned if he's going to put me under his thumb. And if he thinks he can wrap me around his finger with a few kisses, well, he's got another think coming!"

Braiding her hair, she put on her hat and went to the kitchen by the back stairs, avoiding the study and her father. One stubborn man to deal with was enough.

She knew Duncan would follow her, but she had enough of a head start that he wouldn't catch her 'til she reached town. She was not taking for granted their concern for her safety. They forget that she can ride and shoot as well as any man, and better than anyone that John had working for him, including Roy Walker.

She didn't need their protection around the clock. What she needed was some time to think, some time to herself, to be alone with her thoughts.

CHAPTER 13

Duncan followed Catherine to town, going directly to Peabody's Boardinghouse. Mary Peabody just grinned and handed him the key when he told her he and Catherine were married.

He took the stairs two at a time and used the key to open the door. As the door closed, Catherine bounded up, backing toward the far side of the room. He grinned as he came across the room toward her. This could be fun, playing chase, but he would have her.

She looked quickly toward the window. He sensed her about to try for it and just shook his head moving closer all the time.

The old iron bedsprings squeaked when she scrambled onto the bed. On her knees, ready to roll off the other side, he grabbed her ankles, flipped her onto her back and fell on top of her, using his body to pin her. He raised her arms over her head, trapping her wrists in one of his hands.

She squirmed and bucked underneath him. Every movement brought her into intimate contact with him. Finally, he felt her body succumb to his. Whatever resistance she felt was gone. He released her wrists and her arms came up around his neck and she brought her lips to his. She kissed him openly, warmly, thoroughly.

He raised his head and looked down at her. Her smile sent any questions he had straight out the open window into the warm afternoon sunshine.

Duncan could have stayed there, wrapped in her arms forever, but they couldn't, not now. He had obligations and the most important one was to keep her safe. Besides, they had all night, after they got back to the boardinghouse.

He leaned up on his forearms and smiled.. "Before I get too carried away and keep you in this bed for the rest of the day and night, we'd better go do that shopping."

She looked up at him, her eyes glazed over with passion. "Hmm, I suppose you're right but...kiss me again before we go. I like it when you kiss me."

He grinned down at her, lowering his head to capture her mouth. "Any time, Mrs. McKenzie," he whispered. "Any time at all."

*****

Catherine was silent while they walked up the stairs after dinner. She'd been doing a lot of thinking, and when they reached the door to the room they shared, she stopped and looked up at Duncan.

"We don't have to share this room. Mrs. Peabody can give me another," she said quietly, fearing he would accept her offer, praying that he didn't.

"We're married. Do you understand? There's no going back for either of us," he turned to the door and unlocked it, "no matter how much we may want to."

She stopped, her knees shaking. "Want to? You want to go back?" she whispered softly. Catherine's heart shattered hearing his words. He wanted to go back? He was sorry he'd married her?

"What?" He opened the door and ushered her across the threshold.

She lashed out at him, "If you want out of this marriage so badly, if you want to go back, we can always get a divorce. Surely, you're not worried about reputations at this late date."

"What brought that on?" He entered the room behind her, slamming the door. Divorce? *Over his dead body.* "There will be no divorce, not now, not ever. We're married, and on Sunday everyone will know it. You had better get that through your pretty little head. We're stuck with each other."

Then he took a deep, calming breath and said more softly, "Is it really so bad...being stuck with me? I told you once we'll be good together, and we will if you'd just give it a chance."

"I've never considered myself stuck with you." Reaching up she stroked his cheek. "I chose this, you're the one who sounds like you think you're stuck with me. Just tell me this, do you love me?"

He recognized the hurt in her eyes. He'd have given anything to tell her what she wanted to hear, but he couldn't. Even though he'd hurt her, he'd promised never to lie to her. He remembered another time, another woman...Madeline. He'd thought he loved her, given her everything he had to give. She'd betrayed him. The pain was still there, even after eight years.

He turned away, hoping Catherine didn't see the pain her question brought with it. His voice was soft, barely a whisper. "I don't know what love is...if there is such a thing. Don't ask me for what doesn't exist. I can't give it to you."

Her silence made him turn back to face her. She'd wrapped her arms around herself and her lip trembled as she asked, "If you can't give me love, what can you give me? Your name? I have a name. A home? I have one of those, too. So tell me, what can you give me?"

Confident his voice was sure, he said, "I can give you my trust, my respect, my protection, and my children. I don't have much else to offer."

Catherine looked into his indigo eyes. There was honesty there and something else. Something that gave her hope. What it was, she couldn't say, but it was there. She couldn't tell him she loved him, not yet. It would leave her much too vulnerable to tell him, if he didn't love her back.

She made a decision, one she hoped would see her through the long years to come; one she hoped she'd never have cause to regret.

She stroked along his jaw, her hand working it's way up into his thick, black hair. "I guess that'll have to do...for now. No other man has ever offered me his respect or his trust." Smiling she teased, "Although a few have offered to give me their children."

He reached for her. She came willingly into his arms, the tension broken, as she knew it would be.

"Well, Mr. McKenzie, I'm a bit tired and ready for

bed. How about you?"

"Oh, I'm ready for bed, Mrs. McKenzie, but I'm not the least bit tired," he replied, lifting her in his arms.

"We're not alone. They'll hear us. What will people think?" she cried, mortified.

"They'll think I'm bedding my wife, which is exactly what I intend to do. Now, are you going to get out of those clothes on your own, or do you want me to help you?" He chuckled as her eyes flew open wide.

"I didn't bring anything to sleep in."

"You don't need anything. You'll be warm enough, I'll wager, just wearing a smile."

The gleam in his eye made Catherine ache in the center of her being. She moistened her suddenly dry lips. "Yes, well, um, I don't need your help. If you'll just turn your back for a few minutes."

Before the words were out of her mouth, he was shaking his head. He lay down on the bed and crossed his arms behind his head. "I don't think so. I want to see you, sweetheart, in all your splendor."

"You can't mean..." she said, shaking her head. "You mean to just lay there and watch me get undressed! I can't do that." She was shocked down to her toes.

"I mean to do exactly that, Mrs. McKenzie. I want to see my wife and, since that's you, I think you'd better get started before I help you." His voice was stern but his eyes were laughing.

"Well, I never." She spun around

heading to the door.

He was off the bed like a shot. "Wait a minute, sweetheart." He grabbed her by the shoulders, pulling her back against his chest. He rested his chin on the top of her head and closed his arms around her.

Kissing the top of her head, his voice caressed her. "Where do you think you're going? I don't mean to scare you. Don't leave. Neither one of us will get any sleep if you do."

She pulled away from him enough to turn to face him. She leaned back in his arms and wrapped her arms around his neck. "You didn't scare me. You've never scared me. I admit to being a bit shocked, well completely shocked, actually. I've never had a man watch me undress in my life. It's embarrassing. This is all new to me."

She raised her hand to his cheek, feeling the stubble beneath her fingertips. "Try to understand. This is different. Even though we've already made love and seen each other...well...I can't explain it, it's just different, that's all."

"I do understand. It's new to me, too. Sometimes I forget you're so young. Forgive me. I'll never force my attentions on you. I only want you when you're willing." He pulled her back into his arms and began caressing her neck with his lips.

Catherine gave a low moan. "I'm not that young. Besides, all you have to do is touch me and I'm willing. It just isn't fair. My body betrays me. When you touch me, I don't seem to have any will power at all."

With his thumb and forefinger, he raised her chin so

she was looking at him. "Is that so bad, little one?" He smiled at her.

Before she could answer, his lips came down on hers, ever so softly, caressing gently, almost pleading.

Catherine was lost. That gentle ache in the center of her body became a raging inferno. Wrapping her arms around his neck, she kissed him with all the love in her heart.

Working quickly, he removed her shirt and camisole, revealing her breasts to his touch. His thumbs worked magic, caressing and teasing her nipples, which hardened in response. He kissed her jaw, then down her neck. Her head fell back and she lifted her breasts to him. Accepting one perfect peak into his mouth, he continued to tease the other with his thumb.

He sucked her deeper into his mouth, Catherine moaned, and arched her body. Moving his hands downward, he unbuttoned her denim pants, his mouth never leaving her breast. His tongue wove magic circles of increasing pleasure, making her ache for him to take her again into his mouth.

He removed her boots, then her pants, and found her mouth again, the kiss raw and full of hunger. She returned it just as hungrily. Like a drowning man clinging to a life preserver, she clung to him.

Her hands came down his chest and her fingers tangled in his soft, curly hair. Finding her way blocked by his shirt, she pulled at the buttons, ripping first one and then another. He stilled her hands, then he picked her up in his arms and placed her gently on the bed, their lips never parting.

He lifted his head and looked at her. "Darlin', if you don't slow down, you'll have to sew all my buttons on before we can leave in the morning." He stood up and removed his clothes.

Catherine put her hands behind her head and watched him just as he'd wanted to watch her. He was so at ease with his nudity. So comfortable with it. She smiled.

"Now just what are you smiling about, sweetheart?"

"I was just thinking. If you get even half as much pleasure watching me undress as I'm getting now," she moistened her lower lip, "I must drive you crazy."

Duncan rolled his eyes. "You're a minx. You drive me crazier than I've ever been. Are you only now realizing that? And yes, I like looking at you." He finished removing his clothes and lay down beside her. "But I get even more pleasure touching you." He pulled her into in his arms and kissed her deeply.

This was a kiss of possession. No mistake. She was his—body and soul.

He made slow, passionate love to her. He caressed her very soul along with her body, touched her with such tenderness...nothing else mattered. As wonderful as her life was on the ranch, something had always been missing. That something was Duncan. She knew that now.

No one else existed, only the two of them. Only this...only now...and whether he knew it or not, only love.

Duncan came to her in the night and loved her again. His strokes long and slow. Reaching between them, he rubbed her until her tremors began and she moaned from deep in the back of her throat. Then he let himself go and joined her in her climax, shouting her name as she shouted his.

She was a noisy one, his little wife.

Noisy, passionate, and she loved him. He didn't believe in love, but he found himself very pleased that she did. As long as it was with him.

CHAPTER 14

"I won't be able to help with the ranch chores for the next few days. I think I should help Alice get ready for the party. You know there's lots of food to get ready and decorating to do."

James, wide-eyed, said, "You're not planning on cooking are you?"

Catherine, a mischievous gleam in her eye, said innocently, "I thought I might help. I could learn some things, I know how much Duncan wants me to become a good little wife. What better time to try things out than on unsuspecting wedding guests?" She turned and left, her new skirt swishing as she walked.

"Son, you've got to do something." Panic filled James' voice. "Catherine's tried cooking before. I was sick for a week. Take her out on the range, look for strays, go hunting, anything to keep her out of the kitchen. These people coming on Sunday are my friends. I'd like to keep them that way."

"Oh, come on. Catherine told me she can't cook, but you don't really think she'd poison the people at her own party...do you?"

James didn't answer.

"Well, do you?"

Duncan watched James walk away, shaking his head and immediately tried to think of a way to keep Catherine out of the kitchen for the next few days. This was Thursday and the wedding was to take place on Sunday. How in the world was he going to keep her busy?

He knew what he'd like to do—keep her in bed for those days. Just the thought of her in bed, her soft silky skin next to his, made his body react violently. Good lord, what was the matter with him? He never reacted this way to a woman. But then, she was not just any woman. She was *his* woman and by God she would do as he told her to. Duncan smiled; he had the perfect idea to keep Cat out of Alice's hair for a few days. Whistling, he headed up the stairs to his blushing bride.

Duncan opened the door to the bedroom and silently went inside, closing the door behind him. Catherine sat in the middle of the bed awaiting him. She was clad in a filmy nightdress that revealed her creamy shoulders and enhanced her rounded breasts. He sucked in his breath at the beautiful sight she presented. All thoughts of talking to her about cooking went right out of his head. He stood, frozen to the spot, staring at her.

"Are you going to stand there all night?" she asked softly.

"I'm not sure I trust myself to move from here." His voice was a hoarse whisper.

She eased herself off the bed and sashayed over to him. The closer she came, the more he could see what the nightdress revealed. Which was much, much more than it concealed.

His gaze traveled the length of her and back,

settling on her silver eyes filled with unspoken desire.

"Sadie said this would make you take notice." She traced his neck from his Adam's apple to his chin as she turned and headed back to the bed. "Do you like what you see?"

He swung her around, wrapped his arms around her waist and pulled her close, letting her feel every inch of his arousal. "You tell me."

Locking his lips with hers, he swept her up into his arms, laying her gently on the bed, settling his own long body close to hers. He began to remove the flimsy negligee so he could touch her silky smooth skin, when she pulled away from him.

"No, this is my evening." She pushed at his chest until he reclined against the pillows. "I want to make you feel all the things that you make me feel. I want to make you crazy tonight."

Leaning over, she kissed him tenderly on the lips and lightly grazed his whiskered jaw with her fingers, before pushing back and sitting on the edge of the bed.

Duncan smiled and crossed his arms behind his head. "Very well, Mrs. McKenzie, I'm completely at your disposal."

"Come to the edge of the bed, please."

He moved to the side of the bed and sat there. She turned, pointed her shapely derriere at him and lifted his legs one at a time, holding them with her knees, to remove his boots. He reached his hand toward her bottom, and then pulled it back. It was all he could do not to touch that lovely, rounded part of her so nicely presented to him.

"Now, stand up, please." He stood and she unfastened his gun belt and hung it on the bed post. Then she unbuttoned his shirt. Burying her fingers in the dark, curly hair, she fanned her hands across his wide chest, moving up to his shoulders. Then she moved down his arms, lovingly caressing them as she removed the shirt and tossed it aside. Kneeling in front of him, she undid his belt and pants, caressing his legs as she moved the trousers down them.

She watched him struggle to keep from touching her, to keep himself under control. As she unbuckled his pants, his erection sprang forward, but still he resisted. She had him step out of his pants and caressed his legs and buttocks, coming eye to eye with his manhood.

She stared at the appendage before her and couldn't resist running her fingers over the velvety texture. It was soft and silky, but terribly hard as well. He threw his head back and groaned deeply. She moved her head so she could rub her cheek against it, then kissed the tip. Pulling back, she saw the small bead of liquid at the tip and flicked her tongue out to taste him.

That sent him over the edge. He bent down and scooped her up in his arms, tossed her on the bed, landing on top of her, and still managed to keep most of his weight on his arms.

"Are you trying to drive me insane or is this just your way of punishing me for some reason?" His breath came in short pants, his dark eyes pierced her like a dart.

"Umm, do you feel punished?" she said, running her hands through his coal black hair. "Perhaps I should stop, and we can just go to sleep now." She tried to turn away from him, but he wouldn't let her.

"Oh no you don't, you little witch." He lowered his weight onto her, pinning her underneath him. "You started this and I'm going to see that you finish it, even if it kills me," he said hoarsely, then fiercely took possession of her lips with his own.

She let him take her on a magical journey. That was what her couplings with Duncan were, magical journeys. Each one more special than the one before. She couldn't tell him though, he'd never understand her feeling of being carried away. He was always in such control.

She felt wanton, free. Wriggling her hips against his erection, his kiss became more possessive, if that was actually possible. Smiling, she decided, maybe he wasn't always in control. She felt him start to lose his composure, and reveled in the knowledge she could do that to him. Hugging him tighter to her, she grabbed his hair in her hands to press his head even closer.

He moved his lips down her neck, trailing hot, wet kisses all the way. Her nightdress covered her ripe breasts, temporarily stopping his seeking lips. He pulled at the tie with his teeth, never letting his hands stop caressing the silken skin of her thighs.

He found the downy hair that covered her most secret part and gently started stroking it, pressing, making lazy circles with his palm. He parted her nether lips and manipulated her with his finger, very gently, then harder, then gently again.

She tried to wrap her arms around him, hoping to bring him closer to her, but he pushed them away, anchoring them both above her head with one of his hands. All the while, he continued the magical motion of his fingers with the other.

He managed to loosen the tie on her gown but grew frustrated, and he suddenly grabbed it, ripping the flimsy material from her body.

Catherine gasped when his hand left her to grab her nightdress. She ached and her body arched, seeking his hand.

He trailed wet, searing kisses all the way down her body, then slid between her legs. He released her hands so he could tease and play with her nipples and gently knead her breasts with his hands. His tongue made circles and curly-queues in and around her navel and continued on. Then he was there, probing and teasing her with his tongue.

Her eyes flew open. "Oh. My. God..." Her voice trailed off as he continued the pleasurable dance with his tongue.

She dug her hands into his hair and pressed his head closer to her, afraid she would smother him, but afraid if she let go, he'd leave her. She was so close, the burning deep within her and rising to touch every nerve. Her hands were suddenly above her, gripping the headboard, her teeth clamped together to control the scream rising in her throat. The sun exploded and all its rays shimmered down upon her. She bucked and twisted, but his tongue never stopped its sweet torture.

As she began to return to her senses, she was still extremely sensitive and, as she soon discovered, ticklish. He continued to tease her with his tongue.

She smiled and began to move his head away,

but he continued, as if she had not touched him. She giggled at first and then laughed. Soon she was begging for him to stop and laughing at the same time.

He looked up at her. With one brow arched and a devilish grin on his face, he said, "This is supposed to be the most fun you can have *without* laughing." Then he laughed himself.

She continued to giggle and buck under him. He kept to his task and the fires within her built again. She no longer giggled but moaned, begging for him not to stop, screaming his name, as wave after wave of pleasure washed over her.

Lifting himself over her, he plunged into her slick wetness. "God, you feel so good, so right. I don't think I'll ever get used to you." He buried his face in her neck and nipped at her while he stroked in and out of her warmth. She met each thrust, bringing him deeper and deeper. With one last hard thrust, he buried himself deep within her, throwing back his head, shouting her name.

A long while later, after he'd regained his senses, he rolled over, bringing her with him, then pulled her close in his arms and nuzzled her neck. "I've never known anyone like you in my life."

"And you never will, Mr. McKenzie. I'm unique, and you'd better remember that." She cuddled closer, turning herself in his arms so she could feel his chest next to her cheek and closed her eyes. He decided to let her sleep, for now.

*****

Catherine felt wonderful. After the loving she and Duncan did last night, she could take on anything.

Whistling, she went to the barn to start her chores. He'd let her sleep late, again. He and her father were already out culling the herd, pulling out the weaker animals. If there were no signs of sickness, they would be corralled, fed for a couple of weeks, then slaughtered for the smokehouse. Those with symptoms of disease would just be shot and burned or buried so the disease wouldn't spread.

She had an easy day today. She'd already milked the cows and gathered the eggs. Now all she needed to do was feed the horses. After that, she could spend the rest of the day in the kitchen with Alice. She was determined to make dinner tonight and show her father and Duncan that she could cook an edible meal.

Swinging open the barn door, she walked through talking to all the horses as she went. She checked on the cat and her new litter of kittens. The babies were just opening their eyes. The runt was her favorite. He was a gray tabby, so little he fit in the palm of her hand. She picked him up and stroked him then scratched him under his chin.

"Hello, Sebastian. How is my baby kitty today? Hmm?" She set him back at his mother's teat so he could eat. He needed all the milk he could get if he was going to stand up to his brothers and sisters. She reached the double doors on the far side of the barn and swung both doors wide, letting in light and fresh air.

Going back inside, she grabbed the pitchfork and started giving the horses their breakfast. There were twelve stalls, six on each side of the barn. Eight of those still had horses in them needing to be fed. Wildfire was the last. She fed and watered her baby, then gave him the carrots she always carried just for him. That was when family. Some family named Smith adopted Jenny. They couldn't have kids and she was only three and the cutest little thing. All curly blond hair and blue eyes.

"Me? I was ten and harder to place. I got sent to a family that needed labor. Slave labor. That's all I was to them. They worked me 'til I couldn't do anything but fall into bed at night. Then it started all over again in the morning, and when I tried to refuse, they starved me.

"I left, but I didn't get far the first time. They found me and the old man beat me." He came closer, pulled up his shirt and showed her his back. "Cat o'nine. That's what he used. These scars will never go away. They remind me of what I owe Duncan McKenzie."

"Oh my God." Catherine couldn't help h⸍ She'd never seen anyone scarred like that. ⸏ scars over scars over scars. He'd been h⸍ once. "I'm sorry for what happen⸍ not Duncan's fault. It was ⸍ lives, lots of children lost th⸍

His eyes lost their gla⸍ her. "Maybe. Maybe not. It does⸍ way it was because of McKenz⸍ they're going to pay. Shut up. I d⸍ more about poor Duncan." He turn⸍ sitting at the table. "Pete, you got th⸍ hungry."

"Comin' right up, Roy." The little⸍ plates on the table. He sat across from⸍ started eating. It was disgusting, watching th⸍ food into their mouths and then chew so she ⸍ everything. Catherine turned her head away. W⸍ appetite she might have had was gone now.

---

the blow came and she saw stars.

Catherine glanced at the man across the cabin from her. If her head didn't feel like it would explode if she moved, she might've tried to send him into the wall and get free. But as it was, her head hurt so bad, she barely noticed the pain in her wrists. He'd tied her tight. Her legs were still free though; she guessed he couldn't carry her by himself.

He was older, not very tall and was pretty skinny, but she wouldn't mistake that for weakness. He could still be strong as a bull moose. She didn't recognize him, but then she didn't know all of Morgan's men; he could be a new hire. If she could just get these ropes loose... The door slammed open and Roy Walker sauntered in like he owned the place.

"Well, looks like the little princess is awake. Good, I want you aware of everything that happens." He walked over and removed the dirty rag they had used as a gag from her mouth.

"This here's my favorite." He blew his nose into the rag and shoved it in his pocket.

Catherine thought she was going to throw up. That thing had been in her mouth. Uggg!

"What do you want from me, Walker? Dad is never going to sell to John, no matter what. Kidnapping me isn't going to change that." She kept her eyes on him all the while working her binds looser.

"I don't want your land. Never did. I came here to get even with McKenzie."

She drew her attention to her surroundings. The cabin was small, only one room. There were two bunks in one corner on the far side of the door. She was sitting on the floor next to the fireplace, the door only a few feet from her. She didn't know if they'd put her here so she'd be warm, or if it was just the first place they could drop her. The latter she suspected.

The kitchen area, a counter with some shelves above it, was on the other side of the fireplace. The only weapons she saw were the ones the men had strapped to their legs. There was no way she would be able to get one of those. No, when she got loose, she would just have to hightail it out of here and try to get back to the ranch. The only problem, she didn't know where 'here' was.

She could head away from here, go farther into the mountains if possible. They could never follow her, even with her on foot. She knew too well how to cover her trail. Thank goodness they didn't get the knife in her boot. Men never suspected that a woman would be equipped with the same gear as they were. With that she could survive as long as necessary. It would be hard, but it wouldn't be the first time she'd been out alone.

Duncan and her father were going to be furious when they found out she'd taken off by herself. Oh well, they'd just have to get over it. Right now all that mattered was getting away from these two.

*****

"Gone! What do you mean gone?" Duncan roared. "She knew she wasn't to leave this house without me."

"Duncan, yelling isn't going to get us

"Why? What could Duncan have done to you?" She kept working the ties that bound her hands. Were they getting looser? Yes, she could actually feel her blood start to flow again, and with it the tingling pain of feeling.

"Done to me? What hasn't he done to me? He killed my father. In cold blood, he killed my father."

"You're crazy. Duncan's never killed anyone in cold blood."

"Oh, he did all right. He doesn't know that it was my father, but I found out. Even in war there are witnesses. I don't care if they were on opposite sides. He killed him just as sure as he is going to die for it. And killed your father, too."

"Dad? What could he have to do with this?" Then she remembered. She knew how Dad and Duncan met. Duncan had saved his life. By killing a man.

"That was war. You can't seriously hold either of them responsible for something that happened then." She fought her ties harder, knowing that if she didn't get loose, she would die. Walker was crazy and he would kill her.

"Oh but I do. He took everything from ... day. My mother tried. She died trying to pro... and my sister. She worked her fingers ... to hold on to the farm. But it was ...

Catherine watche...
...alked. He was back...
...organ...

anywhere." James was able to keep his temper in check, but barely. He knew it would do no good to have them both yelling at Alice. "Alice, where did she go?"

"She only went to the barn to feed the animals. When she didn't come back, I sent word to you. That's all I know. Wildfire is still here, so she didn't take off on her own."

Alice cried into her handkerchief. "I'm so worried. She wouldn't go off by herself any more. I know she wouldn't."

James took Alice in his arms and held her while she cried. "Hush now. We'll find her."

He set Alice away from him, her tears having stopped. "We better get saddled up and see if we can find her. The place to start is the bluffs, and that is a good hour ride."

"I'm already saddled. You can catch up."

"I'll get some men and meet up with you. Find her, Duncan. Find my baby."

"I will," he said as he rushed out the door into the twilight.

"You'll find her? I don't know what I'd do if anything happened to her." Alice was ringing her hands as she spoke. Her eyes still filled with tears and red from crying.

James took Alice in his arms again and kissed the top of her head. "We'll find her. You know she can take care of herself. She's going to be fine." He said it as much for his own comfort as Alice's.

*****

Catherine watched as the two men lay down for the night. She had to be vigilant, but she was so tired. The ache in her head was now down to a dull roar. Her hands were free, though she kept them behind her back. She would love to bring them out and rub them, but she didn't dare. Slowly, Walker and Pete put out the lamps and turned in. The only light now was from the fireplace, and it was dying.

"Hey, Walker. What about a blanket? It's goin' to get cold tonight." She hoped the blanket would hide her hands as she brought them around and got the rest of the feeling back in them.

"You don't need a blanket. Doesn't matter if the dead get cold." Walker said from his bunk, without ever looking at her.

She shivered at his words. If she didn't escape soon, she never would. Just a little longer. She could wait until they were asleep. Just a little longer.

Her head snapped up in terror. She must have fallen asleep. The fire was completely out, the only light was coming from the moon through the small window above her. That was all she needed. Slowly, she rose from her place on the floor.

Long ago, she had learned to move silently, she would be forever grateful to Gray Wolf for those lessons. She moved around the table to the door, easing the latch up and pulling the door open. Just as slowly, so as not to make any noise, she closed the door behind her. Straightening, she turned to step off the porch when a hand covered her mouth and an arm like a steel band cinched her waist back against a rock hard chest.

"Quiet!" the deep masculine voice whispered.

She immediately relaxed. Duncan. He'd come for her. She kissed his palm where it covered her mouth and his hold on her waist relaxed, became a caress as he gently rubbed her side.

"Follow me."

"Anywhere," she replied silently, her heart singing. He'd come for her, nothing else mattered.

She walked silently behind him to where Jake waited, surprised Duncan made no noise.

He lifted her as if she weighed nothing and swung himself onto the saddle behind her, then settled her comfortably in his lap before he nudged Jake's sides. They rode quietly for a safe distance then Duncan clicked his tongue, and Jake sped up to a gallop. Duncan held her close to him with one hand, guiding Jake with the other.

"It was Walker, not John Morgan." She suddenly remembered what Walker had said. "Duncan, Walker is after you. He said you killed his father and he wants you and Dad. Dead, he wants you both dead."

Duncan slowed Jake to a walk. "How could I have killed his father? I didn't even know Walker until a few years ago."

"He said you killed his father in the war. He doesn't care that it was war. In his mind you took everything from him and made his life miserable. Now he wants you to pay for everything he and his sister Jenny went through."

Catherine continued, "She was adopted by a wealthy couple that couldn't have children. I think he resents it that her life was better than his. He blames you for that, too. We have to get back to Dad and warn him. It's not just John Morgan we're fighting anymore. Walker doesn't care about the money or the land. He just wants you two."

"Right. Let's go." He clicked his tongue again, the sound slightly different and Jake immediately broke into a run. Dawn was just breaking over the mountain, but Jake didn't need the light. Duncan knew he was sure footed and knew the way home.

*****

James and his riders greeted them halfway between the ranch and the cabin Walker had taken her to.

"You found her. We went to the bluffs, but it was too dark to track them. Started again at sun up. How'd you find her?" James pulled his horse, Apache, up beside them.

"An old bounty hunter skill." Duncan said as if tracking in the dark was a skill every bounty hunter had.

James nodded and then turned his attention to Catherine. "Are you all right? Do you have any idea how much worry you put poor Alice through? She's been in tears all night and was still crying when I left. If you were younger, I'd turn you over my knee for scaring her so."

"But, Dad, I just went to the barn..."

"Don't. Don't even start with any excuses. There

is nothing you can say that is going to change my mind. You are going to start acting like a lady from now on. Duncan's here now and can take over your chores. You will start learning to be a lady."

"No, I can't. I have responsibilities. I..."

"Enough." James roared. "Your responsibilities are to the people on this ranch."

Catherine had never seen her father like this before.

"Finally, some peace." James muttered.

She looked up at Duncan, unshed tears in her eyes, then turned away and stared straight ahead.

He understood James' anger wasn't really at Catherine. It was at Walker, at Morgan and at the situation they'd been put in. He was trying to protect her the only way he could, by curtailing her freedom. As much as he may have agreed with James, he knew how she felt. He pulled her close and gave her a squeeze.

"He'll calm down." He whispered in her ear. "He was just scared. Loving someone does that to a person."

She sniffled. "I know. But it still hurts."

She said nothing more until they reached the ranch. As Duncan lifted her down, she said, "Thank you for coming after me, even though I escaped Walker on my own. It was nice to know you cared about Dad enough to come for me."

She turned away from him as he set her on the

ground, but he didn't let go of her arm. Pulling her back to him, he wrapped his arms around her and kissed her senseless.

"I didn't do it for James." He kissed her again and let her go, slapping her bottom as she walked away.

"Oh!" She spun to give him what for, but he was already walking Jake to the barn, whistling as he went.

CHAPTER 15

Duncan planned on going to see if Cassie Morgan would come to keep Catherine out of Alice's hair and especially out of the kitchen. He knew he was taking a chance going into Morgan's territory, but if he could get her away from her brother, he'd be not only saving her, but everyone subjected to Catherine's cooking, as well. He was taking his coffee with him out to the barn when he saw Cassie come through the gate. The fact that she came in a buggy and with a trunk should have alerted him that something was wrong, but he was so pleased that he paid no attention.

"Cassie, I was just on my way to see you." Smiling, he walked over to the buggy.

When he got close enough to see her face, his smile fell. The dust from the ride outlined the paths of her tears. A bruise showed on her right cheek and the split lip at the side of her mouth still bled.

"Good God, girl, what happened to you?" He dropped his cup and helped her down. She clung to him, sobs wracking her body.

"Roy Walker is what happened. He cornered me in the kitchen this morning after everyone else had gone. He tried to..." she cried harder.

"You're safe now. Shhh. You'll be fine. Tell me what happened," he coaxed, holding her in his arms, letting her cry.

"It's not..." she sniffed, "not the first time he's tried to, but it sure as hell will be the last. When I resisted he just laughed. I kicked him and screamed. Then he hit me. When I hit the floor, he realized what he'd done, because he left. John is useless. He says he needs him and I must be exaggerating."

Her body shuddered. He held her and gently stroked her back, calming her as he would skittish colt.

Between sobs she tried to tell him everything. He let her get it off her chest. Some instinct told him it would be best to just let her talk.

"I packed my bags and I came here as fast as I could. It's the only place I can be safe." She looked up at him, her eyes still wild with fear. "Don't you see, if I go to town, John will just drag me back home. I'd rather die than let that man touch me again. I can't go back. I just can't." She burst into tears again.

"Hush now. You're not going anywhere except upstairs." He held her gently but firmly, trying to comfort her.

Wrapping her arms around his waist, she sobbed into his chest. Then she pulled back, looking up at him. "I'm so sorry. I should have left sooner or done something to stop John. I'll do anything I can to help you stop him now. I guess it took this," she said, pointing to her face, "to make me realize just how dangerous John has become."

"I know Catherine is going to be glad to see you,

and you can count on all of us to help you." He hugged her and was about to release her when he heard Catherine.

"Well, what have we here?"

He could hear the jealously in Catherine's voice and was inordinately pleased. Turning to her he said, "Catherine, I—"

"Cassie!" She hurled herself down the steps to her friend. "I am so glad to see you. But what's going on? Why are you here?"

As Cassie pulled back, Catherine saw her face and she wrapped her arms around her. "Oh Cassie, what happened? Are you all right? Come on inside, we'll get something for the swelling and get your lip cleaned up. Duncan," she said over her shoulder, "would you please get Cassie's trunk and take it upstairs to the bedroom across from ours?"

"Sure, and I'll let James know he has another house guest."

Cassie turned back and smiled. "Thank you for letting me cry on your shoulder."

"Anytime."

Catherine ushered Cassie inside and got her coat off. Cassie had put up one heck of a fight with someone. The bodice and sleeve of her dress were torn. Her neck and arm were bruised. Just looking at her best friend made Catherine want to cry.

"What the hell happened to you? You look like you've been in a fight!"

"Oh God! Catherine!" Cassie broke down, sobbing.

Catherine gathered her friend in her arms, holding her, stroking her hair and gently rocking her. "It's okay now. Everything is okay," she crooned as she would to a small child.

After Cassie told her what had happened that morning and what she'd been putting up with for the past few months, Catherine got mad, but she couldn't do anything except help Cassie now.

"I'm so sorry. Dear God, why didn't you tell me sooner what was going on? I would have helped," she said, hugging her friend.

"I couldn't tell you. I was afraid for anyone to know, and he never really hurt me before, he just taunted me. I thought I could handle him. It wasn't until today that I realized I was just fooling myself."

Cassie smiled at Catherine, "I may be slow at some things, but I'm not completely stupid."

Catherine laughed; she couldn't help it. "No one ever said you were. Oh, I'm glad you're here. We'll get you all dolled up and a little powder will cover that shiner. It'll be so much fun."

"I feel safe here. Something I never thought I'd feel again. I've been so afraid. I didn't know what to do."

"You did the right thing by coming here. To hell with that brother of yours. I won't let anyone hurt you ever again, and neither will Duncan or Dad. Don't give it another thought. All right?"

"Thank you."

"No thanks necessary. That's what friends are for."

She finished getting Cassie cleaned up and then took her upstairs to get into a clean dress. When they were through, Cassie sat on the bed and looked Catherine straight in the eye. "So, does Duncan know you love him?"

Catherine sat down beside her and twisted her hands in her lap. "You sound just like Beth and no, he doesn't. I never could keep anything from you though, could I?"

"Never," she agreed. "Who's Beth?"

"Beth Peterson. It's a long story, but she and her husband are staying with us 'til after their baby is born."

"A baby! Oh how wonderful! I do so love babies." Cassie clapped her hands together and smiled. "Oh," she winced and put her fingers to her lip. "Darn it."

Catherine grabbed another clean cloth and handed it to her. "Here, you're bleeding again. And speaking of babies, Sarah and Zeke had a little girl, so you'll get all the babies you want."

Cassie dabbed at her mouth, then held the cloth there. "Good. Between that and you telling me about you and Duncan, I'll hopefully get my mind off what happened. So...tell me about how you met again after all these years, why you married in White Buffalo's village. Everything."

"All right." Catherine got up and paced the room, but she told her everything, from the beginning.

When she finished, Cassie sighed. "Oh, it's all so romantic. But what are you going to do to get him to fall in love with you?"

"Well, I don't know really. I figure I'll just be a good wife and maybe he'll grow to love me. If I could just get him to tell me what happened to him, why he doesn't believe in love anymore, I could...fix it. It must've been something really awful. I just don't believe we can live as husband and wife without loving each other. I have to make him realize that."

"Good luck. From what you said, he's a pretty stubborn man."

"He is, and I'll need all the luck I can get." Catherine laughed, but crossed her fingers anyway. "Come on now, let's go on downstairs and get something to eat. You're going to need your strength, 'cause we're going to be so busy. Alice really needs my help in the kitchen, and you can help too."

"Kitchen?" Cassie choked. "You're going to help Alice in the kitchen?"

"Yes. What's so amazing about that?"

"You can't cook, that's what's so amazing. I think I should help Alice in the kitchen and you should do something else."

"Like what?"

"Anything but cook." Cassie snorted, trying to contain her laughter. She was not successful and winced again in pain.

"Why is it everyone thinks I can't cook? I can cook, and I will prove it to you. All of you."

If she hadn't been trying to comfort Cassie she would have stomped off, but as it was, she kept heading for the kitchen with her arm around Cassie's shoulder.

*****

As Sunday neared, Catherine became more nervous. She and Duncan lived as man and wife under her father's roof, but what if she couldn't get him to love her?

Though she didn't know why she bothered, she put on a soft cotton nightgown. It never stayed on her long. Brushing her hair, it occurred to her that if Duncan wanted, he could just walk away. Marriage or not. She laid down the brush and paced the room. She had to think of a way to keep Duncan with her, even if he wanted to go.

She was still pacing when Duncan came upstairs. He closed the door softly behind him and leaned against it watching her in silence. He looked like he'd never get enough of her. She knew she'd never get enough of him, not in a thousand lifetimes, and she only had this one.

She ran to his waiting arms. "Oh, Duncan, I'm so worried."

"What about?"

"The party. What if no one shows up or they don't have fun or..." *What if you leave me?*

"Sweetheart, why do you let yourself get so worked up?" He squeezed her tight, resting his chin on top of her head. "The party's going to be fine, all your friends are going to be here, and everyone will have a great time. Don't worry."

She nodded. "I'm just nervous and I haven't the foggiest idea why." But she knew. She still had her doubts, but she pushed them aside, for now.

He chuckled. "I've heard it's a normal thing for the bride to be nervous. I always thought it was just virginal brides fearing the wedding night. But we're beyond that and getting to know each other very well." He ground his arousal against her belly.

She blushed. He loved to make her blush. Still wrapped in his arms, he lowered his head to kiss her. He took her mouth hard, grinding his lips against hers. Plunging his tongue into her mouth, it danced with hers. Pulling his mouth away, he rested his forehead against hers.

He picked her up in his arms and carried her over to the bed. Laying her down in the middle of it, he stopped only long enough to take off his clothes and strip off her nightgown, before coming down on top of her.

He made sweet love to her and she felt cherished.

Later, unable to sleep, her mind raced, sure Duncan felt something for her. Did he love her? She felt he did and just didn't know it. What she needed was a way to make him realize it, convince him it was real. She thought of how they'd made love and then Duncan had held her in his arms until he slept. She smiled.

She was still smiling, remembering how wonderful it felt, when he turned his head, took her nipple in his mouth and suckled. She hadn't realized he was awake, and here he was going to make love to her again and she was ready to love him right back.

*****

Sunday morning was finally here. The sun shone bright on the valley. Catherine thanked God Cassie was there. Alice and Beth were busy with the cooking and the decorating. They had no time to help her prepare, so it was a blessing in more ways than one that Cassie had come to stay with them.

Catherine hurried through her normal morning chores then took a long bath with the lavender soap she saved for special occasions. She supposed this was the most special occasion she'd ever have. She washed her hair twice, combed the tangles from it and let it dry. It was naturally wavy and if she didn't braid it, then it would curl and wave all down her back.

Cassie arranged it with loose curls on top and long ringlets cascading down her back. She pulled a few tendrils loose to curl softly around her face. Then she wove her mother's pearls in and out of the curls, spreading them so they swept down her back, carefully pinning them all in place. Some of the ringlets she spread over her shoulders.

Cassie wanted to apply cosmetics to her, but Catherine refused. She finally gave up saying Catherine was pretty enough without it, then she helped her get into the dress.

Cassie hadn't seen Catherine in the deep blue satin dress Catherine had bought the day she saw them in the mercantile. She caught her breath when Catherine turned around. "My God, Catherine you look magnificent. Every woman here, including me, is going to be green with envy when they see you in that gorgeous dress. And the pearls in your hair are a perfect color match to the seed pearls on the dress. Duncan won't be able to take his eyes off you."

"Do you really think so?" she asked shyly. Never having thought of herself as beautiful, she glanced in her mother's full-length cheval mirror.

She was tall and big, but with muscle not fat, well proportioned for her height. Her waist was small, which made her chest and hips look larger, but Duncan didn't seem to mind that she was a big girl. Hell, next to him, she actually felt small.

"Yes, I do," said Cassie. "I've never seen you look so beautiful, and look how long we have known each other."

Catherine smiled, twirled around and gazed at herself again in the mirror.

"Thank you." She took Cassie's hands in her. "Thank you for being my friend and being here to share this day with me."

Cassie's eyes filled with tears. "Oh, I wouldn't have missed it for the world." She hugged her and pulled quickly away, wiping her eyes with the back of her hand. "Now this just won't do. Your eyes will be all red and puffy. If Duncan sees you like that, he'll think you changed your mind."

"But I'm not the one who's crying." They both laughed.

There was a soft knock at the door.

"Catherine, it's Dad. May I come in?"

Cassie went and opened the door wide. James stepped through and froze.

Catherine bent her head, looking at her father, in his best black suit and bolo tie through her eyelashes and smiled a small smile. Her father was so handsome. His eyes were the same silver-gray as hers and with the silver at his temples, they shone bright. Or maybe it was because he was seeing her, ready for her wedding, finally.

"Will I do, Papa?"

"You're beautiful. Daughter, you do me proud." He walked over, hugged her then put her hand in the crook of his arm. "It's time we went down and got this shindig underway."

She thought she saw a tear in his eye as he walked her down the stairs to the parlor, but knew she must be mistaken. Her father never cried.

Her father and Duncan had moved the furniture in the parlor, the sofa and matching chairs they never used, to the side of the room. They formed the aisle that she walked down. Duncan stood with the preacher, the good Reverend Black, at the end. Alice had gathered wild blue and yellow columbines and set them in vases on the tables around the room. It was beautiful, something Catherine would remember for the rest of her life.

Her father took her toward Duncan. She watched his mouth slowly drop open and his eyes grow wide. He took her arm from her father and her heart pounded so hard she thought he might hear it. He only smiled at her, straightened his back and turned with her to stand in front of the preacher.

Duncan was a sight to behold. Dressed in a black suit and snowy white shirt that contrasted wonderfully against his tanned skin. He wore a silver bolo tie at his neck, his hair tied back with a black satin ribbon and a new black Stetson sat at a rakish angle on his head. Catherine had never seen him look so handsome, even including the wedding at White Buffalo's camp, where she didn't think he could get any more wonderful to look at, yet somehow he'd managed it.

James, Alice and Cassie served as witnesses to the ceremony. When Reverend Black pronounced them man and wife, Duncan took her in his arms. He'd intended to give her a gentle little peck, but it turned passionate, as it always seemed to whenever they kissed.

James cleared his throat and Cassie giggled before he pulled away. He tucked her hand in the crook of his elbow and together they greeted their neighbors and friends. James proudly announced their marriage and introduced Duncan to everyone as his favorite son.

The party was loud and boisterous. Alice outdid herself preparing food for the celebration. She'd had James slaughter a steer and slow roasted it over an open pit the day before.

In addition to the beef, she'd prepared fried chicken, mashed potatoes and gravy, pinto beans and cornbread, baking powder biscuits, and fresh peas, carrots and onions from the garden.

Catherine couldn't believe how much food there was. It was a veritable feast, and Alice fluttered among the guests like a proud mama, which in a way she was, as she met and greeted everyone, making sure they all had plenty of food and drink. No one would leave this party hungry, if Alice had anything to say about it.

The wedding cake was Catherine's favorite, white cake with boiled icing covered in shredded coconut, and she was hard pressed not to stick her finger in it to take some of the icing. Only two layers, Catherine cut it in small slices and still there were only sixteen pieces…all of which she wanted to keep. There were lots of other desserts, cobblers, pies and cakes. All the guests got something sweet, even if they didn't get any of the actual wedding cake.

James hired some local musicians to play so they could dance. She loved to dance and was delighted to discover Duncan was an excellent dancer. He even knew how to waltz, which she did not, but he never let her falter, holding her tight, twirling her around and around until she was nearly dizzy.

She'd never felt so wonderful. The day was perfect. When her father danced with her, he held her close and told her again how very happy he was and how proud he was of her. She saw the joy in his eyes. He was happy she'd married, but more so that she'd married Duncan. Now he really could call him son.

The celebration went on all afternoon and well into the night. Catherine was happy and exhausted by the time Duncan came to her side and told her it was time they left. She turned to say goodbye to everyone, but Duncan stopped her.

"They won't even know we're gone. Besides I don't really want a shivery, do you?"

"Lord, no. But shouldn't we at least say goodnight to Dad and Cassie? After all, she just got here and I don't want her to feel deserted. And what about Beth and Tom?"

"They're all fine," he said, pulling her into his arms. "I don't think Cassie will notice, and she certainly won't feel deserted. Haven't you noticed her and Michael seem to be getting along quite well? They've spent all evening together."

She moved away from him, looked for and found Cassie in the crowd. Sure enough, she was standing in deep conversation with Michael, the ranch foreman, who was holding her hand. "Well, I'll be. She's recovering from her traumatic experience rather well, don't you think?"

"Very well. Now come with me. I have a surprise for you."

"What? Tell me."

"If I told you, it wouldn't be a surprise. You'll just have to trust me." He held out his hand to her.

She took his hand and grinned. "I trust you. I married you, didn't I?"

He took her around to the back of the house where Jake was tethered to the hitching post. Behind the saddle, two saddlebags bulged.

Duncan swung up into the saddle, held his arms out to Catherine, and lifted her to sit sideways on his lap.

"Can't be getting your dress all dirty," he said absently. He nudged Jake with his knees and they took off, headed southwest.

"You're taking me to town?"

"Nope."

"Where then?"

"Curious little thing aren't you. You know what they say about curiosity and the Cat?"

"Oh, quit teasing me. Where are we going?"

"Not far. We're nearly there."

As they approached, she saw a small building of some kind, which she didn't remember being there before. She smelled the smoke from the chimney and saw light coming from inside.

They stopped in front of a cabin and Duncan carefully slid Catherine to the ground, then dismounted. She walked toward the door, but he stopped her, gathering her high in his arms. She squealed and wrapped her arms around his neck.

"It's traditional for the groom to carry the bride over the threshold," he whispered, striding toward the door. He bent carefully, turned the knob and crossed into the cabin, closing the door with his foot.

Catherine looked around in amazement. A bed covered with a beautiful wedding ring quilt stood in one corner. A cozy fire crackled in the fireplace. In the center of the room was a round dining table and two chairs. A bottle of wine chilled in a bucket of icy river water. Two wineglasses were on the table, along with fresh wild flowers, more blue and yellow columbines. Catherine figured there must not be any more columbines on their property. They were all picked for her wedding celebration.

"Oh Duncan, it's beautiful. But where...this cabin wasn't here before."

"This is the first room of the house that Tom and Beth are building. Your dad thought the little house on the South Ranch would be too small, with their growing family. I asked if we could borrow it for a couple of days. We can be alone and get to know one another a little better. Do you like it, really?"

"Oh yes. I love it." She turned in his arms and kissed him soundly. "I want us to get to know each other, too, even though we have the rest of our lives to do it. What a wonderful way to start. This is a new beginning for both of us. I never knew you were so romantic."

"There are lots of things we don't know about each other. But we have a few days to explore each other." He gave her a lecherous grin, and then he slid her slowly down his body until her feet touched the floor.

She kept her arms around his neck, her voice laced with false dismay. "Why, Duncan McKenzie, by the look on your face, I believe you mean to keep me in bed for the next few days."

"And if I do, would that be so bad?" He hugged her closer.

"I can't think of anything I'd like more." Then she stood on tiptoe and kissed him.

The next few days were the best Catherine could remember having in a very long time. The whole outside world ceased to exist. There was only her and Duncan, alone. They laughed, loved, and talked, then loved some more.

It was going so well that she decided to broach the subject of his past.

Early on the fourth day of their honeymoon, they laid in bed after making love. Catherine turned to Duncan and ran her fingers through the curly black hair that sprinkled his chest.

"There's something I want to ask you. You don't have to answer, but I hope you do. Beth says that you must have been hurt dreadfully to not believe in love anymore." She felt him stiffen. "Is that true? Please tell me. I really need to know, But I'll understand if you don't want to talk about it."

He wrapped a strand of her hair around his fingers and brought it to his nose, inhaling deeply before releasing it. Sighing, he began, "Well, I guess you might as well know. Then we can put it and this silly notion of love behind us. I met her in Denver. I was twenty-six and getting tired of my life. I wanted to settle down, have a family, and had enough money for a place of my own. Her name was Madeline. She was eighteen, and I thought the prettiest little thing I'd ever seen."

He paused, remembering, "Her father didn't seem to care much for me at first, but I figured I could get around that. Besides, she seemed so perfect. She was blond and petite with a luscious figure. Dainty and soft-spoken. Everything I thought a real lady should be."

Her insides clenched at his words. Dainty, soft-spoken. Everything she wasn't and would never be. Would he ever be able to love her? Duncan's voice broke into her thoughts and she listened again as he spoke.

"We had tea several times, and I courted her. Always properly chaperoned, we never did anything that could be considered improper. Hell, I never did more than hold her hand and give her a kiss on the cheek. I fell in love, or so I thought, I know now that it was just a passing fancy. Lust, nothing more. Anyway, I thought she was in love with me. She certainly told me she was often enough. I was determined to make her my wife and we became engaged and were to marry the next spring. During that winter, her father became ill and died rather suddenly."

He frowned, remembering the changes that had come with Edwards's death. So many changes. So much pain.

"After his death, Madeline changed. She became sullen and secretive toward me. One day I went to see her, unannounced, and found her barely dressed, in the arms of another man. Roy Walker. When I walked in, all she did was look up at me and start crying. She told me it wasn't what it seemed, and if I'd only listen, she could explain. I didn't want to listen or have her explain. I was so angry. I told her she was nothing but a whore, and I'd never marry a whore."

"Oh, Duncan, I'm so sorry." She hugged him closer. "What'd you do then, just leave?"

"I left Denver that same day and headed for Reno. I found out later that she'd been having men for a long time. Roy Walker was one of them."

He rose and sat on the side of the bed. His broad

back to her, he ran his hands through his hair. She knew the memories were hard for him and wanted to stroke his back in comfort, but she stayed her hand. He must have changed his mind, because he laid back down next to her, propping on his elbow so he could look at her.

"Her father left her well provided for. She didn't need a husband for anything but show. Just so her name wouldn't be sullied. I sometimes wonder if her father didn't find out what she was and decided to marry her off to the first person that asked. I don't know. I thought he was a good man and maybe he just did what he thought was best. I'll never know now if he knew what she was or not."

He'd begun to stroke her arm and play with her hair while he told her the story. Catherine didn't think he even realized it, but she did and she was glad that he could share something so painful with her. Now at least she knew the reason he'd changed so from the boy she remembered.

"Oh, Duncan. Not every woman is like her. Surely you realize that."

"What I realize...is that I was a fool to think that I could love her or that she loved me. I won't be a fool again." His voice was hard and she cringed inside. How would she overcome his pain and make him see her? Not as another woman, but as his wife who loved him.

"Well, I understand. Thank you for telling me. I'd claw her eyes out if I could. What a wicked, wicked woman. My God, what she did to you."

There was such vehemence in her voice that he smiled. He gently stroked her cheek with the back of his knuckle. "Madeline was six years ago," he said very softly.

"Don't ever mention that woman to me again. We will not speak of her."

"Do I detect a note of jealousy in your voice? You have no need, you know," his amusement was evident.

"Jealous? Me? Not on your life. I'm angry though, mad as hell. You loved her and she treated you so very badly."

He was a little disappointed. Jealously on her part wouldn't have been such a bad thing, would it?

"I told you I don't believe in love."

"Maybe not now, but you did then. What she did to you, it changed you and how you feel. I tell you if she were here right now I'd…why I'd shoot her myself."

"Lord, you are a feisty little thing, but you shouldn't get yourself all worked up over something like this." He pulled her closer, sensing that he needed to reassure her about this thing with Madeline. "Catherine, I don't know that I ever really loved her. I lusted after her. I was very young then. I didn't know the difference between love and lust."

"So you're telling me, all you feel for me is lust. Right?" She tried to pull away from him.

He wouldn't let her. He pulled her closer and tighter in his arms. "Yes, well, no. Cat, I care deeply about you. It's not just lust. But I just can't see myself in love. Not the way my parents were, or your parents were. That is something very special and very hard to find. It doesn't happen with just anyone, and for me it will never happen. So now that you know everything, why I am the way I am, can we just drop this subject?"

Catherine could feel the tug on her heart at his words. "I understand." But she didn't, really. She loved him with all her heart and soul. She would find a way to break down those walls and make him realize he could feel love for her. He cared about her and she supposed that was as good a place to start as any. She smiled to herself. *Oh yes, Mr. Duncan McKenzie, you will come to love me.* She was sure of it.

CHAPTER 16

They had returned to the ranch after a week in the Peterson's cabin. Catherine thought it was wonderful. Everything, except their discussion about Madeline. That had disturbed her. How could someone treat another person like that?

They learned about each other in many ways, not just physical, but they definitely explored each other's physical side very well.

To get Duncan to see reason about love, Catherine had her work cut out for her. She didn't really have the first idea how to start, except to continue with her plan to be the wife he wanted.

If only she had more time; but she didn't. She still had her duties to see to around the ranch, which didn't leave much time to learn about being a model wife. But she would try; she would recruit Cassie to help her.

Cassie, James, and Alice were in the kitchen having coffee, when the newlyweds returned. When Catherine and Duncan came into the kitchen, Cassie jumped up and ran to Catherine.

"I'm so glad you two are back." She gave her a big hug. "I know you are probably wishing you had a lot more time alone, but I'm still glad you're here."

Catherine hugged her back and laughed "You would think that we had been gone a month with a greeting like that."

Duncan went over to James. "Good to see you," then he whispered, "I would like to speak to you in private if I could."

"Certainly, son. Come on into the study while the girls are otherwise occupied." James turned to the women, "If you will excuse us ladies, we have some business to attend to."

Catherine looked from her father to her husband, "I'll catch up to you later. I want to visit with Cassie and Alice, if you don't mind. Then I'll get going to the regular chores."

Duncan shook his head at her. "Don't worry your pretty little head about the chores. I'll help James, now that I'm here to stay. I think it's time I relearned what kind of life I have gotten myself into anyway, don't you?"

"Yes," she said reluctantly, "I guess it is, and you won't have any better teacher than Dad."

*****

They spent most of their time together. Catherine couldn't completely give up working with the cattle. Cooking and sewing were just not her cup of tea. It didn't matter what she did by the end of the day, she was exhausted, and so was Duncan. But somehow they managed to have the energy to make love, even if that meant just touching each other. Of course, touching always led to more touching, and kissing, and full-blown loving.

Cat learned there are many ways to make love to someone. Sometimes it was gentle and slow; other times they were like wild animals, pulling and pushing at each other, never seeming to get enough.

They both made an effort to learn as much as they could about the other. Cat still had so many questions, and Duncan had almost as many. They spent hours answering them for the other.

Catherine discovered being a wife was not the kind of thing that came naturally. It was work, hard work. She still had her regular chores to take care of, tending the animals, mucking the stalls, eggs to gather, cows to milk, and she had to learn her wifely duties on top of everything else. But she was determined to make it work.

There were so many times she wanted to scream and kick her feet or just take off on Wildfire and never look back. She amazed herself at the restraint she showed towards Duncan. She told herself over and over again that it was necessary and would be worth all the effort when he realized that he loved her. She believed that he did, she just didn't know how to get him to realize that he did. But she was sure she would eventually get him to see things her way, one way or another.

Duncan, in the meantime was also discovering that being married was a lot more work than he thought. His parents had seemed so happy all the time, never fighting. Of course, he knew that they had disagreements, but never in front of him. Sometimes it seemed he and Cat were at odds at just about everything. She was the most spoiled, stubborn, obstinate woman he had ever met. She insisted on trying to do everything that she used to do before they were married and learn to cook as well. Plus they were helping Tom and Beth with their house.

He saw the shadows under her eyes, could see how tired she was, but the more he tried to get her to give something up, the more she was determined to do even more. Sometimes he just wanted to turn her over his knee. He was amazed at the restraint he showed toward her. But he was sure he would eventually get her to see things his way, one way or another.

*****

Catherine couldn't believe her father gave them the piece of land north of his as a wedding present. It was not a large piece, just five hundred acres, but it was good land, fertile land, as was all the land in the valley.

There was plenty of timber in the hills on the east and west. The river provided good water, and there was pasture for grazing the horses. There was even a hot spring in the hills behind a small bluff on the west side that she was sure they could use for bathing and swimming.

Duncan let her decide where to place their home. She chose the small bluff overlooking the entire valley. He designed it so the front of the house would face the river to the east and catch the morning sun. Behind the house would be the barn, corral, and foaling sheds.

She showed him the hot spring and asked if there was a way that they could pipe the water to the house. Maybe they could build a small bathing room, like the ones she had seen in Denver many years before. He told her he thought they could, and began to make the changes necessary to the design.

They worked together on the house, cutting the timber, smoothing it, notching it so that it would fit together tightly. They both wanted the house to be made of logs, not store-bought lumber, and they wanted it to be made with their own two hands, not by hired carpenters. Duncan did most of the cutting of the trees. Catherine hooked the logs to the mules and dragged them down to the house site.

Catherine discovered Duncan was a good carpenter. Just one of the many occupations he had done over the years to support himself.

He may have designed the house, but he asked her opinion on everything. Thrilled he consulted her, she didn't hold back on what she wanted in her house. They didn't agree on everything, like how many bedrooms there should be; he wanted three bedrooms, she said there had to be at least five. When he asked her why, she kissed him and said that she intended on having lots of children, so they should just keep on practicing as often as possible. He couldn't argue with that, so the house had six bedrooms. He wanted lots and lots of practice.

They worked on the house as often as time would allow, but the cattle, stopping Morgan, and getting Tom and Beth settled were the most important things. So their house took much longer than they would have liked. Catharine hoped that after everything else was settled they could have a barn raising, only this would be a house raising.

Duncan tied the last of the logs they'd felled together, ready for the horses to drag them to the site. Suddenly, there was an explosion. A large ponderosa pine fell towards Catherine.

"Run! Get out of the way!" He shouted and ran toward her.

She saw the tree and moved as fast as she could but it still caught her.

Duncan heard her scream. Then all was silent. "Oh God! Please let her be okay. Please let her be okay!" He prayed over and over as he ran to the place where he last saw her. His heart was in his throat. *Please God let her be alive, please.* He frantically tore at the limbs of the tree, finding her underneath them, thankfully and not under the trunk.

He broke the limbs as much as he could, away from her still body, then knelt down and gently turned her toward him. He could see that she was cut and bruised. There was blood matted in her beautiful hair, but she was breathing. Catherine groaned and slowly opened her eyes. She reached up and brushed a tear from his cheek as it fell. Duncan wasn't even aware he was crying. He was too relieved that Catherine was alive, to be aware of anything else.

CHAPTER 17

Duncan carried her to where Jake was standing and slowly mounted. It was difficult with Catherine in his arms, but somehow he managed. He wanted to gallop all the way back to the ranch, but knew it would jar her too badly and he still didn't know the extent of her injuries. So he walked Jake and brought her down from the mountain as gently as he could, holding her tenderly in his arms.

When he arrived, Alice came out from the kitchen and started crying when she saw her baby unconscious in his arms. She ran over to him, tears streaming down her face.

"What happened? Is she...?"

"Calm down, Alice. She's not dead. She's unconscious. She got hit by a falling tree. She's badly bruised and may have a concussion. Bring some hot water, towels, liniment, and iodine if you have it. If not, get me some whiskey to clean her wounds. And send one of the boys for Doc."

As he barked out orders, he walked past Alice into the house, up the stairs to his and Catherine's bedroom. After he laid her on the bed, he gently removed her moccasins and clothes. He saw bruises already forming on her arms and face. The tree limbs had scratched her beautiful face and there were pine needles and sap in her hair.

He gently examined every part of her for major injuries. He found some deep cuts on her back, but hoped that they wouldn't need stitches. Her head and unconscious state were what worried him the most. He felt a large knot on the left side of her head. The bruising was becoming more pronounced on her left cheek and temple. He'd known men who took hits to the head and never woke up. It scared the hell out of him.

Alice came bustling into the room, arms loaded with everything he had asked for.

"We don't have any iodine, but I have a bottle of good whiskey that should work for cleaning those wounds. And I brought some butter to get the sap from her hair. Now you go on and let me take care of her."

"No, I'll do it," he said firmly, but not unkind. "I need to do it. Find James."

Duncan bathed all her wounds, used the butter on her hair, and then bandaged the worst of the cuts. He rubbed some liniment on her shoulders and legs, places he knew she would be sore. Then he tucked the blankets up around her chin and kissed her forehead.

She looked so pale, so fragile, lying there in the big bed. He spread her hair around her on the pillow to dry, then pulled the rocking chair next to the bed and began his vigil. He would not leave her until he was sure she would be all right.

The doctor came early that evening. He apologized for not making it sooner, but he had a baby to deliver and couldn't leave. He tried to get Duncan to leave the room while he worked on her, but Duncan refused. He stood next to the bed as the doctor examined her, commenting on how well the cuts had been taken care of. He still ended up stitching a few of the deeper ones on her back and one on her chest. Duncan grunted and watched as the doctor poked and prodded Catherine's unconscious body.

The doctor checked for internal bleeding and examined the large knot on her head. He shook his head and stood back, surveying the woman.

"She is an extremely lucky young woman. The bump on her head isn't serious, I don't think, but she may remain unconscious for a couple of days. When she does wake up, she should rest and take lots of fluids. Make sure she doesn't have any excitement for a while either." He shook his head again, as though bewildered. "I'm just amazed that she didn't lose the baby, having an accident like that. Everything seems to be fine, but..."

"Baby? What baby?" Demanded Duncan, not believing he'd heard the doctor correctly.

"Her baby. Your baby. Catherine's pregnant. Didn't she tell you? Well, probably not. She may not even realize it yet, being her first time and all. But yes, son, she is pregnant and going to have a baby. Early spring would be my best guess."

"A baby! I'm going to be a father!" He went over to the doctor and pumped his hand. "Thanks, Doc! Thanks a lot."

The doctor started to leave when Duncan stopped him. "Hey Doc, don't say anything to anyone about the baby. We'll tell everybody when she's well and able to. Okay?"

"Sure, son, whatever you say. It's not my place to tell anyone anyway. Doctor-patient privilege, that sort of thing." The doctor added, "I wouldn't tell her too soon either. I don't think the excitement would be good for her until she's better. I'm going to be honest with you, Duncan. There is still the possibility that she could lose the baby. Her body has been through one hell of a beating and, well, we'll just have to wait and see."

"Sure thing, Doc. And thanks again."

Duncan couldn't believe it. He was going to be a father. Catherine was having his baby. Well, he supposed that was to be expected, considering how much time they spent making love. But still...A baby. He looked down at her pale face and smiled. Tenderly he stroked her cheeks and her lips. She lay very still, but the doctor assured him she would be fine.

She would be a beautiful mother. He could picture her with the babe in her arms, cradling it to her breast. Then later, trying to teach a small...small what? Boy or girl? Did it really matter? She would teach the child the same whatever it was. Everything she knew. They would teach him or her together. Teach them about ranching, about life, and about loving.

Good Lord. He loved her.

He didn't know why he'd been so determined that what he felt was not love. All the loving they did could have been so much better, if he'd not been so stubborn and spoken with his heart.

*****

Catherine didn't awaken that night. James tried to get Duncan to come down for dinner, but he refused to leave her side. James finally sent Alice up with a dinner tray.

Duncan wasn't hungry. It went back untouched. He stayed by her bedside, sitting in the rocker. He held her hand, stroked it with his thumb. Praying to any and all gods that she'd wake up.

"Cat, I don't know if you can hear me or not, but you can't leave me now. We have to finish that house and fill it with kids. There is so much we still have to do. Come back, Cat. Come back to me." He didn't know if it would make a difference or not, but he felt better talking to her.

"I'm going to find the people who did this to you. I'll make them pay, Cat. I'll make them pay for nearly taking the most precious thing I have from me before I have a chance to tell her just how much she means to me. Don't you see, you can't leave yet. You have to hear me, hear what I need to say to you." Duncan lowered his head to the bed, resting his lips against her hand.

The next morning, James again tried to get him to come downstairs to eat. He again refused. Catherine still hadn't awakened, she'd moved very little, even in her sleep, and Duncan worried. He feared the doctor was wrong and knew the longer she remained unconscious, the less likely it was that she would ever awake.

That night, Duncan had just nodded off when he felt her grasp his hand, then she cried out. She began moaning and thrashing in her sleep.

He was on the bed next to her in a flash. As gently as he could, aware of her wounds, he held her to his chest, murmuring, "It's all right sweetheart, I'm here.

I won't let anything happen to you ever again. It's all right." He held her and softly spoke to her until she finally relaxed against him.

Her lids fluttered open. Her eyes dazed, questioning.

"Duncan, why are you holding me? I'm very warm, open the window please."

He smiled down at her and held her a little tighter. She knew him. His relief was so great, all he could do was grin at her.

"What's the matter? Why do you look so happy? Please, let me go and open the window." She struggled weakly against his chest, trying to get out of the warmth of his arms and the covers that engulfed her.

He put his cheek to her forehead. She was warm. Fever was setting in and he knew from experience that it could kill just as easily as that bump to her head.

"You need a shave."

"Probably." He laughed, sounding strained even to his ears. "All right. I'll open the window, but stay under the covers. I don't want you to get a chill."

Laying her back on the pillows, he tucked the covers up under her chin. He went to the window and opened it just part way, just enough to let the stale air out and a fresh breeze in.

Turning to look at her from the window, he could see the weariness on her face. Even in the dim light, he could see the telltale brightness in her eyes, and her cheeks flushed with fever. This was not good. He must get the fever down and fast.

"I'll be right back, sweetheart. You rest for a minute, okay?"

"Yes, I'm very tired..." Before she finished the thought, she was fast asleep.

Duncan ran down the stairs to the kitchen. He took a block of ice from the icebox and began chipping it into small pieces. Pumping water into a pan, he added the ice, then grabbed some cloths from the pantry and headed back upstairs.

James met him at the top of the stairs in his dressing gown.

"I thought I heard Catherine. Is she awake?"

"She was. She has a fever. I have to get it down." He walked brusquely past him into the bedroom.

James followed. "Let me help you, son. She is my daughter as well as your wife."

"There's no..." He stopped and looking into his father-in-law's eyes saw sadness and fear. James needed to know she would be all right as much as he did. "All right, pull up a chair on the other side of the bed and take some of the cold cloths. Start bathing her arm and neck. I'll do this side. If we can get her cool quickly enough, maybe the fever won't take hold."

James quickly did as he was asked. Duncan could see the pain in James' face, seeing his beloved daughter so pale and so very ill. Watching James fret over Catherine brought back memories of when Catherine's mother had died, but he quickly pushed the thoughts away. This was Catherine. She was not her mother, she was not fragile. She was strong, she would make it. He willed her to make it.

He and James gently bathed the woman that was so important to both of them.

Alice got up, made coffee and brought them both a cup, then stayed with them. Cassie soon came in as well, tears in her eyes.

None of them said a word.

CHAPTER 18

Catherine opened her eyes. Duncan was holding her and seemed very happy. She tried to move, but pain hit her like a freight train. She couldn't help the moan that escaped her.

She poked Duncan in the chest with a finger. He smiled down at her. "How do you feel?" he said softly.

James, Cassie, and Alice were all sleeping in chairs around the bed. She replied just as softly, so as not to wake the other occupants of the room. "I am very thirsty and hungry and confused. What are they doing in here?" She nodded toward the sleeping people.

"Ow. Remind me not to do that again," she said after nodding her head.

He smiled at her and pulled her closer, taking care not to hold her too tightly. He held her gently and she cuddled against him, rubbing her cheek against the soft chambray shirt he wore.

"They've been worried about you. We all have." He kissed the top of her head. "Actually, you scared me half to death."

"Why? What happened? I don't remember..." Then she did remember. She was suddenly back there, saw the tree falling. She ran to get out from its path, but couldn't.

Yes, she remembered it all. She turned her face into his chest, she started to cry.

"Hush now. You're going to be fine, just fine." He wiped her tears from her cheek with his thumb and kissed her forehead. "We should wake these three up. They want to see you almost as much as I did. James, Alice, Cassie wake up. Our girl is back among us."

James' head popped up. "What? What did you say?" Then he saw Catherine smiling at him from her husband's shoulder.

"Hello, Papa. I'm sorry I gave you a scare."

There were tears in his eyes. "Oh, my baby girl, you're all right. For a while there, I thought we were going to lose you. We all did." Then more sternly, but with a smile still in his voice and tears in his eyes, he said, "Don't you ever scare me like that again." He dramatically grasped his chest. "The old ticker couldn't take another one like that."

Alice took Catherine's hand, tears streaming down her face. "Oh, my baby, you're back. Thank God and your husband. He never left you. He was determined you'd be all right, and here you are all smiles and back with us." She got up, wiped away her tears with the back of her hand and said, "Well, I best get moving. My baby has got to be near to starving, not having eaten for nearly two days." She walked to the door, turned and looked back at Catherine. She smiled and left the room.

Cassie jumped up. "I think I better help Alice." She raced from the room but not before Duncan saw the tears in her eyes, too.

James cleared his throat and walked around to her

side of the bed.

"I love you, daughter. I'm very glad that you had the good sense to rejoin us." He kissed her tenderly on the forehead and left, leaving them alone.

She tried to push away from Duncan and get out of bed. He refused to move. Instead, he held her close, resting his head on top of hers.

"How are you really feeling?" He asked, his hand smoothing her hair.

"Sore. I feel like I got caught in a stampede and every cow walked across by body and through my mouth. I need some water."

He chuckled. The sound surprised him. Until she woke, he hadn't so much as smiled in the last two days, and now he was chuckling. God he loved this woman. He didn't know when it happened or how it happened, but it happened. He loved her with all his being. It had taken nearly losing her for him to realize it, but he finally did.

He wasn't immune to love. She'd worked her way into his heart. It was as if he hadn't been whole until now. Until she had come back into his life, he'd been a shadow of a man.

He thought Madeline had killed everything inside him, killed his ability to love. But Catherine had seen through to his very soul. And she loved him. That was even more precious to him.

She gave him back himself.

Never in his adult life had he felt like this. So

content, so happy, and it was all due to Catherine. His stubborn, obstinate, loving wife. He wouldn't change her for anything. She was perfect just as she was. And he had nearly lost her. He hugged her tighter to him.

She groaned, bringing him out of his reverie, scattering his thoughts to the wind.

"Hmm?" he responded, loosening his hold on her.

"Water. You were going to get me some water, or have you changed your mind about letting me out of this bed so I can get my own?"

He grinned at her. "Yes, water. And no, you are not to set foot out of this bed until I say so." He sat up, poured a glass of water and handed it to her.

The glass slipped from her hand, too weak to even hold it, and spilled down the front of her. She gasped as the cold spring water ran down her chest.

He took the glass, refilled it, and held it for her, letting her drink her fill. "Sorry. I should have realized that you have no strength. Would you like a bath? I'll wash your hair for you."

"I think I just had one." She laughed and laid back on the pillows. "I would love a real bath, and to have my hair washed for me would be heaven. Though after this, you might never offer to do it again." She closed her eyes. "I'm so tired. I'm just going to rest awhile."

"Fine, you rest and I'll get the water started. When it's hot, I'll bring the tub in and give you your bath in here."

"Wonderful," she murmured sleepily.

He left the room and walked down to the kitchen. James, Cassie, and Alice were there, sipping hot coffee, as though it was nothing out of the ordinary for them to be sitting around the table in their nightclothes.

"She wants a bath," he announced cheerily as he entered the room.

"Thank God she's all right. I've never been as scared in my life as I was last night. I thought sure we were going to lose her." James gripped his coffee cup so tightly his knuckles were white.

Duncan walked over and clasped James on the shoulder. "She's too damn stubborn to die, thank God. You of all people should know that."

"Yes, I guess I should. But it's hard seeing your child like that." James shook his head speaking so softly that Duncan could hardly hear him. "I never ever thought she might die before me. It scared me so bad."

"I know, but she's going to be fine. Healthier than ever, just wait and see. She's sleeping again now, but when the water is ready, I'll take it up and give her a bath. I even told her I'd wash her hair." He winked at his father-in-law. "She said after this time, I'd never volunteer again. What do you think she meant by that?"

Alice and Cassie both laughed.

"She knows what trouble her hair is. It's so thick and wavy that it is nearly impossible to get a comb through it after she washes it," Cassie said.

Alice agreed. "Yes. It's so much work she knows you won't like doing it."

"Now there you're wrong. I used to help my mother wash her hair when she was ill, and it was just as bad. But I loved it and I love Cat's hair just as much."

James smiled at him. "I know exactly what you mean. I used to wash Elizabeth's when she was pregnant and couldn't do it by herself." There was a far off sadness in his eyes; one Duncan didn't ever want to experience himself.

*****

Catherine was still sleeping when Duncan slipped into the room with the long metal tub. He set it in the middle of the room and closed the window, then went to get the buckets of hot water to fill it. He had to make several trips before he got water deep enough for his liking. Bringing in the last two buckets, for rinsing her hair, he set them by the fire to keep warm. As he set them down, she woke up.

She stretched, winced and tried to sit up.

"Hi there," he said, crossing to the bed. "Ready for your bath, my lady?"

"That I am, my handsome knight. But I am going to require your assistance. My body doesn't seem to want to respond to me without pain."

He pulled back the covers, deftly removed her nightgown, lifted her in his arms, and carried her to the tub. Gently he stood her in the hot water, where he removed the bandages covering her more serious wounds, then helped her to sit.

"I hope it's not too hot. It may sting a little on some of your cuts, but the heat will help your muscles relax.

Just lean back and soak for a few minutes."

He placed a folded towel on the rim to cushion her head. She leaned back and closed her eyes.

"Umm, this feels wonderful."

"I'm glad. Cat, do you feel like talking." He sat backwards in the chair by the tub and rested his arms on the back. "What do you remember of the day this happened?"

Without opening her eyes she said, "I remember the explosion, then the tree falling and trying to run out of the way. Guess I didn't quite make it. What was the explosion, dynamite? Why would somebody be using dynamite?"

"I believe it was, and I believe they wanted to kill us. It would have looked like an accident. Do you remember seeing anybody?"

"No. We were both so busy and working so hard to get the trees down to the house site. Anyone could have done it. But we both know who was behind it. Morgan."

"I don't know. From everything you and James have told me, I don't think so. This has the earmarks of Roy Walker's handiwork and I'd bet Morgan didn't know about it."

"You're defending John? Why?" Her eyes popped open.

"Because I've learned to trust my instincts, and this doesn't feel right. It doesn't seem like something he would do. What do you think? Gut reaction."

"You might be right. I don't think John wants me dead. He's wanted to marry me too long for me to believe that. But why would Walker go against John and do something like this?"

"Think about it. He's already selling the ranch. There's no telling if he's sold property to anyone besides Tom and Beth, but if he has, then he'd want to get us off here quick. And, if I die in the process, all the better. He's getting impatient. That makes him careless."

She closed her eyes again, the water was getting cooler and she was very tired. He wouldn't question her anymore today.

She sighed, "I don't think I like what I think you're thinking. Will you wash my hair for me before this water gets too cold?"

He let her change the subject and washed her hair. He soaped it twice with her lavender soap, and then poured both of the extra buckets over her to rinse it, wrapping the long length in a towel when he was through.

She took the washrag and soaped it up to start washing her body, but he grabbed it from her hand.

"Let me. I'm your lady's maid until you're able to take care of yourself." With that he gently rubbed her body with the fragrant cloth. Taking extra care to be gentle over her cuts and bruises. He washed her back and shoulders first, then down her arms and chest, taking his time when he was at her breasts, using his hands not the cloth, to wash and caress them.

She leaned back and sighed with pleasure. Her nipples tightened under his tender touch. He put the cloth back in his hand and washed her belly, legs and feet. Then he put his hand between her legs and washed her there.

"I've missed you," he said hoarsely.

"You have?" She said lazily, enjoying the feel of his hand between her thighs. "Did you really stay with me the whole time, like Alice said?"

"Yes."

"Why?"

"I was worried."

"Why were you worried?"

"Because you were hurt."

"I've been hurt before."

"Never like this. I was so afraid I'd lose you if I left, and I couldn't let that happen." He removed his hand and rinsed her off with the cloth. He shouldn't be doing this to her now. She was too sore and too bruised for any kind of lovemaking, even this.

"Done. You are officially clean now, my lady." He tried to keep his voice light and teasing. "Let's get you out of that tub and dry that hair of yours. I've been warned that it's a handful."

"It is, and you won't like doing it because it's such a mess, but I'll love having you comb it for me. Were you really afraid you'd lose me?" She asked quietly.

"Of course. I'm your husband. I'm supposed to protect you, but I didn't do a very good job." He brushed aside the tender feelings. Now was not the time. When she was better, he'd show her just how much he loved her.

"You're wrong about your hair. I love it and I'll love taking care of it for you. I'll be very gentle. You'll see." He knelt by the tub so she could put her arms around his, then easily lifted her out of the water, as though she weighed but a few ounces. She'd lost weight in the last two days, he could feel it as he lifted her.

Setting her on the side of the bed, he knelt in front of her with a towel. He rubbed her feet and legs dry, then took her hands, massaging as he dried them.

"Stand up and put your hands on my shoulders." She did, but was a little wobbly. He caught her by the waist and steadied her. "That's right. You okay?"

She nodded.

"Now spread your legs a little bit so I can dry all of you."

She did and he rubbed the towel up her inner thighs, then across her silky down, and around to her backside, stopping just a moment to give her a gentle squeeze.

It was just a moment too long. Her legs collapsed, and she fell over his shoulder.

"Maybe this wasn't such a good idea," he mumbled into her belly.

"I think you're right. I need more strength before you bathe me again." She laughed and tried to straighten her legs. He patted her bottom again and rose moving her into the cradle of his arms.

"What do you say we tackle this hair of yours, because much as I have missed you, you're too weak for me to make love to you now. I don't trust myself and I sure as heck don't trust you with that twinkle in your eye and husky voice of yours. I think your hair is safer for both of us right now."

She reached up and touched his unshaven jaw. He moved his face against her hand, loving the feel of her fingers against his whiskers.

"Yes, that would probably be much safer." She licked her lips.

There was passion in her eyes and her voice was deep and sexy but it was her touch that nearly did him in. He was rock hard from wanting her. He wanted to reassure himself that she was safe and alive, but he controlled himself and gently set her down on the big chair in front of the fire. Now was not the time for passion. Later, he told himself; later when she was stronger.

He began to untangle the flowing mass of damp hair with his fingers, working from the ends to the scalp, just as he had with his mother. When it was mostly untangled, he reached for her comb and did the same thing with it. He gently pulled the comb through it again and again until it was dry. Then he took her brush and brushed it until it crackled in his hands.

It was glorious. He loved her hair; loved the way it smelled, the way he could wrap his hands in it; loved the way it floated over them when they made love; loved waking up with it tangled around them in the mornings. Would he ever get used to this woman? Lord, he hoped not.

He lifted her up from the chair and settled her on the bed, then he helped her into a clean nightgown, remembering the pretty little thing he had destroyed, telling himself he would get her another one. He might destroy it too, but he would just keep buying them for her, because she was so damned beautiful, she deserved beautiful clothes. Even if they didn't stay on long.

He carried her downstairs to the kitchen so she would be with the family and they could see for themselves that she was all right. He knew they needed that as much as he did.

Alice and Cassie had cooked up all of Catherine's favorite breakfast foods. There were scrambled eggs, bacon, sausage, pancakes with maple syrup, biscuits with honey, and lots of coffee. There was enough food on the table to feed an army.

When Catherine saw the massive amount of food laid out on the table, she started laughing. Duncan looked down at her, then back at the table and laughed with her.

Alice put her hands on her hips, pretending to be irritated at their laughter, then joined them. Soon everybody was laughing.

Duncan sat her in a chair and started dishing up a plate with some of everything on the table. Then he sat next to her, picked up her fork, and started to feed her.

She stopped his hand, smiling. "I think I have enough strength now to feed myself."

He felt himself blush, much to his embarrassment, but gave her the fork. "After the incident with the water earlier, I wasn't so sure. I didn't think you would want another bath so soon." He winked and gave her a knowing grin.

She laughed. Lord, it was good to hear her laugh. He wanted to hear that every day for the rest of his life.

"No, I don't think I could survive another bath just yet." Then she winked back at him and laughed some more.

CHAPTER 19

Catherine was tired of being in bed. Duncan hadn't let her up by herself since that first night she woke up. He carried her everywhere, to eat, to the bathroom, much to her embarrassment, and then back again. He never let her walk on her own two feet. That was three nights, and she was ready for some exercise. Her muscles ached and she needed to walk out the soreness and get back her strength. Besides, she needed to use the chamber pot and didn't want to have to call him every time. A woman needed some privacy.

Duncan had left her to rest and went to help James with the ranch work. Now was her chance. She put her legs over the side of the bed. Weak and wobbly, she tried to stand, but needed something to hold onto. She sat back on the bed and scooted to the foot of it, grasped the poster and stood. If she went really slowly, she could do this. One step and then another and another until she made it to the corner where the chamber pot was kept.

When she was finished, she rose and started to go back to the bed. She had just taken a couple of steps when her stomach suddenly and viciously cramped. She doubled over with the pain and curled into a ball on the floor.

"Duncan!" she screamed as another cramp

seized her.

Duncan heard her from the study, where he was going over the latest cattle prices with James. He leapt out of the chair, toppling it, and ran up the stairs. Slamming open the door, he saw her lying on the floor, blood pooling beneath the lower part of her body.

She was losing the baby. His heart twisted at the thought. Oh God, why now? He went over to her and picked her up in his arms, scared out of his wits at the sight of all the blood. Carrying her to the bed he gently laid her on it, then he grabbed up the towels next to the wash basin. Spreading her legs, he held the towels there firmly to help stem the flow of blood. He didn't know if it would help, but it seemed like the right thing to do. Lying down next to her, he held her close with one arm and kept the pressure on her with the other hand. His heart broke over the babe, but the fear of losing Catherine overshadowed even that ache.

Tears streamed down her cheeks. She looked up at him, "It hurts so much. What's the matter with me?"

He brushed the hair out of her eyes and gently kissed her forehead. "Cat, you're losing a babe. You'll be okay, but we have to stop the bleeding."

"A baby! But I can't be…I would have known." She cried harder. "I should have known. What kind of woman am I not to know? It's my fault. It's *all* my fault." She buried her face in his chest, sobbing.

"Hush, now, love. It's not your fault. It's all right. There will be other babies. Don't worry. Just get better. I couldn't bear to lose you, too." He just held her and let her cry.

Catherine was crying so hard that she hadn't heard his tender declaration. Just as well, he thought. She needed to heal, now wasn't the right time.

James appeared in the doorway, breathless from having rushed up the stairs. Duncan hoped he hadn't heard about the baby, he didn't want to deal with that now.

"We need the doctor." He kept his voice soft and reassuring for Catherine's benefit.

He nodded his head and silently mouthed "fast".

When Alice came running up the stairs, James said, "Catherine is losing a baby. I'm going to get the doctor."

Duncan knew he would bring the man no matter what he was doing. He would not let his girl, their girl, bleed to death.

Duncan looked up at Alice when she came in and gave her a silent nod of thanks. He saw her tears and her fear, but she was in control of herself by the time she'd gathered more towels and came back to the room.

He held Catherine to him as she softly cried. She wasn't racked with pain as she had been, because her body had relaxed against him.

Alice was very efficient. Between the two of them, they had stripped Catherine out of the bloody nightgown and cleaned her up in no time. Then she changed the towels between Catherine's legs, telling Duncan to keep firm pressure on them. The first towel soaked through in no time. Another and another replaced it. By the fourth towel, the bleeding had mostly stopped.

Together they dressed her in a clean nightgown and let her rest in the bed, but he continued to apply pressure until the doctor arrived.

The doctor arrived sooner than expected. "Good evening, Duncan. I could do without seeing you this often."

"I know, Doc. No offense, but I would be delighted not to ever see you again."

"None taken. James filled me in on what happened. I'm very sorry. I'm going to check to see if the bleeding has stopped and make sure there is nothing left to cause an infection. That's the greatest threat to her now."

After checking her, the doctor turned to Duncan. "All you can do now is to make sure she gets plenty of rest for the next few days. Then get her up and have her start walking, slowly, to build up her strength. She's lost a lot of blood and will need fluids more than ever to help replace it. See that she has a drink in her hand at all times, and get her to eat as much as you can, if her stomach can handle it. Beef broth is the best to start with. Build her up to solid food as soon as her stomach will accept it."

Catherine was sleeping, James and Alice both occupying the same chairs they had just a few days ago. The doctor took Duncan aside. "Son, she's going to be in a bad way for a while. Physically she'll be just fine in a few weeks, but it may take longer for her to heal in here." He pointed at his head. "Be gentle with her."

"Thanks, Doc. She'll be okay. We'll take all the time she needs to get better."

"You do that. And send for me if she gets worse or doesn't improve in the next few days, or if she develops a fever. Otherwise, I'll come back out next week."

"Sure, Doc, thanks." Duncan went to the bed, laying beside her, taking her once again into his arms. She seemed to know he was there, that she was safe, curling closer to him. He went to sleep like that, with her wrapped safely next to him.

He awoke to fingers curling in his chest hairs. He opened his eyes and looked down at Catherine. She was twirling the hairs on his chest around her fingers and looking up at him expectantly.

Bending his head, he kissed her gently. "Hello, love. How are you feeling?"

"Sore. Thank you for holding me." She suddenly burst into tears. "I'm so sorry for losing the baby. If I'd listened to you and stayed in bed..."

He laid his fingers gently on her lips. "Shh. It was nobody's fault. You didn't know you were pregnant and neither did I, until Doc told me. Do you think I'd have let you work on the house, felling trees, lugging supplies, if I had known? God, Cat, I am so sorry. But there'll be other children. Doc said that losing the baby isn't unusual, considering the shock your body took from the accident. Nothing either of us did or didn't do, could've prevented the loss of the baby. It's not your fault."

"I understand," she whimpered, "but I still feel guilty. What kind of woman am I to not even know...that...I was carrying."

"You're a young woman, who's new to being married. And I have kept you rather busy." He grinned at her. "We shouldn't be surprised you got pregnant."

She smiled and laid her head on his chest. "You're right. We'll just have to try again."

CHAPTER 20

Madeline Connor got off the stage looking around her at the little town of Creede. She was disgusted by what she saw. Dirt streets with boardwalks. Clapboard houses and no stores, other than one small mercantile. This was definitely not her kind of town. She'd be glad to just get her money and get the hell out of here.

Where was Roy? He was supposed to meet her, wasn't he?

Madeline was a woman to be envied, she thought as she checked her reflection in the window of the mercantile. She lived her life the way she wanted, with no man telling her what to do. She'd always had her pick of men.

Except one.

Duncan McKenzie.

He'd discovered her in bed with someone else, admittedly a mistake on her part. Then he had looked on her with nothing but disgust. He wouldn't let her explain, not that she could have explained, but then he had called her a whore. She was not a whore. Those women who worked in the saloon were whores, not her. She'd told herself over and over that she was not a whore, often enough that she almost believed it.

Duncan had decided he would not marry her, thought she was a trollop, and had said as much. He'd been nothing but a gunslinger and small-time gambler and he'd had the nerve to tell her she wasn't good enough for him. Well, now was the time of reckoning. Now she would make him pay dearly for how he had treated her.

Madeline checked into the boardinghouse. She would have preferred the hotel, but the boardinghouse was cheaper and included meals. She was short of money, which was one of the reasons she was here.

After freshening up a bit, she headed out to see what kind of town this was. After all, she was planning on being here for a while and needed to familiarize herself with the surroundings.

Roy Walker was waiting for her as she left. He took her elbow and walked her into an alley where they wouldn't be seen together.

"Glad you got my message and decided to join me here," he said as he pulled her close for a kiss.

She put her hands on his chest to keep some distance between them and purred, "Well, of course, darling. I would never miss a chance to get even with Duncan McKenzie, but then you know that or you wouldn't have brought me here, now would you?"

"You're still a fine looking woman, Maddie, if you'd just learn to control that tongue of yours, we'd make a mighty fine team," he said, still holding her close.

"Don't call me Maddie. You know I don't like it."

Only Duncan had ever called her Maddie. Somehow, from him it seemed right. Almost an endearment. She'd lost Duncan then because she couldn't stay away from Walker. But she could now. Oh, yes, she'd gotten control of herself. She no longer needed the excitement, the danger he provided.

"And don't get any ideas, Walker" she said as she pushed him away from her. "I'm here on business, and unless I say so, that business doesn't include taking up where we left off."

"Still a bitch, aren't you, Madeline?" he said, releasing her.

"You don't know the half of it. I've learned a lot since I saw you last." Brushing her hands on her skirt she said, "Now let's talk business. Why have you brought me here?"

"Not enough time now, darlin', but I'll tell you tonight. What room you in?" He winked at her, his smile more of a leer.

"Who said anything about you coming to my room? We can talk here and now."

She really didn't want him to come to her room. He was dirty and he smelled, but the thought of having sex with him still excited her. What she saw in him, she still didn't know, but she wanted him. Even now, dirty and smelly, she wanted him. On her terms, not his. She needed to have the control.

"Not if you want to know all about your ex-fiancé. Besides, if I don't, you won't get that money you so desperately need, now will you? But if you'd rather just get on the next stage back to Denver, be my guest." Stepping back to let her pass, he gave her an exaggerated sweeping gesture with his hand.

If she hadn't been a lady, she'd have hit him. Damn the man, he knew she needed that money. "You're scum, Roy. Unfortunately, I don't have a choice and you know it. Room six. Be there at nine and don't be late. I don't like to be kept waiting."

"Neither do I. I'll be there." He took her by the waist and brought her against him for a kiss.

She pushed away and side-stepped passed him, carefully straightened her skirt and stepped back onto the sidewalk.

*****

Walker came to her room that night at nine o'clock on the button. He'd changed his clothes and even bathed, much to Madeline's surprise and relief. She knew she would bed him; she didn't really have a choice if she wanted his cooperation. She loved him, or at least lusted after him. She wasn't sure that it was love, but it was definitely something. She just wanted to make sure he knew it was her decision, not his.

Walker laid out the plan for her. All she had to do was to get Duncan to become involved with her, maybe even fall for her again, then Catherine would seek a divorce and John Morgan could marry the bitch like he wanted to. He said his boss was a patient man and there was five thousand dollars in it for her, if she succeeded.

Madeline was incredulous. She laughed. She

couldn't help herself. "You brought me down here for that? Are you insane? Duncan McKenzie would just as soon spit on me as look at me, because of you. Do you really think *he* would want me again, just because you do? Some men have principles. They're built of stronger stuff than a weak bully like you!"

As soon as she said it, she knew she'd gone too far. Her eyes got wide and she backed away from him. But it was too late. Walker hit her with his closed fist, and that was all she would remember. Thank God!

Mary Peabody heard Madeline's scream and went upstairs just in time to see Walker leaving by the backstairs. She went to the Connor woman's room. Knocking on the door, she waited for an answer. When there wasn't one, she used her key and entered. It was a good thing she was made of strong stuff, because a weaker willed woman would have fainted at the sight of what that man had done to this young woman.

Madeline was lying face up on the bed. She'd been badly beaten. Her face was swollen, so much as to be almost unrecognizable. The lovely blue dress that Mary had admired, was ripped to her waist, in shreds and bloody. Even through the blood she could see the cuts on her face, shoulders and breasts. Bruises were already beginning to show. Mary couldn't do much for her except cover her up before she went for the doctor and the sheriff.

Doc Wright grimly started the task of trying to clean the young woman up so he could assess her wounds. It was not an easy task for him. He hated seeing a woman treated this way. She was lucky though. She was young and strong, and would probably pull through, but he knew that she'd never be the same. They never were.

She'd probably been a beautiful woman, but even after the bruising and swelling went away, she would never again be beautiful. It looked like there were probably fractures in her face, her cheeks might be shattered, and her jaw broken. He just couldn't be certain until the swelling went down and the woman awoke.

The cuts on her chest and breasts were not life-threatening, but would definitely leave scars, both physical and emotional. Yes, this young woman would be changed forever. He finished his task and shook his head sadly.

"Mary, there's not much more I can do for her. Keep her warm, give her water and call me if she comes down with a fever. I'm leaving some laudanum to help with the pain. Give her four drops in each glass of water, whether she's awake or not." Looking back at the young woman, he sighed. "Such a damn waste."

"Thanks. I'll do what I can for her." Mary followed him down the stairs. "I didn't have a chance to go to the sheriff but I'd appreciate it if you'd stop by there and tell him about this." She nodded her head up towards the ceiling and Madeline's room. "I don't want any trouble, but I saw Roy Walker slinking off just after I heard her scream."

Doc took Mary's hands in his, his eyes gentle and comforting. "I'll tell him, Mary. You call me if you need anything."

"I will, Ben."

He squeezed her hands and left.

Mary sat with Madeline, watching her, dribbling water on her lips, hoping to see her wake. Madeline was restless in her sleep; she moaned and called for Duncan.

Mary knew only one Duncan, Catherine's husband. What would this woman want with him? Maybe they were friends. She wrote a note to Duncan and found one of the Jones' boys to take it out to the ranch. Then she made some tea and returned to her vigil.

*****

Duncan received the note from Mary telling him about Madeline. He didn't want to go, couldn't imagine what she could be doing in Creede, but felt that he didn't have any choice. If she was as injured as Mary said and was calling out for him there had to be a reason and he wanted to know what that reason was.

He hoped that Catherine would understand. It had been more than a month since she'd lost the baby and was completely, healed according to the doctor. She was back to her normal routine, spending every other day out with the ranch hands, and the others in the kitchen with Alice. Her cooking was improving immensely, and she was trying so damned hard. Almost every meal she fixed was edible, with only a few minor mistakes. Thankfully, Alice was a patient teacher and they'd not had to endure too many horrible meals.

Today hadn't been a cooking day. It was branding season and Duncan would have been out there with her, but James wanted to talk to him about some future plans. Duncan was thankful for that at first. He didn't know if he would ever get used to the smell of branding cattle. Now he wished he had been there. He didn't like leaving this way, but he had no choice. He had to find out what was going on. Roy Walker and Madeline both in town was too much of a coincidence to be overlooked.

After reading the message, he just told James to tell Cat that he had to go to town and didn't know when he'd be back. He didn't explain to James either, since he'd told no one but Catherine about Madeline and, thankfully, James didn't ask any questions.

Catherine returned from the range just before suppertime. She looked forward to seeing Duncan and finding out how his days were going. Was he learning ranching? Did he like living here? Would he stay?

They really hadn't talked too much about that. He'd been very attentive and tried to be with her every minute since the accident. They were still building the house, but he kept her well away from the trees and anything else he thought might be dangerous to her. But she still had doubts. He still hadn't told her that he loved her. But he did, didn't he? Surely he wouldn't have stayed by her side during her illness if he didn't love her. He wouldn't treat her so kindly now, if her didn't love her, would he?

Was he really going to stay and build a life with her here, or was he going to go back to bounty hunting? He said that he was done with that life and wanted to settle down, but that was before he was forced into marrying her. She couldn't bear it if he left, but she knew she couldn't follow him into the kind of life he'd had. So many questions with no real answers.

She ran into her father on her way upstairs to clean up and change for supper.

"Hello, Kitten. Did you have a good day? You

didn't wear yourself out now, did you?"

She hugged him. "Dad, I'm just fine, really. You and Duncan need to stop worrying about me. I'm completely well now and back to normal. Well, as normal as I ever was."

James smiled at her and hugged her back. "Okay, okay. I'll try to stop worrying so much, but never completely. Oh, by the way, Duncan said he had to go to town. He didn't say when he'd return."

"Did he say why he was going? Was there something we needed for the ranch?" She was disappointed, but she wouldn't let it show.

"Not that I know of, but he didn't say. See you shortly, at dinner." He turned and went to the kitchen telling Alice to set one less plate at the dinner table.

Catherine didn't think much more about Duncan's absence, until she was lying alone in their bed and he still wasn't home. There was lots of conversation at dinner with the Petersons and Cassie there, keeping her occupied, though she ate little and continuously watched the door for him to come through it.

Now that she was alone. All her nagging doubts came back. Was he gone for good? Had he received a bounty that he couldn't pass up? Would he be back for her?

Beginning to make herself crazy with worry, she paced and then stopped to read a novel. When she couldn't concentrate on that, she got up and paced again.

So it went all night long. Duncan didn't return that night. When dawn came, she was worn to a frazzle with worry. Her imagination had run wild until she decided she'd go to town and see if she could find him. If he was going to leave her, she had to stop him. She dressed and slipped out of the house, leaving a note for her father so he wouldn't worry.

She couldn't get to the barn fast enough. She didn't even bother to saddle Wildfire, just bridled him, swung up on his back, and took off at a gallop for town.

She arrived at Peabody's Boarding House just before breakfast. Mary was just setting the table when Catherine walked in.

"Hi, Mrs. Peabody. I bet you are surprised to see me so early in the morning." Catherine gave her a little smile. It was all she could manage, given how worried she was.

"Not at all." Mary continued setting the table as if seeing Catherine at seven o'clock in the morning was an everyday occurrence. "Expected you sooner, as a matter of fact. Duncan is upstairs, room six."

"He's here?" She tried to keep the relief out of her voice. "What's he doing here? All he told Dad was that he was coming to town and didn't know when he would be back. I've been worried silly."

"Well, stop worrying. He's just fine, but as to why he is here, I guess he'd better explain. You go on up. Just remember, he's a good man and your husband." With those cryptic parting words, Mary left the dining room.

Catherine ran up the stairs, stopping before the door to room six to catch her breath and restore her composure. She knocked lightly on the door.

"Come in," called that deep voice she loved.

The room was cast in shadow. The drapes had not been opened, even though it was now daylight. Duncan was sitting beside the bed, holding the hand of its occupant.

"Catherine," he said, slowly released the woman's hand, came to Catherine and took her in his arms. "You shouldn't have come, but Lord, am I glad you did." He kissed her soundly almost making her forget her worries.

"Duncan, I came looking for you. When you didn't come home last night..." Her eyes strayed to the bed. She could see now that the occupant was a woman. A badly hurt woman. Duncan hadn't been dallying, and it certainly didn't look like he was going to leave her. But what in the hell was he doing here. She looked back at Duncan, the question, clearly in her eyes for him to see.

"Mary sent me a message that she," he nodded towards the bed, "had been calling my name. Mary didn't know what else to do but to send for me."

He walked over to the bed, Catherine's hand firmly linked in his. "Cat, this is Madeline. Someone, probably Roy Walker, beat her severely. She hasn't awakened yet, but the doctor says she'll be all right. He's giving her enough laudanum to keep her sleeping for a few days and let the healing begin."

"Oh Duncan, I am sorry." Catherine looked up at him and saw the worry there. Was it for this woman? Did he still care for her? Silly question. Of course he did. Didn't he say that he had loved Madeline at one time?

"Cat, I can't imagine why she's here, but I need to know. She lives in Denver and Creede is definitely not the kind of place she would travel to by choice. I also want to know who did this to her. No matter what she did to me, she never deserved this kind of treatment. I can't leave her until I know what happened. Do you understand?"

Catherine wrapped her arms around his waist and hugged him close. She didn't really care now why he was here in town, as long as they were together.

"I'm just so glad you're here and didn't leave me." Oh lord, what was she saying, she never meant to tell him that. She rushed on. "I wouldn't care if there were a dozen women in that bed. Madeline is very lucky to know you, but I'm luckier because I married you."

"Leave you? Why on earth would you think I would leave you?"

He looked down at her, seeing her looking up at him, tears forming in her beautiful eyes. He wrapped his arms tighter around her and held her close, nuzzling the top of her head. She smelled so good, fresh and clean. Lavender. She smelled of lavender, just like on their wedding night.

"Well, you didn't come home and I didn't know why you came to town and my mind just sort of took off on its own, thinking about bounties and your old life and..." She lowered her head and buried her face against his chest.

Caressing her face with his fingers, Duncan raised her chin until she was looking at him.

"Catherine, sweetheart. I am *not* going to leave

you. We're married now. For better or worse, remember?" he said tenderly.

She nodded. "I remember. Oh, Duncan, I feel so foolish. I'm sorry for not trusting you, for thinking that you would leave without telling me goodbye."

"There will be no goodbyes. Not between us. I'm not going to go back to bounty hunting, ever. I love it here, in this valley, with you."

"You do?" Her eyes were glossy with tears.

"Yes, I do." He smiled down at her even as his arms tightened around her. "I know we've only talked a little about the future, but I don't really think I'm cut out to raise cattle."

"I know." She sniffled. She was trying so hard not to cry anymore.

He rested his chin on the top of her head so he wouldn't see her reaction to his next words. "I would really rather raise horses. I've always had a dream of raising the best Arabians west of the Mississippi. What do you think? Can you give up cattle for horses?"

"Oh, Duncan." she cried, hugging him tighter. "I'd raise pigeons if that's what you wanted to do. Anything, as long as we do it together. Actually, I have to admit, I would love to raise horses. It has always been a sort of dream of mine, too. At least, since I got Wildfire."

"What does Wildfire have to do with raising horses, beside the fact that he's as beautiful a piece of horseflesh as I've ever seen?"

"Well, Dad let me break and train him all by myself. I found out I'm really rather good at it." She blushed and lowered her eyes.

"What!" He bellowed as he set her away from him, out of his arms. "Is James crazy? Doesn't he have any idea how dangerous it is to saddle break a horse? You could have been killed."

"Quiet. You'll wake her up." She nodded to the bed where Madeline lie.

Running his hands through his hair he began to pace. "No wife of mine is going to be breaking horses. If there is any bronc busting to be done, I will do it. Just the thought of you up there on a wild bucking horse is enough to make my hair turn gray. Why the thought..."

She put her fingers gently to his lips, scattering his next words to the wind. "Duncan, don't get yourself all worked up. There is plenty of time to discuss this later"

"There will be no discussion," he muttered through her fingers.

"Besides," she continued, "I think our patient is waking up."

She glanced over at Madeline, who was trying to open her eyes. One of them was so badly swollen that she probably wouldn't be able to fully open it for a few weeks. The other was not as swollen, but she wasn't able to open it much either, probably because of the effects of the laudanum.

"Water, please," she croaked out.

Duncan went to her, raised her head and put a glass to her lips, letting her take a few small sips. He remembered nursing Catherine just a few weeks ago. and his chest constricted at the memory. So close, he had come so close to losing his wife.

"Madeline, it's Duncan. Can you talk? Can you tell me who did this to you?"

She nodded her head, and then looked at Catherine as if to ask who she was.

Duncan saw her gaze land on Catherine. "This is Catherine, my wife. Catherine, this is Madeline Connor."

Catherine came forward and took Madeline's hand. "I'm pleased to meet you, Madeline. Don't you worry; Duncan will take care of everything. You just concentrate on getting better, do you hear?"

"Duncan, I am so sorry," she whispered, barely able to talk, tears falling from her eyes. "I treated you so badly, and I came here to do you dirty. Then what do you do? You take care of me. Most men would have turned away and never looked back if I'd treated them like I did you. I'm so ashamed." She cried harder, making her one good eye all red and swollen.

Duncan was at a loss. Here was the woman who had played him for a fool, crying her eyes out in the same room with his wife, who, it looked like, was going to cry herself.

Catherine went over, sat on the edge of the bed, and took Madeline's hand. "Now, now, don't cry. Everything will be all right, Madeline. You're going to be just fine. The doctor says so, and he's a really good doctor. Every bit as good as any you'd get in Denver. Come on now, don't cry."

"I'm so sorry. You're both being so nice to me and you don't have to. I just don't know what to say."

"Madeline, why don't you start by telling us what the hell happened to you," suggested Duncan.

"Well, I came into town," she stopped; it was taking great effort to speak. Duncan thought her face and mouth must hurt terribly. "What day is this?"

"It's Wednesday."

"Oh, God. I got here on Monday. I've been out for more than a full day. Anyway, I came to town because I got a letter from Roy Walker, saying there was money in it for me if I would help him with a little plan he had." She looked away from them to the windows. She couldn't face Duncan and say what she was about to say. "He didn't tell me what the plan was, just that it would get even with you, and there was $5000 in it for me."

Looking back at Duncan, she said, "I needed the money. I've gone through everything Dad left me. Bad investments, over indulgence, stupidity. Having revenge on you for not marrying me was a bonus."

Duncan's jaw clenched. This was hard for him to hear. It was bringing back memories he didn't want to remember. Things he thought he'd put behind him. "Anyway," she continued after another sip of water, "he sent me a stage ticket and said that if I was interested, he would tell me the rest when I got here.

"He came to my room the night I got here. I

knew what he wanted. I haven't changed," she said bitterly. "He said I was to try to get you to fall in love with me again, so Catherine would divorce you and somebody named John Morgan could marry her."

Catherine gasped.

Madeline was continuing to speak. "I laughed when he told me that. I told him that you were a man with integrity, with principles, not some mealy mouth little bully like he was. As soon as those words left my mouth, I knew I'd made a mistake. Walker is a dangerous man. His face got all red and he hit me so hard, I must have blacked out. I don't remember anything after that."

Duncan was silent for a long time. He couldn't imagine having anyone except Catherine as a wife; loving anyone else. His mind stopped. Loving Catherine. He loved her with every fiber of his being, and he still hadn't told her. He should tell her, let her know, but it was hard to put into words. Every time he wanted to, they got distracted by each other and ended up making love. Now certainly wasn't the time but he would tell her. Soon.

His mind went back to what Madeline was saying. Morgan! He still wanted Catherine. Wanted her to divorce him, so he could marry her himself. How far would he go to see that happen? Would he make her a widow? He might try, but a lot of men had tried to kill him and failed. That was before he had something so wonderful to live for. Before he had Catherine.

Catherine didn't say anything either. She was trying to digest everything that Madeline had said. John still wanted to marry her. She'd refused him so many times, and now she was married to Duncan. Since the incident with the tree, things had been so quiet that she figured that he had finally given up. Not a chance. He was just biding his time until he could put this latest scheme of his in place. Duncan's voice brought her out of her musings.

"Catherine, it's not safe for Madeline here. I think we should take her to the ranch as soon as she is well enough to travel, and let her recuperate there."

Catherine looked up at him as if to say something, but he held up his hand.

"Hear me out. You, too, Madeline. Morgan is still plotting to have you, Cat, and your ranch. He might figure that Madeline will talk, especially after what Walker did. He might send Walker back to make sure she doesn't say anything. And Walker may decide to take care of her for his own reasons, like avoiding jail. In either case, it's not safe for her here. Do you agree?" He looked at each woman, judging her reaction.

Catherine was the first to speak. "I agree. It sounds to me like John is getting more and more desperate. No telling what he'll try next."

Duncan was so proud of her, he wanted to take her in his arms and kiss her senseless. She was putting her fears, her insecurities aside to protect Madeline.

Madeline was slowly shaking her head, trying not to move too much. "I can't put you two in danger. Walker will likely have left the country, fearing that he already killed me. Leave me here. In a few days, I'll be well enough to return to Denver."

"Don't be silly." said Catherine, giving her hand

a little squeeze. "You may have come here for the wrong reasons, but you've admitted your mistake. I give folks a second chance. Besides, from what the doctor told Mary, you won't be able to travel any time soon."

Madeline started to cry again. Then she looked over at Duncan "Can ever forgive me for hurting you like I did. I won't blame you if you can't, but I'd like to leave here as friends. I can see that you love your wife and she loves you. I could never come between you even if I wanted to. I know that now."

Duncan walked to the window. He smiled and kept his back to the women. Madeline knew that he was in love with Catherine. Did it show that much? Did Catherine realize it? When they were next alone, he would make slow, gentle love to her. He would show her just how much he loved her.

He was dragged from his reverie, by a movement in the shadows across the street. He saw Charley Sloan shift his position against the building. He was watching the boardinghouse. Waiting to get Catherine alone or was he waiting for them to leave Madeline alone? Duncan didn't know which, but he didn't like either choice.

CHAPTER 21

Roy Walker knew he had to leave, and rode into the mountains west of town. Even in this far off backwater, he couldn't get away with what he had done to Madeline. She'd just made him so mad. Comparing him to McKenzie, calling him a weak-minded bully. She deserved what she got, but he couldn't just let her blab her fool head off. That could ruin everything for Morgan, but that didn't matter to Walker. He didn't care about the money or the land, or the woman anymore. He wanted McKenzie. He had to pay for this, for making him run again.

He spit tobacco juice onto the ground and stared into the campfire. He could hole up in these mountains for a long time. No one would ever find him if he didn't want to be found. He smiled to himself, thinking how he would enjoy seeing McKenzie on the ground, writhing in pain from the gut shot that Walker would give him. Yes, it had to be a gut shot. They were the most painful, and a man with a gut shot took a long time to die. McKenzie needed to live for a long time with that pain. Oh, yes, he'd get McKenzie and make him pay.

Then he'd finish that bitch, Madeline, if she survived, that is. He'd enjoyed that. If he hadn't heard that old lady coming up the stairs, he'd have finished her that night and gotten a little something for his trouble. But he couldn't. He'd had to leave unsatisfied when old lady Peabody came up. It didn't matter; he could get his satisfaction some other time. There was always another woman who needed to be taught a lesson. And he was just the man to teach them.

*****

Walker didn't realize that he was being watched. White Buffalo knew the trouble his friend James Evans was having, and knew this man was part of it. There was little he didn't know about what went on in the surrounding mountains and valleys. He had to know, to keep his people safe. His warriors watched the town and the Evan's ranch. They kept him informed of everything that happened, yet he did not allow them to get involved. It was bad medicine to mix in the white man's troubles, and James could handle his trouble himself. He just wanted to make sure that their trouble didn't spill over to his people.

Now there was this man here in his mountains. Why would he leave the safety of the Morgan Ranch? He was alone, and he looked to be hiding. All of his gear was on his horse, but he didn't appear to be traveling anywhere. His camp was made in a place that would be hard to see, if you didn't know where to look. It was beneath an outcropping of rocks that were sheltered on all sides by thick forest.

No, this man was definitely hiding, but why? He would have to find out before he decided what to do with him. Gray Wolf would get the information he needed.

White Buffalo returned to his camp, leaving two warriors to watch the evil white man. Then he sent Gray Wolf to speak with James. He would find out what this man was doing hiding in his mountains. Then he, White Buffalo, would decide what to do with him.

*****

Morgan was still determined to get Catherine, and that scared Duncan nearly to death. He needed to let James know what was going on, and he had to get all of them back to the safety of the ranch. But how?

"We're being watched." He said finally, turning away from the window. "Charley Sloan is out there keeping an eye on this place. We're going to have to be careful getting back home. For now, I think it would be best if we stayed here. We need to tell Mary and see if she has a bigger room. I don't want to leave you alone," he said to Madeline before turning to Catherine, "and I can't let you go back to the ranch by yourself. Damn, I wish James was here."

Duncan sat down in the chair next to the bed and ran his hands through his hair, as if that would help him think of a solution.

It was Catherine who came up with a plan.

"We could have Mrs. Peabody take a message to Gordon Jones. He often delivers out to the ranch, so Charley wouldn't think anything of it if he took a wagon load of supplies out there. Mrs. Peabody is always going to the general store, so he wouldn't think anything of that, either. Dad and some of the hands could come into town to escort us back. John wouldn't try anything then."

Duncan could have kissed her. Hell, he got out of the chair and did kiss her. Hard. Not as long as he wanted to, because now was not the time or the place.

Catherine either didn't remember or just didn't care that they weren't alone. Her legs went weak and she held on to Duncan for support as she kissed him back. Madeline's discreet cough brought them back to the present.

Catherine pulled away from Duncan and blushed to her toes. Madeline laughed, then groaned as a wave of pain hit her.

"Well, before you two get too carried away, you'd better get started with the plan. I'll try my best to be ready whenever you say." The laudanum appeared to be helping and she was talking better. At least he and Catherine didn't have any trouble understanding her.

"You're not going to be able to travel, even the short distance to the ranch, for a few days. Then it is still going to be hard on you. I don't think you realize what kind of shape you are in." Duncan said matter-of-factly.

"He's right," agreed Catherine. "We should have Dad come to town in a couple of days. The rest will help you more than anything, and you're going to need it. It's a couple of hours to the ranch in the buckboard. Gordon needs to go out today so Dad doesn't come into town to find out what's going on. We'll tell him not to come here until Saturday. We want to keep everything as normal as possible for Charley's prying eyes."

While Duncan went to get Mrs. Peabody, Catherine sat down and penned a note to her father, explaining in as few words as possible what was going on and what they needed him to do. When she was done, she went over to give Madeline a few drops of the laudanum in some water to help ease her pain.

Madeline gratefully accepted. "Why are you

helping me? Duncan must have told you about me. I treated him very badly. So why?"

"Well, yes, he's told me about you. You did hurt him, and I wanted to hurt you because of it. Actually, what I really wanted to do was to skin you alive."

Madeline made a muffled noise that could have been a stifled laugh or a groan. Not that it mattered either way. Catherine smiled at her.

"I would've done the same, if I was in love with him." Madeline felt her eyes fill with tears.

"Yes, well, that was my first reaction, then I saw you there, lying in that bed after what Walker did to you, and I just couldn't be mad anymore. No one deserves what happened to you, no matter what they've done. And Duncan is obviously worried about you. I had to help you." Catherine shrugged. "Does that make any sense to you at all?"

"Yes, it does. You're good a person. Like Duncan. I don't know how I'll ever repay you. The two of you have given me back my life."

"I'll tell you how. Take your life and make something good out of it. I think you know how, I just don't think you have cared to try before." Catherine laughed and shook her finger at her, "And you keep your paws off my husband."

Madeline laughed.

Duncan returned with Mary Peabody. Both of them were carrying trays. At the site of food, Catherine's stomach growled. Very loudly. Everyone laughed.

"Goodness me, Catherine, if I'd known you were that hungry, I would've sent something up sooner." Mary walked to Madeline and set the tray on the small bedside table. "For you, my dear, I have some wonderful beef broth and some hot tea. Nothing more substantial for you for a while. Now here, let me help you."

Duncan set his tray on the round table in the corner of the room. Catherine sat down in one of the three chairs at the table. She was famished, her stomach rumbled again. She hadn't eaten much at dinner last night and nothing this morning, because of her worry.

"Dig in before your stomach decides to come out and start on its own." He chuckled and handed her a plate piled high with eggs, biscuits, sausages and bacon. He poured them both a cup of coffee and sat across from her. "Start eating, or Mary is going to decide I'm a poor excuse for a husband because I'm starving my wife."

She grinned at him and shoved a forkful of fluffy eggs between her lips. Then she rolled her eyes and made sounds that let the cook know she enjoyed it.

Mrs. Peabody shook her head and smiled at the two newlyweds.

"Mary, do you have a larger room, one with two beds?" Duncan asked between bites. "As I explained downstairs, we'll be staying for a while and I don't want to leave Madeline alone."

"Well, I have a suite. I usually save it for families. Its two rooms, connected with a door. The smaller of the two used to be a dressing room, and doesn't have windows or an outside door. I think that might be best."

"That's perfect. No one will be able to get past us, even if we're sleeping." Then he looked at Catherine, a twinkle in his eye, and said for her ears only, "And I'll be able to hold my beautiful wife in my arms, even if I can't make love to her, because she shrieks like a banshee."

Catherine choked on her coffee, nearly spitting it at him. But she didn't say a word, instead giving him a dazzling smile, letting him know that she *would* get him back.

*****

James arrived on Saturday, as if nothing was amiss, except that he had six men with him, all armed to the teeth. He was driving a buckboard and pulled it up in front of the boardinghouse. As he pulled up, one of his men rode over to the sheriff's office.

Mary had been watching for him and yelled to Duncan that he was here. Duncan carried Madeline out to the wagon and gently laid her in the back. He and Catherine climbed in beside her. James had made sure that there were plenty of blankets and pillows to cushion Madeline.

He wasn't taking any chances on getting them all back safely. He sent one of his men to ask the sheriff for escort, just to make sure that Morgan didn't try anything like an ambush. He wouldn't dare, with the sheriff along. He might mess with the cattle and the fences, but he wasn't going to do anything to overtly draw the attention of the law. Not unless he was desperate, and hopefully, he wasn't yet.

*****

Charley Sloan watched it all happen and knew there was not a thing he could do about it. They were going to get back to the JC Ranch and he couldn't stop them. Well, his job had been to watch and let his boss know when they left, so he rode back to the Morgan ranch to tell him what had happened.

Mr. Morgan was not going to be a happy man. Charley almost wished he could just ride out and never look back, but he knew that Roy Walker would kill him if he did. No, he was not looking forward to telling them this bit of news.

*****

Duncan was glad the trip back to the ranch was uneventful. Even if Charley had told Morgan, there was little he could do without risking the involvement of the law. As they rode out of town, White Buffalo and ten of his fiercest warriors surrounded them, making sure no one could get close to them. Morgan, in his lunacy, might decide that the sheriff was not a problem, but he would never take on White Buffalo. Not if he wanted to live for any length of time.

When they got to the ranch, most of the warriors went on, but White Buffalo stayed and went inside with the rest of the family. He wanted to see what plans they had and how he could help James.

He already knew that Roy Walker would bother no one again. After James had told him what Walker had done to the woman, White Buffalo had ordered Walker's death. It was an easy thing. It angered him that any man could treat a woman that way. Women and old people were to be protected by warriors, not abused by them. His people believed this and so, he knew, did James

277

Evans.

He felt it best not to tell James what he had done. James would've wanted Walker to be punished by the white man's law. White Buffalo had little respect for the white man's law or their word. Except for a few honorable men, like James Evans, he had never had a white man keep his word. No Indian had. White Buffalo made his own decisions and dispensed his own punishment. Walker would never hurt anyone, man or woman, again.

*****

Madeline took additional laudanum to make the trip, but she was beginning to heal nicely. Doc Wright came to see her that morning and pronounced her on the mend. The swelling in her face had gone down enough so he could determine that no bones were actually broken, but she did have a few loose teeth now. He told her no solid foods for at least a week. She said that was okay with her, it hurt enough to talk, she couldn't imagine trying to chew.

Duncan carried her upstairs to his old room. The Petersons were now staying in their cabin, and Cassie was occupying the guestroom.

James announced they were now officially out of beds, so they better not find anyone else who needed their help. At least, he amended, until they sorted out the messes they already had.

Once Duncan got Madeline settled in the bed, Catherine came in and shooed him out of the room so she could wash her and get her in a clean nightgown. Then she gave her some more laudanum and let her go to sleep. The doctor had said that sleep was the best medicine now. It would help her to heal, so she was to get as much rest as possible and lots of beef broth to build her strength.

After Madeline awoke Catherine sat on the chair next to the bed. She looked at the pretty woman, who, despite all of her injuries was still attractive and would probably once again be beautiful, when she healed. The doctor had been wrong. He said that she would never be beautiful again, but Catherine could see that she would.

Catherine looked down at her hands. "Madeline, I told you that when I first heard what you had done to Duncan I wanted to kill you."

Madeline closed her eyes and rested her head against the pillows. Without opening her eyes, she responded, "I suppose if I had loved him as much as you do, I'd feel the same way. I never set out to hurt him, though I did come here for revenge."

Catherine looked at her, "How could you? How could you do that to him? He loved you. I would give anything if he loved me like he loved you."

Madeline opened her eyes and stared at Catherine. "He loves you. I see it in his eyes, the way he looks at you, the way he touches you. He never looked at me like that. He never touched me like that.

"You asked me how I could hurt him. I never meant to hurt him, I just didn't care. I never loved him. My father accepted when he asked for me, because father had discovered that I was sleeping with someone else. Someone I thought I loved."

Catherine looked at her, "But Duncan said that he found you in bed with Roy Walker. How could you

279

think you were in love with Walker?"

Madeline gave her a little smile. "Love does funny things to the heart; makes us blind to the truth. Maybe it was because he seemed so dangerous. Maybe it was because Roy wasn't kind and gentle like Duncan. I know now that I didn't love Roy, but I lusted after him. I slept with him after convincing myself that I did love him. But obviously he didn't love me, doesn't love me. Someone who loves you couldn't do this to you." She pointed at her body, at her face. "Duncan had a reason to leave me. He had a reason to be hurt, and I am sorry for that. More sorry than I can ever express."

Catherine didn't interrupt her, but let her get it all out; let the emotional healing begin.

Madeline continued, "I was angry at first when he left, because it ruined my plans. But I understood why he did. He may have been infatuated with me, he was young, but that was all. He loves you."

Catherine stood and went to the bed, taking Madeline's hand, "Thank you for being honest with me. I know it wasn't easy for you. I meant what I said before. I believe in giving people another chance. You've been given a second chance, don't waste this one."

Catherine went downstairs to find everyone in the kitchen, including Tom and Beth, who'd come up when they saw the wagon pass by their place. Alice had a big pot of coffee and some fresh baked sugar cookies for them.

All the chairs were taken, so Catherine just stood by the stove with her coffee, until she saw Duncan grin at her and pat his lap for her to sit.

She shook her head at him.

He patted it again, then crooked his finger at her.

She shook her head again.

He calmly rose, walked over to her and picked her up in his arms.

She shrieked.

Everyone else laughed. He ignored her, walked back to his chair and sat down, settling her in his lap.

"I was just fine where I was," she hissed under her breath.

"I like you better here." He grinned at her.

"Children, enough foolishness." James' voice was gruff but he had a smile on his face. "We have to make plans. Tom, I'm glad that you and Beth came. This involves you two as well. I don't think that you should be staying in the cabin for a while. You're too isolated if something should happen, especially with Beth expecting and so near to her time. I think it best if you move back here for a while, until all this is settled. I'll move to my study and you can have my room."

"Do you really think it's necessary?" Tom protested.

"I sincerely hope not, but I don't want to take any chances. John's had his plans foiled this time but good, and I doubt he's very happy about it. I don't know what he'll try next, but we need to be ready for anything."

Duncan agreed. He told them what Madeline

had said, and how the boardinghouse was watched so they couldn't leave. "I know it seems like we're prisoners, but this is the best way to protect everyone. At least for the time being."

Everyone nodded agreement.

"Well, other than having everyone together, what else are we going to do?" Catherine asked to no one in particular.

No one answered her. She knew there was no answer for her. They had to wait until Morgan made his move, and then hope they could counter it. That was all they could do. For now.

*****

The ranch was being watched. Duncan knew it as sure as he knew his own name, but they couldn't just sit around and wait for him to strike. There were still cattle to see to, chores to be done, and Tom and Beth's house to finish. Too many things to be done and not nearly enough people to do them. He made sure there were always several men on guard around the house. He was taking no chances.

Duncan was afraid Morgan knew now would be the best opportunity he would have to make a final strike against the Evans. He wished he knew what Morgan was planning. The wait was almost worse than the knowing would have been.

*****

John Morgan knew this was the perfect time to strike. He could get them all. He would get even for all the insults, all the wrongs, and all the grief that James and Catherine had caused him.

He was far beyond just wanting the ranch and the gold. Oh, he still wanted them, but since Catherine's marriage to Duncan, he wanted more. He wanted revenge on the man he saw as having everything that was rightfully his. More than anything, he wanted Duncan dead. Dead and buried.

*****

They didn't have to wait long for Morgan to make his move. Zeke was recovering well from his injury during the stampede. His splint was off and he only used one crutch now. He was one of the regular guards, but he still managed to do some of his chores as well. He stayed around the main ranch most of the time, occasionally taking the supply wagon to town or up to the north camp.

It was on one of his trips to the camp that he saw the smoke. A tall, gray plume rising from the hill above the camp. All the cattle were there in that pasture; they had been moved there to try to keep them out of harm's way. Most of the cowhands were there with the herd. He needed to warn them fast.

Zeke slapped the reins. "Yehah, giddy up you nags." He continued slapping the reins until the horses were running. When he got close enough to the camp to see, he prayed the boys were there.

He started yelling "Fire! Fire on Mount Baldy!" He stood up, ignoring his leg, and pointing towards the hill. As the wagon came barreling down the road, the cowboys looked to where he was pointing, saw the smoke, and ran for their horses. They had to get the cattle out of there before they smelled the smoke and began a stampede.

If they could get them moving away from the fire, back toward the ranch, they would be all right. Zeke watched the cowboys ride fast and furious to get to the back of the herd without stampeding them. When they were in place, they started yelling and shouting, shooting their weapons in the air to get them going. They didn't really care if they stampeded now, as long as they moved in the right direction.

*****

At the ranch, they also saw the smoke. Everyone was running to get their axes and saws. The only way to stop the fire was to cut a firebreak. Water was too far away and too hard to bring to the fire to fight it. All but two of the men, including Duncan, James, and Tom, went to fight the fire.

Catherine stayed at the ranch. She, her Colt, and the two cowboys were the only defense for the women now.

Beth had still not given birth. Alice had told Catherine she was afraid all this excitement would send Beth into labor. And she was only too right.

Beth's labor started almost as soon as the men left. She was in the kitchen, fixing coffee, when her water broke. She doubled over in pain, and dropped the coffeepot.

"Catherine! Catherine, help me! My baby is coming."

Catherine ran to her, helped her to her room, got her undressed and in the bed. Alice and Cassie prepared the hot water and gathered towels.

Hard labor began quickly, and Beth screamed in pain. Alice made Catherine and Cassie leave. She said she didn't want them to be frightened by what they saw.

Catherine at first refused. "I've helped with the calving and just about every other birth on this farm. I can help, Alice. You know I can."

"I know, but this is not calving. This is a woman giving birth. Just as you will someday. This is not something you should see now. Not yet. Besides, Cassie is too young and unmarried. Do you want to scare her from ever wanting to have children?"

Catherine gave in. She knew Cassie had never worked on the ranch like Catherine did. She'd never seen a birth of any kind, and this would be very traumatic for her. She went to the kitchen.

Cassie, sitting at the kitchen table, was pale and wringing her hands. When Catherine entered, she looked up.

"Did you hear her? Beth is in such pain. I've never heard anyone, never thought... I don't think I will ever be able to go through that!"

"Sure you will, Cassie. When you get married, you're going to want a ton of children."

"Catherine, what about you? How do you feel, having lost one babe? Do you really want to get pregnant and go through what Beth is going through now?"

"Yes, gladly. I will try and try until we have our own children. I am sorry I lost the first babe, but I didn't even know I was pregnant. I didn't have time to get attached, to grow to love it. If Doc hadn't told Duncan, we might never have known."

"Do you wish you hadn't known? I know it's been months now since it happened but have you thought about it?"

"Sure I have. I think about it all the time. But I was only a few weeks pregnant." Her menses were late now. It may be too soon, but she was pretty sure she was already pregnant again. She smiled a little secret smile and touched her belly. "I wonder what it would feel like now, growing in my belly. Would I be showing yet? How in the world would I get into my buckskins? Silly things."

Another wail from the bedroom above stopped her rambling. They both raised their eyes again to the ceiling, glad it wasn't them up there.

Cassie shuddered. "I don't think I'll be able to stand it. I'm not good with pain."

"You will too. Stop saying that. You won't even remember it after you get the babe in your arms." She went to Cassie and held her. "Now, we need to make sure that Alice has everything she needs. We still have to prepare food and water for the men, so what do you say we get busy?"

"You're right. Let's get to work. I'll do the cooking." She looked at Catherine and they both laughed, knowing that Catherine was better, but still a terrible cook.

Hours later, they were frying up the last of the chicken, when they heard a baby wail. They both shouted and ran for Beth's room. There they found Alice putting the new baby in Beth's arms.

Beth looked up at the two of them and smiled. "I have a son." She took Alice's hand. "Thank you, Alice."

Alice smiled back, squeezing her hand, "You did all the work all I did was catch him."

Beth looked at the face of her newborn son and gently kissed his forehead. "I never thought I could love anyone this much, but you, my little man, mean more to me than anyone. You are so beautiful and so precious." She looked up at Catherine. "Tom and I already talked about this, and we'd like to name him James Duncan. They've both been so good to us, and we just don't know what we would've done without either of them. Or you. Do you think they'll mind?"

"Mind? They'll both be tickled. Can I see little James?" asked Catherine

"Of course. Here you go, my little man. Go to your Aunt Catherine."

Catherine took the little bundle from his mother. He was so small and so perfect. His eyes were open. They were blue, as most babies were, or so she'd been told. He looked at her, blinking those beautiful eyes of his. He opened his mouth and she thought he was going to cry, but he just stuck his fist in and started to suck it.

Catherine looked up, smiling, "Alice, you better get Beth cleaned up, I don't think this little man is going to wait too much longer for his first meal."

As if to emphasize what she had said, little James Duncan Peterson took his fist out of his mouth and hollered. There was nothing wrong with this little one's lungs, that's for sure.

*****

John Morgan made Charley Sloan start the fire, while he watched the ranch himself. He told him to set the fire far enough away that it wouldn't threaten the house but would get the men away from it for a long time.

He'd wanted Roy Walker, to start the fire but he'd disappeared suddenly, after that Connor woman had been found nearly beat to death. He figured Walker had done it, but he didn't really care. John assumed he'd left town. That didn't bother him either. The man made him nervous from the start, and if he hadn't been afraid to, he would have fired him long ago.

Now, though, everything was working out perfectly. It would have been easier if Cassie was still at home. He'd have said Cassie was sick and needed her. Catherine would come running. She'd do anything for Cassie. Now, though, he'd have to catch her alone. All he had to do was wait. He hated waiting, but he had no choice if he wanted Catherine. And he did want her. Badly.

The men had been gone most of the day, when he saw Catherine go out to the barn. Leaving his vantage point, he sneaked down to the barn behind her.

Entering quietly, he heard her cooing to Wildfire. "Hello boy. How is my sweet boy?"

"He's much better, now that you're here."

Catherine swung around, reaching for her colt.

He was ready for her, his gun already drawn. "Oh, no you don't. Put your gun on the ground in front of you, then kick it over to me." She did what she was told. "That's a good girl."

She lifted her chin, looking straight at him. "You're not going to get away with this, John. Dad and Duncan will hunt you down if you kill me. There won't be anywhere on earth you can hide that they won't find you."

He sneered at her. "My dear, I'm not going to kill you. Quite the contrary, I'm going to marry you. I'll get the land that I need that way. The land with the gold on it will be mine." He laughed, but there was no humor in it.

"You've lost your mind, John." Contempt dripped from every word she spoke. "Utterly and completely lost your mind. If you are talking about the land you tried to buy, there is no gold. It's fool's gold, John. Only fool's gold, for the biggest fool of all. You."

"You lie. The gold is real. I saw it myself."

"I don't lie, and I will never marry you. I'm already married to the man I love. I'll never divorce him."

"Ah, I see the Connor woman told you of my previous plan, but I didn't say anything about divorce, now. Did I?" His sneer turned to a smile, an evil smile. "I intend for you to be a widow, my dear, and very soon."

"You can't be serious. Duncan is much faster than you are. You'll never beat him in a fair fight!"

He laughed. "I don't intend it to be a fair fight. I'm not stupid! He'll meet with a tragic accident while fighting this fire. It's so sad, my dear, but you may already be a widow."

Catherine fell to her knees, feeling like someone had kicked her in the gut. She wrapped her arms around her waist trying to ease the intense pain. "No, oh, please God, no."

From behind Morgan she heard the deep, familiar voice she so loved. She raised her head, her face streaked with tears.

"No. Not today Morgan. Now drop your gun, unless you want to die here and now."

John Morgan just laughed. "I don't think so, unless you want your pretty wife here to die with me. If I don't hear that gun drop to the floor, she's dead..."

Duncan didn't give him a chance to finish what he was saying. He looked at Catherine, told her with his eyes to roll to the right, and fired. His shot hit John Morgan in the right shoulder, as he intended. Morgan's gun went off at the same time, the bullet landing harmlessly in the ground, where Catherine had just been.

Morgan wasn't through, though. He fell to the floor, rolled over and fired. Duncan never took his eyes off of Morgan, saw him roll and fired at the same instant, hitting him square in the chest. He was dead.

Morgan's desperate last shot had caught Duncan in his left shoulder, though he didn't feel it. He ran to Catherine, knelt beside her and took her in his arms and cradled her there. He realized just how close he had come to losing her, again. He'd been so scared when he entered the barn and saw Morgan with his gun aimed at Catherine. Thank God, he had seen the strange horse and went to investigate.

Now he held his beautiful wife in his arms, safe, close to his heart. He held her, letting her cry. He relived the moments when he thought he might lose her, and his heart ached with the pain of what could have happened. Coming so close to losing her, he couldn't think of the right words. Yes, it was true. He loved her. He knew it in his heart, in every fiber of his body. The revelation made him hold her even tighter.

Catherine's sobbing subsided to small sniffles. She pulled back and looked up into his gorgeous blue eyes. Eyes she thought she might never see again, and saw a change in them. There was a softness in them, a smile she had not seen before.

"Oh Duncan, I was so frightened. John said he would have you killed and that you were probably already dead. I thought I'd never see you again."

"I heard, but it's all right now, my love. Everything's all right. He won't be bothering us ever again." He kissed the top of her head, then lifted her chin and kissed her lips. It was a gentle, tender kiss.

She kissed him back, but not gently. Her kiss was ferocious, hungry, raw. She needed his passion, his touch to wipe away the ugliness of what had just happened. She grabbed at his shoulders and hit his wound. He winced and she broke the kiss.

Her fingers were sticky with his blood. She saw his arm then and tears came back to her eyes. "Oh my God, Duncan! You're wounded!"

"It's nothing. It didn't even hurt until now. Guess I didn't move quick enough. I must be getting old." He grinned. "Come on, let's go on up to the house."

"Okay." She stopped and looked up at him. "What are you doing back here? What about the fire?"

"I came back to get supplies and to check on you. James and I didn't think this fire was a coincidence. We also wanted to let you know not to worry, the fire isn't as bad as we first thought and..."

His explanation was cut short by Cassie slamming open the barn door. "What's going on?" She was breathless from running from the house. "We heard shots." She stopped and saw her brother lying dead on the floor. "Oh God. John." She walked over to him and slowly knelt beside his body. "What have you done?"

Catherine went to her. "Cassie, I am so sorry, but..."

"Oh, John, what have you done?" Cassie looked up at Catherine, tears streaming down her cheeks. "He wasn't always bad, you know. You remember, Catherine, we used to have a good time together, the three of us. It was after he hired Roy Walker, that things really got bad. Walker filled John's head with all these ideas. I never thought he would take it this far. I never thought..." She dropped her head and wept for the brother she had loved, but not the one who was dead.

"Cassie, honey, it's all right. You couldn't have known. Nobody could have. Come with me now. We'll leave John here for the sheriff." Catherine grasped the smaller woman by the shoulders and gently tugged her to her feet.

Cassie looked at Catherine and then at Duncan, "You're wounded. I'm so sorry. This never should've happened. He really was a good boy you know, he just turned into a bad man."

"I know, Cassie. Now you go along to the house with Catherine. I'll be up shortly." He nodded toward the door, silently telling Catherine that he would take care of John.

Catherine took Cassie back to the house. She held on to her and wished that things had been different. Alice was on the porch waiting for them. Before she could ask, Catherine said, "John Morgan is dead. Duncan had to shoot him. We'll have to send for the sheriff."

Duncan came up later, after having covered John. His arm was really beginning to hurt. The shock was wearing off, and he knew he'd lost some blood. He went in by way of the kitchen to clean up. All of the women were there, even Madeline.

Catherine took one look at Duncan's pale complexion and nearly fainted herself. He was white as a sheet and there were small beads of perspiration on his forehead. She went to him, put her arm around his waist, and his good arm over her shoulder to support him while she helped him to a chair at the table.

"Alice, bring me some of that hot water you were making for tea, and get me some towels. Cassie, go get my sewing kit, you know where I keep it. Beth, you just sit there and don't do anything except take care of that sweet baby."

"Baby? Beth, you had your baby? Congratulations! What variety do we have?" asked

Duncan.

"A boy. His name is James Duncan Peterson and he is the most beautiful baby I've ever seen. Of course, I could be a little prejudiced since I am his mother." The baby squeaked and they all laughed.

Duncan sat at the table and Catherine undid the buttons on his shirt and removed it. He leaned down and whispered in her ear, "Do you think this is the proper time, Mrs. McKenzie? In front of the ladies and all?"

He grinned lecherously at her. She slapped his leg. "You just keep your mind on not passing out Mr. McKenzie and let me worry about what is or isn't proper in front of my friends."

Alice set the pan of hot water, along with some lye soap, towels and a bottle of whiskey on the table in front of Duncan.

"I thought he might need this. You know, for the pain."

"Thank you Alice, I..." he reached for the bottle.

Catherine moved the bottle out of his reach. "He won't need that, at least not yet. But I will. You just sit there real nice and be a good boy. I've got to clean this wound and I don't need you drunk just yet." She started cleaning the wound and saw that the bullet had torn through his arm, missing the bone but was still lodged in his shoulder. She'd have to get it out or it would poison him.

"Well, my love, it looks like you do get that whiskey after all." She handed him the bottle. "Drink up now. The bullet's in your shoulder and it's got to come out. It's going to hurt," she paused, "a lot."

"Well, give me the damn bottle and then get after it, there are still the supplies to get to the men." He took a long drink from the bottle.

"Alice, you know the drill, you hold his arm for me. Cassie, why don't you take Madeline, Beth, and the baby back upstairs. They both need rest and it sounds like little James needs to be fed...again." She winked. Catherine knew that Cassie had been through all this before, but she doubted Beth or Madeline had been. Given their weakened conditions, now was not the time for them to be introduced to the intricacies of bullet removal.

As they left, Catherine took the whiskey and poured some of it over her knife. While Alice held his arm, Catherine cut into his shoulder making an inch long incision crosswise through the wound. After pouring some whiskey on her hand, she told Duncan to take another drink. Then she put her finger into the wound and felt around, looking for the lead.

"Good God, woman, are you trying to kill me?" he shouted as the pain tore through him.

"You're lucky it's not too deep." She took the lead out with a long pair of tweezers, made just for such an occasion and dropped it on the table. Taking the whiskey bottle from Duncan, she poured some into the wound. He groaned, but stayed in the chair and let her do what she had to do.

Catherine took her knife and went to the stove. She removed one of the top burner covers and stuck the blade directly into the flame getting it almost red-hot. Then she walked over to Duncan. "This is going to hurt me a lot more than it hurts you." She laid the knife on the open wound to cauterize it, so the bleeding would stop.

Duncan clenched his teeth and wanted to scream, but no sound came from him.

"You can let him go now, Alice. Thank you."

"Anytime, dear. I'm just glad it wasn't James this time, no offense Duncan. I've just patched that man up too many times."

Alice smiled and said to Duncan, "I think you're in good hands now. I'm going to go check on the girls and let them know everything is fine."

Catherine told him, "I'm going to sew you up now. It's going to hurt but I'll be as quick I can."

"This isn't the first time I've been shot you know." He looked down at his shoulder. "You did a pretty good job." Then he frowned. "Hey, wait a minute. I thought you said you couldn't sew."

"I can't sew a dress, but I'm pretty good at stitching up people. Things happen now and again out here. Now drink some more of that whiskey and let me finish." Twenty minutes later, he was stitched, bandaged, in a sling and a clean shirt.

"Now don't you feel better? You're going to have to take it easy for a couple of weeks though while that heals." He certainly looked better to her. His color was returning, along with his stubbornness.

"I wish I could, Cat, but I still have to get those supplies to the men, wounded or not."

"We'll get them there. Cassie and I did a lot of cooking while Alice helped Beth birth little James, so we already have some of the supplies ready to go.

"That's why I was in the barn when John found me. Getting the wagon. I'm so glad he made his move here. I don't know what would've happened if he'd gotten to me in open country." She hugged him tightly. "Anyway, I'll go with you. Someone has to tell Tom he's a new father and I don't want you to hurt yourself anymore. I'll drive, you can ride shotgun. Deal?"

"Yeah. I like the idea of spending a little time alone with my wife." Then he looked her in the eyes and very softly and seriously said, "We make a great team, you know."

"I know. I'm just glad to know you realize it, too. Now, sit down right there and eat some of Cassie's delicious stew." She got him a bowl and filled it from the big kettle on the stove. "I'll go get the wagon and she'll help me finish loading it. Cassie needs to be busy right now; this has been real hard on her."

He grabbed her around the waist with his good arm, hauling her onto his lap. "You're the most amazing woman. After all you've been through today, you're still thinking of Cassie and what she needs. What do you need, Mrs. McKenzie? A little of Mr. McKenzie, I hope."

She took his face in her hands, "I have everything I need right here." Then she kissed him gently, "My knight in shining armor, my rescuer, my lover, my husband, and the father of my child." Smiling, she let him go and walked out to get the wagon.

Duncan was in a haze, between the liquor and

the pain in his shoulder, he could have sworn she said the father of her child. Child? As in baby? Catherine was going to have a baby!

He jumped up, nearly fell down, got his footing again and went out the door after her. She was just pulling the wagon around by the kitchen door.

"Baby!" He shouted at her. "You're pregnant. As in I'm going to be a father? You're sure? It's so soon. You're really going to have a baby?"

The look on his face was priceless and she couldn't help but smile as she jumped down from the wagon. "Yes, a father! Sometime around April, best as I can figure. Guess it doesn't take much with you and me."

She walked up the porch steps to him. "You are happy aren't you?" She asked shyly, while holding her hands behind her back and kicking at something with her foot.

"Happy? I'm the happiest man alive! When you lost the first baby, I knew you were upset, but I was so scared that I'd lose you, too, I tried not to let it show how much I hurt." He threw off the sling, wrapped his arms around her waist and swung her around, unmindful of his injury. "None of that matters now. I'm going to be a father and I'm married to the woman I love, what more can a man ask for?"

Catherine laughed and hugged Duncan back as they danced around the porch. Then it hit her! He loved her. She stopped laughing, stopped dancing and looked up into his face. He was smiling.

"You said you married the woman you love. Duncan, you love me?" There were tears in her eyes, she was so afraid he would take it back and say it was just the excitement of the moment.

But he didn't. He wrapped his arms around her, "I do love you" he said seriously, then laughed. "I wondered if you heard me."

"I heard you. I was afraid I was hearing things."

"You weren't. I love you so much, sometimes I can't think about anything but you."

"When? When did you decide that you loved me?" She knew she shouldn't ask, but she wanted to know.

"Well, I was pretty sure I loved you after your accident. It scared me so much. Then when you came to find me in Creede, I was certain. But, I didn't know just how very precious you are to me, until I saw you in the barn with John Morgan's gun on you." His body shivered at the memory.

"My blood ran cold. I could have lost you forever. I have never been so scared in my life. Maybe I've always known. I was just too pigheaded to admit it."

He shrugged. "I kept telling myself I just cared about you because you were James' daughter and I knew you as a little girl. I told myself I had no choice but to marry you, to save James, to save you. But I was saving myself." He shook his head, seeing uncertainty in her eyes, knowing what she was thinking.

"I was saving myself from losing you. I knew I didn't have to go through with the ceremony at White Buffalo's camp. I knew the chief wouldn't kill me. But when I heard you tell him that you loved me, I couldn't let you go. The thought of you with someone else, of losing you, I couldn't face that. I think I loved you even then, but I couldn't admit it. Can you forgive me?"

"Oh Duncan! I love you. I've loved you my whole life." She wrapped her arms around his neck and kissed him soundly. Opening herself to him and showing him all the love that was in her heart. He winced as he pulled her tighter, but didn't let her go.

"Hey, I'm a wounded man." He teased as he held her close.

She laughed, "Well, we should get this wounded man to bed. I think he needs some tender, loving care, or at least some tender loving."

"What about the wagon, the supplies?"

"I'll get Cassie to take them. She won't mind. It will give her a chance to visit with Michael. You don't worry about her; you just come with me Mr. McKenzie." She looked up at him. Love shining in her eyes.

"My husband, forever my love," she said as she gently stroked his cheek.

He wrapped his arms about her, pulling her close, "My wife. Forever, my love."

EPILOGUE

Duncan walked into the kitchen just in time to see a little black haired boy grab a cookie off the counter and scamper out of the room. His mother turned after him, shouting, "Ian McKenzie, you put that cookie back. You'll ruin your supper."

Duncan caught her from behind and pulled her close, his arms resting above her swollen belly. "Let him go. What will one cookie hurt?" He nuzzled her neck with his cheek and kissed her softly.

She turned in his arms. "You spoil him. You're almost as bad as his grandparents!"

James finally married Alice two years ago. It had taken him months to convince her. She kept saying that she was just the housekeeper, not good enough to marry him. He kept up his courtship until she'd finally given in.

He laughed. "No one could spoil him as much as those two."

"Well, maybe, but still he shouldn't be having treats before dinner." She pouted, trying to move out of his arms.

"What about his father? Can he have treats before dinner?" He pulled her back into his arms and kissed her again.

She softened. He could always do that to her, make her give in, just by kissing her. "His father can have all the treats he wants. Whenever and wherever he wants." She pushed a wayward lock of hair off his forehead and took his face in her hands. "I love you so much." She kissed him.

"I love you, too." He pulled her closer and kissed her again, then got kicked by her belly.

He grinned down at her and smoothed his hand over her swollen stomach. "I guess she doesn't like me arguing with her mother."

"You shouldn't argue with her mother." She laughed and put her hand over his on her, just as another little foot kicked out at him.

"By the way, she's going to have another cousin. I was over at Michael and Cassie's today. He told me they're expecting," said Duncan. "She and Ian are going to have plenty of playmates in this valley."

"What if she turns out to be a boy? Are you going to be disappointed?"

"Never. But I know this baby is a girl." His eyes glittered with mischief. "Only a girl could be that ornery, besides I'm never wrong." He grinned.

Catherine swatted his arm in mock anger. "Girls are not ornery, we're smart. You men are just too dumb to realize it."

He chuckled, picked her up in his arms and carried her to their bedroom. "Why don't you convince me?"

Their laughter could be heard all through the house.

*****

Elizabeth Cassandra McKenzie was born one month later. A squealing, wriggling bundle of joy with red-gold hair, just like her mother and grandmother before her.

When her father picked her up, the first thing she did was kick him.

CYNTHIA WOOLF

ABOUT THE AUTHOR

Cynthia Woolf is the award winning and best-selling author of more than thirty historical western romance books and two short stories with more books on the way.

Cynthia loves writing and reading romance. Her first western romance Tame A Wild Heart, was inspired by the story her mother told her of meeting Cynthia's father on a ranch in Creede, Colorado. Although Tame A Wild Heart takes place in Creede that is the only similarity between the stories. Her father was a cowboy not a bounty hunter and her mother was a nursemaid (called a nanny now) not the ranch owner.

Cynthia credits her wonderfully supportive husband Jim and her great critique partners for saving her sanity and allowing her to explore her creativity.

WEBSITE – http://cynthiawoolf.com

NEWSLETTER – http://bit.ly/1qBWhFQ

TITLES AVAILABLE

BRIDES OF SEATTLE
Mail Order Mystery

CENTRAL CITY BRIDES
The Dancing Bride
The Sapphire Bride
The Irish Bride

KINDLE WORLD BOOKS
A Family for Christmas
Kissed by a Stranger
Thorpe's Mail-Order Bride

HOPE'S CROSSING
The Hunter Bride
The Replacement Bride
The Stolen Bride
The Unexpected Bride

AMERICAN MAIL-ORDER BRIDES
Genevieve, Bride of Nevada

THE SURPRISE BRIDES
Gideon

THE BRIDES OF SAN FRANCISCO

Nellie
Annie
Cora
Sophia
Amelia

THE BRIDES OF TOMBSTONE
Mail Order Outlaw
Mail Order Doctor
Mail Order Baron

DESTINY IN DEADWOOD
Jake
Liam
Zach

MATCHMAKER & CO
Capital Bride
Heiress Bride
Fiery Bride
Colorado Bride

TAME SERIES
Tame a Wild Heart
Tame a Wild Wind
Tame a Wild Bride
Tame a Honeymoon Heart

BOXSETS
The Tame Series
A Touch of Passion